To Margie, Gus, and Paul

A MOMENT IN TIME

Miss Saint-Clair handed the pianist her music. Too disgusted to watch, Lord Rune went to stand by the open window, looking out over the dark garden. She was going to sing the recitative; it was going to be long.

"In quali eccessi, o Numi . . ."

Lord Rune spun around, for the voice was a remarkable one with a taut brilliance that made his hair stand on end. He stared at Miss Saint-Clair as if she had undergone a metamorphosis.

Her voice rose and fell, reaching the high notes without the slightest effort, navigating the embellishments with an almost insolent ease. She stood erect, but supple. Lord Rune almost breathed with her.

At last the song drew to a close. She sang the last words and bowed her head. A light patter of applause followed. Lord Rune started forward. The applause hushed and then increased as he caught Lucy Saint-Clair's hand and pressed it to his lips.

A GYPSY AT ALMACK'S

CHLOE CHESHIRE

HarperPaperbacks
A Division of **HarperCollins***Publishers*

This is a work of fiction. The characters, incidents, and dialogues are products of the author's imagination and are not to be construed as real. Any resemblance to actual events or persons, living or dead, is entirely coincidental.

HarperPaperbacks *A Division of* HarperCollins*Publishers*
10 East 53rd Street, New York, N.Y. 10022

A hardcover edition of this book was published in 1993 by St. Martin's Press.

Cover illustration by Bob Berran

First HarperMonogram printing: April 1994

Printed in the United States of America

HarperPaperbacks, HarperMonogram, and colophon are trademarks of HarperCollins*Publishers*

10 9 8 7 6 5 4 3 2 1

1

Lord Rune was indisposed. The servant in rumpled livery repeated this allegation for the third time, hoping to discourage the middle-aged lady at the door. His hopes were dashed; the lady shut her parasol with a snap and stepped over the threshold.

"He is always indisposed at this hour," retorted the lady, disapprovingly. "It's his own fault."

The servant stepped back, a trifle embarrassed by so forthright a judgment of his new master's habits. The lady took advantage of his discomfiture, brushing past him and entering the vestibule. The sight of this chamber served to exacerbate her displeasure. The carpet lay crooked, the hall table was dull with dust, and the silver card-tray had two sticky rings on it, where a bottle and wine-glass had rested.

"Madam—" The servant bowed slightly, and the lady turned to him.

"Of course. You don't have the slightest idea who I am, do you? I thought you were Mulespaw—Ernest's last butler—but he was bald, and you aren't, quite, are you? Ernest is always changing servants, and it muddles me dreadfully."

The servant, eyeing her with aversion, replied, "Just so."

"I'm Mrs. Theale," continued the lady, briskly. "Ernest's sister. His favorite sister, I believe, for he never could abide Edith, and dear Agatha is dead. Tabitha," she volunteered, raising her voice and speaking with painstaking clarity. "I'm Tabitha. If you tell him I'm here, he'll rouse himself." She smiled, the smile of a woman who has determined that she is going to get her own way and who, moreover, is going to remain pleasant during the enterprise of getting it. "Where shall I wait?"

The servant, giving up all hope of getting rid of her, allowed himself an unprofessional sigh as he showed her into the morning room.

Alone in the morning room, Tabitha opened the shutters, dusted a Grecian chair with the cylindrical cushion from a matching sofa, and tossed the cushion away with a sniff of disgust.

A less critical observer might have been surprised by so harsh a judgment of the room's character. It was a room of harmonious proportions—Lord Rune had a discriminating eye—and the silver-striped hangings were unmistakably new. The furniture was arranged with mathematical symmetry, and the clear morning light gleamed across satinwood and mahogany, serpentine marble, and parquet floors. Tabitha's inspection, however, was not cursory, and her housewifely instinct was seldom at fault. The room had a neglected look that was subtly depressing; the windows were streaked and the air was stale. Even the bronze Mercury, eternally jubilant as he danced on one leg, had a chilly naked look. Too naked, thought Tabitha darkly; she had instilled delicacy of mind in four lively daughters and had inevitably corrupted herself in the process.

The door opened, and a second servant entered, bearing a Sèvres tea-pot and a gold-rimmed cup. Tabitha nodded regally, and the servant set the tray before her and poured her a cup of chocolate. Tabitha began to think more kindly of her brother, for a fondness for chocolate was among her weaknesses and the Sèvres breakfast service was one of the gems of Lord Rune's collection. She dismissed the servant and spent a very agreeable half-hour sipping the chocolate and composing an address that would awaken Ernest's servants to the sense of shame that ought to be their portion in life. This oration was receiving its finishing touches when the clock struck two, the doors opened, and Ernest came in.

Ernest Howard, Lord Rune, had been a strikingly handsome man fifteen years ago, and his admirers were fond of saying that he had not aged in the least. His detractors—and so singular a man must have many— were even fonder of saying that he looked ten years older than a man of thirty-five ought to look. The curious thing was that both claims rang true. Lord Rune's way of life was dissolute, and his face had absorbed a wide variety of emotions. He could look both weary and dissipated, but there were also times when he cast aside his years, seeming to take up his old beauty as if it were a cloak he had let fall. The beauty of the youth still haunted the man, although the man was not aware of it.

This afternoon he wore a dressing-gown of Oriental silk, embroidered with dragons—outlandish, thought Tabitha appreciatively—and a faint scent of cedar soap clung to him. His light brown curls were damp but beautifully brushed, and he winced at the sunlight like a man just awake. In the bright room the shadows under his eyes looked bruised, but he smiled at his sister and Tabitha set down her cup and went to his arms.

"Ernest, dear, have you been ill?"

She felt the vibration of his laughter as he cuddled her against him. "Deathly ill—and not half an hour ago." His smile broadened as he felt her stiffen, and he pulled her closer, rubbing her back. "Don't condemn me, Tha! The morning is sufficient punishment for any sins the evening may have committed—I believe there may have been one or two." He released her and went to the windows, closing the shutters that Tabitha had opened. "Was the chocolate good? I told Pettibone that I would tear him limb from limb if it didn't please you."

"It was very good," Tabitha answered—reluctantly, for the the prospect of a mauled Pettibone held a strong attraction for her, "but—"

"Was the cup warmed?"

Tabitha looked at his face, as anxious and melancholy as a bloodhound's, and felt a twinge of irritation. It was just like Ernest, she felt, to live in this slovenly house and then fuss over a warmed cup. "Yes," she replied, "but I don't like your new butler one bit, Ernest. It took him four rings to come to the door, and his linen isn't clean."

Ernest looked amused. "He isn't very prepossessing, is he? But then, neither was Mulespaw, and Mulespaw drank my champagne. Now this fellow has a stomach ailment." He saw his sister frown, and laughed. "Never mind, Tha! In another week or so I'll fly into a rage and sack the lot of them. I can feel it coming on."

"Ernest—"

He sat down beside her. "You're going to tell me that a better master would have better servants and that I drink too much, aren't you?"

"I am."

"I know, my dearest. I know." He poured the last few drops of chocolate and handed her the cup. "But that isn't what you came to see me about, is it?"

She was taken aback, not for the first time, by his discernment, and she studied the curve of the cup handle instead of answering. "Ernest, where were you?"

"Budapest."

"Budapest!" Tabitha gave the word its full measure of xenophobic significance. "What on earth were you doing in Budapest?"

He sighed, shoving his hands deep into his pockets. "I didn't do anything—I never do anything. You know that. I was desperately sick of London. I had friends of a sort in Budapest, and—Tha, you don't really want to know any of this. It was all rather sordid and a great bore. I'm sorry I didn't write, and I'm sorry I didn't call on you when I returned to London, but I was ill, and I didn't want to see anyone. I'm sorry."

He had always been good at apologizing, Tabitha thought, with a touch of resentment. In the dim light he looked very haggard indeed, very vulnerable. She heard herself say crossly, "You're always being ill," and was shocked by how rude it sounded.

Lord Rune gave a shout of laughter, his quicksilver features suddenly those of a debonair lad not out of his teens. Tabitha stared at the transformation for a moment and then laughed in spite of herself.

"You're a dreadful man."

"I know it." His complacency ruffled her. "But you didn't come here to tell me that, did you?"

"No." Now that the time had come to bring up the subject of Lucy, she was less sure of herself and less sure of him. "I did want to consult you about something, Ernest, but if you're not well—"

"I am as well as I ever am. Speak." He saw her hesitate. "Tabitha, I got out of bed to see you. The next time you want to consult me, I may be incapable of such a sacrifice. Speak."

"It's about Lucy Saint-Clair." Lord Rune looked puzzled and his sister grew irritated again as she saw him mentally reviewing the ladies—and nonladies—of his acquaintance. "Fanny's daughter."

"Fanny?"

"Fanny Hollins—my old school friend. You remember Fanny, Ernest! She had black curls, and she married the vicar of—oh, I never can remember the name of the place, but it's in Yorkshire somewhere, and Lucy is Fanny's eldest daughter, and my god-child, and she's been living with us for the last three Seasons."

"Oh."

"Fanny sent her to me to make her come-out with Angelica, and I brought them out together. And, of course, Angelica married Scarbridge—she's increasing again, by the by, Ernest, and hoping for a girl this time—"

Ernest nodded politely. Among his more infuriating qualities was his lack of ability to remember which of his nieces was which. Tabitha continued breathlessly, "Then Lizzy came out, and of course, Lizzy is a Beauty." She spoke dogmatically, and Lord Rune blinked at her and then nodded. "I'm afraid dear Lucy was cast into the shade. But she's a very good-hearted girl—much more so than Fanny ever was—and she never seemed envious or made any fuss, so I persuaded Fanny to let her have another season. With Cassy."

"Is Cassy the rabbity one?"

Tabitha drew herself upright. "Ernest!"

"I'm sorry. Grace is the rabbity one, isn't she?"

"I haven't got a rabbity one," Tabitha retorted coldly, aware that her words sounded less dignified than she might have liked. "All of my daughters have very pleasing countenances."

"I didn't say they weren't pleasing," responded Ernest, with deceptive mildness. "I said that one of them had a rabbity look about her, and I rather thought it was Cassy. I had no wish to disparage the girl. Indeed, I have always numbered rabbits among the most graceful members of the rodent family."

Tabitha took a deep breath, remembered that she had come to ask a favor, and decided to ignore his response. Ernest continued, encouragingly, "So you brought Lucy to town for her third Season, with Cassy—"

"With Cassy. Yes." Tabitha leaned forward and placed the cup on the breakfast tray. "Cassy, you know, is rather shy and perhaps the least striking of my girls." She avoided his eyes. "I feared that she might find the Season trying, and I was very glad to have Lucy accompany us. And indeed, it was Lucy who first noticed Mr. Bloomsbury."

"Mr. Bloomsbury?"

"Cassy's intended. A most estimable young man. Dear Cassy is in transports! He is just two years older than she and quite pleasing in appearance, although I have a premonition that he will be fat when he is forty—"

"Tabitha. Please. You will cast me into transports, too, and I am scarcely awake."

"It was in the *Gazette*," concluded Mrs. Theale and she leaned back and looked at him expectantly.

"Well?"

"Well, but you might congratulate me, Ernest! It's really a very good match. He adores Cassy, and he has a very tidy little income. And if Lucy hadn't taken a hand he would never have approached Cassy, because Mr. Bloomsbury is every bit as shy as Cassy herself! And really," she continued, warming to her subject, "it was Lucy who persuaded Lizzy that that auburn-haired fortune-hunter was not the thing."

"I am delighted to hear that she did. But I am beginning to lose sight of the point of this charming colloquy. Are you trying to be subtle about the fact that I haven't sent Cassy a wedding present?"

"Oh, no," Tabitha denied blithely. "There's plenty of time for that—the wedding's not until Christmas. It's Lucy I wanted to talk to you about. Didn't I say so?"

"You did. And apparently she is a benefactress to all match-making mammas. But I, who do not match-make and am not maternal, can perhaps be pardoned for wondering what she is supposed to do for me."

Tabitha did not answer at once. She looked down at the brown sediment in the brightly glazed cup, and knit her brows. "Actually," she began, "it's a question of what I would like you to do for her." She did not catch the look of distrust that crossed her brother's face.

"Because, you see, Angelica and Lizzy are married, and Cassy is engaged, and Lucy—" She sighed. "Lucy hasn't even had an offer. And Fanny wants me to send her back to Yorkshire so she can send me Mina and Letty."

"Mina and Letty," repeated Lord Rune, in a melancholy voice.

"Lucy's sisters," explained Tabitha, automatically. "Twins. Fanny wants me to bring them out before their fronts grow any larger, and really"—she cleared her throat, discreetly—"I think she is wise. Lucy is a fine-looking girl, in her own way, but she *is* a trifle stout, and she looks so matronly for a young girl! And of course the fashions of today only make matters worse, with the waists just below—" She cleared her throat a second time, aware of her brother's lack of response. "Well, what are you looking so mulish about, Ernest? I haven't even asked you yet, and already you're looking as if you're planning a bilious attack."

"Tabitha, I do not wish to marry."

For a moment Tabitha stared at him; then she laughed. "You? Marry Lucy? Good heavens, Ernest! That would never do!"

Ernest laughed, too, the comfortable laughter of relief. "I thought you intended Miss Saint-Clair for me."

"Oh, no. You're too old," Tabitha answered breezily, effectively quenching her brother's laughter. "Although perhaps Lucy would take better with an older man. She is a little inclined to be bookish, and, of course, even an elderly husband would be better than none at all. Have I told you, Ernest, that Fanny has turned pious?"

"No. Not yet."

"Well, she has, and she writes tracts, Ernest—only

fancy how horrid! And then that vicar of hers is always shooting birds and stuffing them and strewing them round the house. The whole vicarage is full of eyes—glass eyes, I daresay, but I don't like having vulturey things watching me when I'm trying to eat my luncheon."

Ernest kicked a footstool into place and leaned back. "It does sound unsavory," he said languidly, "but surely the girl is accustomed to her family's peculiarities. She might even prefer the vultures to an elderly husband. Are you certain, Tha, that she wants to marry?"

Tabitha sniffed. "She says she doesn't care—" She frowned down at the Sèvres breakfast set, as if it, and not Lucy, were guilty of making exasperating remarks. "I know she dreads going home," she said slowly. "Fanny writes the dreariest letters, all about Christian humility and penance and blessed virginity and I don't know what all."

Ernest nodded. His memories of Fanny Hollins were vague but unpleasant; he remembered a shrill voice and a merciless tongue. "Can't you keep the girl as a companion?"

"Not if I am to bring out Mina and Letty. No, the only thing is to find dear Lucy a husband."

"Is that what you are asking me to do?"

"No." Tabitha looked flustered. "Although if you know of anyone who would suit, that would be splendid, of course. But what I was thinking was"—she favored him with a brilliant smile—"was how *kind* it would be if you were to bring Lucy into fashion." She held up her hand as he began to speak. "You could, Ernest! I am persuaded that you could! Why, your epigrams are still quoted at dinner parties, and you've been

away from London for years and years! You're an arbi-
trator—an arbitrer—"

"Arbiter."

"That's it." Tabitha nodded vigorously. "An arbiter of taste. Why, only think of the season when you
disparaged Lavinia Darleigh's recipe for macaroons.
They were good macaroons," she went on, "but you
wanted to give her a set-down, and after you did, nobody had the courage to go near them, let alone enjoy
them. I was quite out of temper, I remember, because I
was increasing—Grace, I think, or perhaps it was Cassy
—and I had a particular yearning for macaroons, but, of
course, nobody served any for the rest of the Season,
because you had disparaged Lavy Darleigh's." She
lapsed into silence for an instant and then spoke.
"That's what Lucy needs."

"A macaroon?"

Tabitha eyed him wrathfully. "Don't be so provoking, Ernest! Of course not! She needs someone with
influence to pay court to her. And you are rich," she
raised her voice, daring him to interrupt her, "and well-
dressed, and well-mannered when you're not being
rude, and high-in-the-instep, and frighteningly fastidious—"

She stopped. Lord Rune had risen and crossed to
the shuttered windows. His movements were anything
but abrupt, but Tabitha rose and took a step to follow
him. She had a sudden, familiar suspicion that she had
wounded him in some manner too obscure for her to
comprehend. "Ernest?" she said tentatively, and then
impatience overwhelmed her, and she snapped, "For
heaven's sake, Ernest, what is the matter?"

"I dislike it, that's all."

"Dislike what?" There was a note of genuine outrage in her voice. "I don't know what's the matter with you, Ernest! You're always disliking something or other, and it never makes any sense to me. Would you be happier if I had said that you were vulgar and repellent and boorish and ill-bred?"

Lord Rune spun around, his countenance illuminated with delight.

"You're so volatile," complained his sister, "and it muddles me. You never say what you mean."

"I mean that I dislike society."

"Nonsense!" retorted Tabitha, with a good deal of spirit. "You don't! Why, except for being ill, I doubt that you pass an evening alone twice a month!"

Ernest shrugged. "That proves only that I dislike my own society even more."

"But—" Tabitha faced him, and for a brief moment the resemblance between them, usually fugitive, was pronounced. Two pairs of green-blue, gold-flecked eyes met, and it was Ernest who first looked away.

"Tha—" Lord Rune's voice was suddenly weary, and he dropped into a chair with a strategic display of lassitude. "The time is gone when I could condemn a man to social ruin by lifting an eyebrow, and I would not bring it back. I am thirty-five, I am no longer an Adonis, and my reputation is far from spotless. Even if I wanted to, I doubt that I could shed much reflected glory over your protégée. Have you never considered that if she has failed to attract any notice in the course of three years—"

"Fiddlesticks," interrupted Tabitha. "She's a dear good girl and perfectly presentable. She has no fortune, of course, but there's no reason why she should have to sit and watch while the other girls dance, night after night." Some quality in his sister's voice made Ernest look at her sharply, all affectation of exhaustion gone. "She has never had a bouquet, and the men who do dance with her don't trouble themselves to call, and Grace receives five invitations for every one of Lucy's. There's no justice in it and no logic."

Ernest did not answer at once. He knew that she was thinking of her own debut, for Tabitha had not been popular. Two long and tedious Seasons had passed before rescue, in the shape of Benedict Theale, had appeared. There had been times when she feared that she was doomed to live the life of an eternal debutante, attending one boring ball after another, dancing exclusively with her brother. She had been too well-bred, and too well-dowered, not to be invited everywhere; she was too plain, and too shy, not to be ignored once she had come. Ernest had been much younger, his star just beginning to rise; but he had seen his sister's misery very clearly and had fought for her with the energy of a young man and the subtlety of a much older one. It had been Ernest who had fanned the flames of Mr. Theale's phlegmatic admiration into an ardor that could face the hymeneal altar; it had been Ernest who had taken the planning of the wedding out of his sister's hands and turned it into one of the most brilliant affairs of the Season. Tabitha had vowed that she would never forget her brother's kindness, and it seemed, Ernest thought sadly, that she never had. He opened his mouth to protest and said, "What do you want me to do?"

Tabitha brightened at once. "Why, just meet Lucy," she answered, in such dulcet tones that Ernest's heart sank, "just meet her in public, and look splendid, and talk to her and admire her. It will do her a great deal of good to be seen attracting attention, and if you could contrive to make her feel that she is a pretty girl—

which she is, really, you know—it would benefit her immeasurably. And perhaps you could stand up with her once or twice—"

"Once," qualified Ernest. "I will meet her once and dance with her once." He added, with martyred air, "Almack's?"

"Oh, no, not Almack's," Tabitha reassured him. She had already decided that to choose Almack's as a backdrop would counteract any charms Lucy might be able to muster. "I know you dislike Almack's, and I wouldn't dream of asking you to go there. No, Lady Gratham—you know her, Ernest, she was Ianthe Lowell —is having a dinner-party and musicale on Thursday night, and that, I know, will be something that you will enjoy." She caught a glimpse of Ernest's face and rushed on. "Ianthe always sets a good table, and Lucy is at her best at a musicale. She sings much better than any of my girls."

"I hope so."

Tabitha eyed him askance, but forebore; she understood that since her will had prevailed it was Ernest's prerogative to be as difficult as he liked during the remainder of the interview. She rose and kissed her brother on the forehead. "I'll have an invitation sent round," she promised.

Ernest had resumed his air of tortured weariness. He did not rise to escort her, but tugged at the bell-pull instead. The pair waited for several minutes, Lord Rune lost in a vision of himself courting an ox of a girl while Ianthe Lowell, now Lady Gratham, warbled the latest Italian aria. Tabitha's visions were more agreeable; she was composing a letter to Fanny Saint-Clair, announcing Lucy's engagement to a man of property. Since this last figure was a shadowy one, Mrs. Theale came to herself after a moment or two. She strode to the door, grasped the doorknobs with impatient hands and found them sticky. "Oh, Ernest! Do sack the servants!" she cried, and she slammed the doors behind her.

2

It was Thursday night, and Lucy Saint-Clair crouched by the fire, warming her bare arms and shoulders.

Outside the spring air was damp and a milky sky was darkening. Mrs. Theale, always solicitous of her daughters' health, had ordered a fire in the girls' bedroom. Ten years ago Benedict Theale had died of a severe chill. Since then, his widow had maintained that her daughters were susceptible to draughts, and she sought to protect them with furs, fire, and quilted petticoats. Her vigilance was rewarded; in spite of their fragile appearance, the girls seldom caught so much as a cold. Now Cassy fretted over her hair before the mirror, ignoring the cashmere shawl her mother had set out for her, while her sister Grace waltzed up and down the room, admiring her new slippers. It was Lucy, and Lucy alone, who shivered and brooded.

It was partly because of her dress that she was so cold. Lucy had rejected the rose-colored crepe that Mrs. Theale had recommended in favor of a gown of straw-colored gauze. The sleeves were tiny, exposing Lucy's broad shoulders and well-rounded arms, and the frills of filmy lace over the bosom were modest rather than warming. Celestine, the lady's maid, had been rather surprised when Miss Saint-Clair asked her to press the gauze, for not two weeks ago the young lady had declared that nothing would induce her to wear that horrid fright again. Nor had Celestine argued with her, for the gown had grown very tight during the last year, and Celestine had cherished hopes that that it might be handed down to her. She had pressed it with a heavy heart and taken her revenge on Miss Saint-Clair's hair, which had been crimped, braided, and pinned into unbecoming submission.

Now Lucy put her hand to her scalp, remembered in the nick of time not to scratch, and tugged at the bands on her sleeves instead. Already the skin under the bands was reddening, and Lucy scowled and chafed her arms. Grace, seeing the gesture, paused in mid-glide. "Come dance with me, Lulie. It'll warm you."

Lucy shook her head.

Grace tapped her foot irritably and turned to the mirror for consolation. There was a strong family likeness among the Theale girls—they were all fair-haired and blue-eyed, as slender and delicately curved as crescents. Cassy had the longest and the prettiest hair, of a rare flaxen shade, but her eyelashes were very pale, and her nose was inclined to be pink, which gave her a lapine look. Grace's hair was more brown than golden, and her nose was snub, but her eyes were round and clear, her mouth was sweet, and her lashes were bless-edly dark. She was pretty; satisfyingly, undeniably pretty—prettier than Cassy, much prettier than Lucy. She gave a spin of pure pleasure, jarring her sister's elbow as she spun.

"Grace!" A flaxen curl had fallen, and Cassy wailed, "Now look what you've done!"

"You shouldn't have fussed with it after Celestine finished," retorted Grace, and she gave another spin. In the mirror, Cassy's eyes met Lucy's, and the two exchanged the long-suffering look that is the birthright of elder sisters and venerable friends. Lucy laughed, her countenance relaxing, and she came and took the hairbrush from Cassy's hand.

"Lucy, are you sure—"

Lucy's fingers darted in and out of the mass of curls and rosebuds that Celestine had engineered, removing hairpins and unplaiting braids.

"Oh," breathed Grace, surveying the wreckage with relish. "Cass, she's taking it all apart. Celestine will be wild with rage.

Lucy took a hairpin out of her mouth. "Celestine," she pronounced dogmatically, "has no taste."

There did not seem to be any response that could be made to this. Cassy closed her eyes submissively and hoped for the best. Lucy's fingers, cold and deft, removed the last of the rosebuds and began to brush the limp curls into a smooth coil. Grace hovered beside them, intrigued.

"It's pretty," she was able to say at last, and her sister opened her eyes and saw that she spoke the truth.

"Here." Lucy handed her the silver mirror. "Check the back—the effect is rather good, I think."

Cassy obeyed, admiring the twisted coil with its single pink rosebud, and observed that her friend's low spirits seemed to have lifted. Lucy had been silent all day, and Lucy—who was by physiology and temperament a noisy person—was capable of a resounding silence. The absence of running footsteps on the stairs, of slamming doors, of trills and scales in the music room, was a dreadful thing. It made Cassy feel as if someone was ill. She had noticed, too, that her friend scowled more often than usual that day, although it was hard to tell. Lucy's eyebrows were very thick and dark: her countenance, in repose, was ferocious. By contrast, her smile was unexpectedly sweet. Cassy, sharing that smile, sought for a topic that would make it linger.

"What are you going to sing tonight, Lucy?"

Lucy swept the left-over hair pins into her palm and considered them. "The 'Mi Tradi,' " she answered, at last. "What will you?"

"I'm not going to sing at all." Cassy's smile was blissful, almost a grin. "Arthur—Mr. Bloomsbury— says he has no ear for music and he doesn't mind if I never sing in public again." She blushed faintly as she uttered her fiancé's Christian name, and Lucy was obliged to suppress the thought that this marriage was indeed made in heaven: the bridegroom's ear matched the bride's portion of skill.

"I'm going to sing 'Batti, batti,' " announced Grace, without looking up from her slippers.

"You shouldn't," Lucy advised, "you'll come to grief over the runs." She bent her head to hide a smile as Grace took an indignant breath.

"I will not!"

"You will if Lucy says you will," retorted Cassy. "I always did, and you're worse than I ever was. 'Ah, vous dirai-je, maman,' that's your lot in life."

Grace pouted, one eye on the mirror to ascertain

whether the pout was becoming. "I don't want to sing that babyish thing if Lucy's going to sing the 'Mi Tradi.'"

Lucy dropped the hairpins into Cassy's jewel-box and went to Grace, kneeling for a moment to shake out the scalloped hem of her friend's white dress. "It's better to sing something simple and sing it well than to bludgeon your way through something difficult, Grace. And besides"—she rose and faced the younger girl—"who will care what you sing, when you look so lovely?"

Grace hesitated, torn between gratification and a sense of injury. "I don't bludgeon," she said, petulantly.

Lucy exchanged glances with Cassy again and then turned back to Grace. "You ought to wear my pearls," she stated, almost absentmindedly, and reached behind her neck for the clasp. "There! Try them!"

Grace obeyed rapturously, her face alight as she fastened the pale gems around her throat. "Oh, Lucy, may I?"

Lucy grinned. "You may if you sing 'Maman' and leave my poor Mozart alone."

"Lucy, you oughtn't." Cassy turned away from her sister's preening and looked at her friend with anxious eyes. "She's vain enough already, and she might lose them." She glimpsed the outrage in her sister's face and tried another argument. "Besides, you were going to wear them."

Lucy shrugged. "I was. They don't show to advantage, though, with all this frippery lace. I could wear a noose on top of this gown, and no one would pay any heed to it." She surveyed Grace critically. "Anyway, they look better on Grace than they do on me. Her neck's not so thick."

Cassy and Grace, diagnosing this last as a piece of

self-criticism, spoke almost in unison. "Your neck's not thick!" they exclaimed.

"It's thicker than Grace's," answered Lucy, coolly. "I don't mind it. It's probably what gives my voice more resonance than hers—not that anyone really cares about music."

The scowl was back. Cassy and Grace looked at one another; Lucy's opinion of the ton's musical acumen was familiar to them both. Cassy ventured, "You were much applauded at the Curry's musicale."

"So was the oboist—and he needed a new reed," retorted Lucy. "The hired soprano sang the most vulgar embellishments I've ever heard—and Lady Curry didn't even bother to have the harpsichord tuned. And everyone was applauded—everyone." She faced her friends challengingly. "People scraping their spoons round their ice dishes, and champing on biscuits, and groveling all over their chairs—and muttering stupid on dits when they could be listening to Mozart." She concluded, sweepingly, "It's infamous."

Cassy was silent, aware that further protestations would engender a development of this theme. Lucy studied her friend's face for a moment and then extended her hand. "Oh, never mind, Cass! I'm out of temper tonight, that's all! I hate—" She did not finish her sentence, but squeezed Cassy's fingers hard and then pulled away, resuming her place by the fire.

"Hate what?" asked the perplexed Cassy.

"She hates Uncle Ernest," answered Grace.

"Uncle Ernest?" Cassy shook her hand, entirely at sea. "But Lucy has never met Uncle Ernest."

Lucy shot a resentful look at Grace and turned to face the fire, the lion-headed footstool scraping the floor expressively. Cassy stared at her younger sister, torn between delicacy and curiosity.

"He's coming to the musicale tonight," Grace responded. "He's going to bring Lucy into fashion, and she doesn't like it."

She spoke matter-of-factly; there was nothing in her voice to further exacerbate Miss Saint-Clair's irritability. Nevertheless, Cassy looked apprehensively at the hunched figure by the fire.

"Bring Lucy into fashion?"

Lucy rose, almost knocking over the footstool in her agitation. "We overheard. That is, we began by overhearing and ended by eavesdropping."

"It wasn't eavesdropping," argued Grace. "It isn't eavesdropping if you hear your name and have to hear what people are saying about you."

Lucy ignored her. "Godmamma was telling your Aunt Edith that your uncle was in town. And she said that she'd arranged to have him come to the musicale tonight, so that he could talk to me and seem to be my—my admirer. And later he's to dance with me." Her voice was muffled, and her cheeks were scarlet. Lucy seldom blushed.

"He's going to bring her into fashion," repeated Grace. "Mamma says he was an arbiter of taste when he was young, and, oh, Cassy—" her voice quivered with laughter, "Cassy, she and Aunt Edith started prosing on about when they were young, and Aunt Edith said that all of the girls of the ton were in love with him, because he was so handsome, and then Mamma said he still was! Handsome! Just fancy, Uncle Ernest!"

"He is handsome," replied Cassy. "He just—" She hesitated, unable to put her feelings into words. "He just doesn't look *new*."

Grace giggled again. "Well, when he was new he was splendidly handsome, and Mamma says he's still a very clever man. And she says that if anyone can help Lucy—" She stopped, the picture of consternation. "Oh, Lucy, I'm sorry! I didn't mean it!"

For a moment Lucy did not answer. The two sisters looked at each other uncomfortably. Then Lucy growled, "Oh, hush, Gracie," in a tone of voice that made Cassy sigh with relief. She ventured, "It's true that Uncle is too old for you, Lucy, but there's nothing that should give you a disgust of him. His manners are very distinguished and his clothes are perfectly beautiful. He won't shame you, if that's what troubles you, and I'm sure Mamma meant—"

Lucy interrupted her. "That's not what troubles me." She bit her lip, as if she meant to say no more, but two puzzled faces interrogated her. "It's so humiliating. As if I were beyond hope."

"Beyond hope?" Cassy echoed, blankly.

"As if—" Lucy considered, and then went on. "If I were a dying man—no, if I were a man who was very ill—"

"But Lucy," Grace shook her head, "you're not a man at all."

"A woman, then," Lucy amended irritably. "If I were a woman, very ill, and I didn't know if I were very ill, or only a little ill, and I overheard someone send for a priest to give me the last rites, that—" She contracted her brows savagely, "That is how I would feel. I mean," she corrected herself, "that is how I feel now. I feel now the way I would feel then, if I were ill and I overheard . . ." Her voice trailed off. "You know what I mean," she finished.

Cassy was not at all sure that she did. She picked

up the comb and the hairbrush, ran the comb through the bristles, and looked helplessly at the hair in the comb. "I daresay Mamma only meant—"

"She didn't compel anyone to dance with you, or Lizzy, or Angelica," Lucy flashed back.

"No, but—" Cassy searched for an argument and found none. She was far too tender-hearted to remind Lucy that she was in her fourth Season, and that the three older Theale girls had found husbands in their first. She cast an imploring look at Grace, who was staring at Lucy's gown with narrowed eyes.

"Why are you wearing that dress?"

Lucy froze, half-embarrassed, half-defiant.

"You can't bear that dress," continued Grace mercilessly. "You said it leaves marks on your arms and that the color makes you look like an old cheese. Why are you wearing it tonight?"

Cassy chimed in. "Celestine did your hair, and you always say she has no taste—"

"No more she has," asserted Lucy, "and so much the better. If I am to be an antidote, I shall look like an antidote."

"Lucy—"

"I shall," declared Miss Saint-Clair, passionately, "and I won't be Lucied out of it, either. It's an abominable thing to have some odious stranger pretending to like me, and I can't and won't endure it."

"Lucy, Uncle isn't odious!"

"He may not be odious by nature," argued Lucy, "but he is odious by function. That is, he is going to be odious by function if he does what Godmamma asks. And I mean to stop him." There was a martial light in her eyes. "I will *not* be groomed and trained and trussed up in muslin and lace, and I will *not* be brought into fashion! And if your uncle dares to act as if he admires me," she concluded, "I will *blister* him with rudeness!"

The Theale girls were too shocked to protest. Lucy was moved to qualify her statement. "Subtle rudeness," she amended.

This idea seemed to appeal to Grace. "Subtle rudeness?" she repeated, in a voice that was by no means condemnatory. "How do you do that, Lucy?"

Lucy surveyed an imaginary arsenal of subtleties. "There are a good many ways. Of course, I can't do anything that would disgrace Godmamma, because however ill-chosen this course of action may be, she has been good to me. But there are certain things . . ." She waved her hands, vaguely. "Looks, for example. A haughty look, delivered in just the right way, can make a man writhe."

Grace nodded, but without much interest. She had hoped for something more exotic than a haughty look, and she could not imagine her uncle Ernest writhing at a musicale. Lucy sensed her disappointment and tried to think of a more drastic subtlety. In this pursuit she was interrupted; Mrs. Theale's footsteps were heard in the hall.

"Mamma," Cassy said, in a relieved tone of voice. "Your music is on the mantel, Grace, and here's your shawl." She reached for Lucy's hand and gave it a squeeze. "Thank you for fixing my hair."

Dinner was over. Lord Rune set down an empty wine-glass, and allowed his gaze to wander to the china clock on the mantel. With the cruel exactness of mechanical things, it informed him that this evening, which he had already classified as interminable, was, in fact, in its early stages. He looked next at Lucy, who was also consulting the clock and was, he considered, glaring at it. Lord Rune smiled at her, endeavoring to neutralize her frown. Lucy shrugged one shoulder, and deliberately turned away.

Ernest found himself wishing that he could slap her. He had known Miss Saint-Clair for three hours and seventeen minutes, and she was attaining a lofty rank in the hierarchy of persons he disliked. When Tabitha introduced her, he noted without surprise that she was unbecomingly gowned, and his aesthetic sympathies were piqued. With compassion, he examined the mangled coiffure and the over-tight dress. And then his eyes met Miss Saint-Clair's. The indignation in her gaze took him aback, and his compassion ebbed away.

Thus an acquaintance had begun unpropitiously, and three hours and seventeen minutes had done nothing to reform it. Loyal to his promise to his sister, and confident of his power to charm, Lord Rune had made periodic attempts to entice Miss Saint-Clair into the banalities of conversation. For this blameless behavior, he was snubbed—blatantly, persistently snubbed. Lord Rune was not accustomed to being snubbed when he had committed no fault, and he did not care for it. Nor did he understand that what he considered incivility was in fact a subtle hauteur, Lucy's subtlety being of a coarse-grained variety.

Lady Gratham rose, casting a benevolent smile around the table. It was time, she declared, for the ladies to leave the gentlemen, but the two sexes would mingle again and all would enjoy the refreshment of music. The ladies rose. Unwillingly, Lord Rune's eyes followed Lucy. He saw his youngest niece draw close to her, whispering, and for the first time he saw Miss Saint-

Clair smile. For a moment Ernest glimpsed his sister's "dear, good-hearted girl," and the transformation baffled him. Then Grace erupted into a fit of giggles, and the door swung shut behind them.

Two glasses of port and a few minutes free of Miss Saint-Clair's abrasive presence relaxed Ernest, and he determined to make one last effort to converse with his sister's protégée. He found her seated beside the pianoforte with his nieces. The rabbity one nudged Lucy, as if to warn her of his approach, and the younger one looked as if she wanted to giggle again.

"I gather you are going to sing for us tonight," Ernest greeted them. "Are you very fond of music, Miss Saint-Clair?"

There was a moment of silence, during which Miss Saint-Clair sought for a subtlety that would crush Lord Rune. She found none.

"Yes," she answered.

"She dotes on it," Grace informed him, simpering.

Cassy looked at her younger sister without approval. "We all like music," she said, in a colorless little voice.

"Lucy sings the best," added Grace.

Lucy bent her head over the keyboard and was mute.

It occurred to Lord Rune that perhaps Miss Saint-Clair was not so much rude as shy. He inquired, in his gentlest voice: "What are you planning to sing for us, Miss Saint-Clair?"

Lucy raised her head and frowned at him ferociously. "I shall sing 'Mi tradi quell'alma ingrata,' " she declared, and her voice carried. Around her, conversations stopped, giving her reply the character of an announcement.

"And a very pleasant beginning that will be," rallied Lady Gratham. "Everyone must find a comfortable seat, and then you must favor us, Miss Saint-Clair."

Her guests resigned themselves to this course of action, and a nervous-looking young man with a fair mustache came and sat down at the pianoforte. Miss Saint-Clair handed him her music, and he glanced over it while she stood and shed her all-encompassing scowl upon the assembly. Too disgusted to watch, Lord Rune went to stand by the window, looking out over the dark garden. The open phrases of the recitative issued from beneath the pianist's unskilled fingers, and Ernest's sense of grievance increased. She was going to sing the recitative; it was going to be long.

"... 'In quali eccessi, o Numi—' "

He spun around. For the voice was a remarkable one, with a taut brilliance that made his hair stand on end. He stared at her as if she had undergone a metamorphosis, and she continued without missing a beat.

"—'in quai misfatti orribili, tremendi—' "

Two dowagers on an acid green sofa were whispering. Lord Rune lowered a glance against them, and they shushed.

"—'e avvolto il sciagurato!' "

Sciagurato was *wretch*—as polyglot Lord Rune knew very well. Lucy articulated the words in his direction, and Lord Rune bowed.

" 'Misera Elvira' " The recitative slowed; the voice softened as Mozart's heroine grew pensive. "... 'perchè questi sospiri? e questi ambasce? ...' "

There was a pause, during which the pianist turned a page. Lord Rune caught Miss Saint-Clair's eye and held it. In that brief pause she recognized his admiration

and accepted it. Then she took a deep breath and began
the aria.

" *'Mi tradi quell'alma ingrata—'* "

Her voice rose and fell, reaching the high notes
without the slightest effort, navigating the embellishments with an almost insolent ease. The rigidity of her
posture had softened; she stood erect, but supple. Lord
Rune all but breathed with her.

At last the aria drew to a close. She sang the last
words and bowed her head. The pianist tapped out the
last notes, and a light patter of applause followed. Lord
Rune started forward. He was not quite sure what he
was going to do, but he sensed that the suddenness of
his movement had piqued the crowd's attention. The
applause hushed and then increased as he caught up
Lucy's hand and pressed it to his lips.

For a split second, he had to work to contain a
smile; like a trained actor he knew that his gesture had
captivated his audience, and like an actor he was delighted with himself. The he felt the hand within his
tremble, and he realized that Lucy, as well as the audience, was caught in his spell. She was smiling radiantly
and her dark eyes were full of tears. Lord Rune looked
into them and knew, with a sinking heart, that Miss
Saint-Clair had fallen in love with him.

3

He could not shun her. Lying in bed, with a
glass of brandy in one hand, he realized it. Exactly what
the assembled crowd had surmised from his impulsive
action he could not guess, but he knew there would be
speculation about his intentions. To leave town—his
first claustrophobic impulse—would expose Miss Saint-
Clair to ridicule and would undo what good his gesture
had done.

For it had done Lucy some good; he did not doubt
that. After the music was over, a great many people
flocked to her side, eager to ape Lord Rune's admiration. In a scornful undertone Lucy hissed to him that
half of them had heard her sing before and not cared a
rap for it. No matter; Lord Rune's recognition had lent
her performance artistic validity and a faint, intriguing
aroma of scandal. Lady Gratham's guests took pains to
flatter, and Lucy exerted herself to respond with grace.

From time to time she glanced hopefully in Lord Rune's direction, as if to see if his approbation lasted.

For a while he stayed by her side, lending her countenance, and then he went in search of his sister whom he found eating macaroons with an insouciance that galled him. He recommended that she take Lucy home, and she agreed.

Ernest reached for the decanter beside the bed and poured himself another drink. The sincerity with which Miss Saint-Clair had hoped to see him again lingered in his memory and made him uneasy. Lord Rune was not unused to feminine admiration, and as a rule accepted it ungrudgingly, but he could see no good in encouraging Miss Saint-Clair. He was old enough to know what he desired in a female companion, and the stout, gauche, and virginal Miss Saint-Clair did not embody it.

Her clothes. Ernest all but shuddered at the thought of them. Why on earth hadn't his sister bought Lucy some presentable clothes? He shoved his pillow closer to the headboard and leaned back to contemplate the problem. He had never thought much of his sister's taste, but she ought to have known better than to deck a shelflike bosom out in frills. And yellow! Ernest swore. It was true, as Tha said, that the girl had a lovely complexion, but couldn't she see that so transparent a skin was bound to reflect bright colors? Miss Saint-Clair had looked as sickly as a broad-shouldered, buxom young woman could look.

By the time dawn whitened the windows, Lord Rune had mulled over the problem of his sister's protégée so thoroughly that he was sick of it—but he had constructed a twofold plan of attack. He would continue to sponsor Miss Saint-Clair into society, and he would persuade his sister to refurbish her wardrobe. He would also—the latter plan was born of the last glass of brandy—behave in such a way as must give any romantic girl a disgust for him.

Mrs. Theale was ill at ease. There was a flutter in her household that she could not like. Nor did she like the look of her daughters: they had a sleek, bright-eyed, avid look, as if they had a secret.

They did not have a secret. Mrs. Theale was not an Argus-eyed parent; as long as her daughters seemed happy and healthy and respectable, she left them alone. Nevertheless, she was no fool. Only a fool could have failed to see that dear Lucy was smitten with poor Ernest. And only a fool could have failed to see that Cassy and Grace meant to collaborate in a campaign to win him for their friend.

Poor Lucy! Always she had been full of common sense, capable of fending off fortune-hunters and coaxing shy suitors out of alcoves. Now she had a rapt and distracted look, and Tabitha guessed that she was recalling the Gratham musicale and the moment when Lord Rune kissed her hand. Tabitha sighed. She had enjoyed having a sensible person about. However, it was Lucy's right, by reason of her age, to be silly, and Tabitha did not begrudge it. She could only hope that it would not be long before Lucy realized that Lord Rune was a fish that would not bite.

The said fish—an apt metaphor, for Lord Rune was born under Pisces—deigned to call at his sister's three days after the musicale, by which time Lucy was looking more distracted than rapt and had taken to singing "Dove sono" with too many appoggiaturas. Lord Rune, hearing her, stared up at the ceiling in surprise.

Tabitha did not notice. "Of course she has clothes," she said fretfully. "I see to it that she has the same sort of clothes my girls have."

Ernest nodded. "I thought as much. No wonder she looks so devilish."

"Ernest!"

Lord Rune leaned back in his chair, trying to avoid the afternoon sunlight that poured between the draperies. He was never at his best in his sister's house, which was decorated in the Egyptian style, with vivid colors and unyielding furniture. "You can't tell me that yellow thing became her."

"It was straw-colored, not yellow," defended Tabitha, "and it cost me forty guineas. I don't deny that it has grown a little tight—"

"It has grown very tight," interrupted Lord Rune. "Moreover, it's the worst possible color for the girl. Good Lord, woman, have you no eye?"

Mrs. Theale's sensibility was not excessive, but so hideous an accusation daunted her. "She's dark," she offered, as a plea for understanding. "Dark people often wear yellow."

"She's not dark," Lord Rune answered unforgivingly. "She's pale. Her hair is dark. Which reminds me—"

"Celestine did her hair," asserted Tabitha, eager to disclaim responsibility.

"It looked like a particularly bulbous pincushion," said Lord Rune. "I'd get rid of that woman if I were you, Tha."

Upstairs the singing stopped.

Tabitha nodded toward the ceiling. "There, do you see?" she said accusingly. "Now she'll come downstairs, and I won't have said any of the things I intended to say to you."

"What did you intend to say?"

Tabitha listened for a moment. "She'll probably change her gown," she said to no one in particular. Then she turned back to her brother with an artificial smile. "I wanted to tell you how grateful I was, of course. Mind you, the hand-kissing wasn't what I would have chosen—"

"It was a moment's fancy. I admit it." Lord Rune gave his sister a speculative glance. "Am I the cat among the pigeons?"

For the first time that day, Tabitha regarded her brother with appreciation. "Yes, that's just it," she answered. "I don't want to seem ungrateful, Ernest, but you know what girls are. I'm afraid that poor Lucy has developed a tendresse for you, and Cassy and Grace—"

"Do you mean to say that they are in love with me, too?"

"Of course not. You're their uncle. Do be serious, Ernest. Cassy and Grace have decided that you are to marry Lucy."

The expression on Lord Rune's face was so appalled that Tabitha began to laugh. "I see you don't know what girls are," she submitted, after she regained control of herself. "Girls, my dear Ernest, are very resourceful. They can make a marriage out of almost anything. And of course the hand-kissing was really very affecting. You do that sort of thing so well."

"Tabitha, you pierce me to the heart. I am weighed down with guilt and apprehension."

"I wouldn't worry so much as that," Tabitha said dubiously, not sure whether her brother spoke sincerely. "But it would be a good thing if you were a little more careful. Remember, they're like sharks. Once they've smelled blood—"

"Pray do not continue."

"It will be different when Lucy has other admirers," said Tabitha, switching tactics. "Because, Ernest, I am persuaded she will have others. Why, already Baron Baumfalk—"

"Baron Baumfalk! Good God!"

"Yes," agreed Tabitha, rather sadly. "He called after the musicale. I'm afraid the girls do not respect him as they ought."

"As they ought." Lord Rune enunciated each word separately. "Good Lord, Tabitha! He's a thousand years old and a dead bore and has egg in his beard."

"Is that what it is?" Mrs. Theale asked, looking revolted. "I thought it was some kind of snuff. Not that a man ought to have anything in his beard, but still, dry is better than wet . . . He called Friday, and the girls have been doing imitations of him ever since. Lucy's imitations are particularly unkind."

A smile crept to the corners of Lord Rune's lips. "Are they, by God?"

"Yes, they are, and you're not to encourage her, Ernest! Such behavior is far from ladylike, and really"— Tabitha said, without conviction—"I suppose she might do worse."

"No, she mightn't," contradicted Ernest. "Even the vicarage full of dead birds couldn't be worse."

The light through the curtains cast an amber shade onto Lord Rune's face, making it difficult to see him, but his tone of voice told Tabitha something she was glad to know. "Why, Ernest, I believe you are beginning to like my Lucy."

Lord Rune opened his mouth to deny it, and changed his mind. "You're right. I am."

"I knew you would," said Tabitha, who had known nothing of the kind. "Not that you ought to encourage her attachment, of course."

"On the contrary."

The faint smile with which these words were uttered did not appear to ease his sister's apprehensions. "You're not going to reject her in public, are you, Ernest? Because—"

Lord Rune's smile reversed itself. "Do you consider me a boor, Tabitha? No, I'm not going to reject her in public. Good Lord, I thought we had agreed that I was to be her benefactor."

Tabitha endeavored to look meek and succeeded tolerably well. "I'm sorry, Ernest," she apologized. "It's such a difficult thing to repel a young girl, especially if you have scruples about hurting her feelings. I can think of no way—"

Ernest, considerably mollified, raised his hand with the air of a magician. "I can."

"Why, Ernest, what?"

Ernest grinned at her, changing unexpectedly into a young man again. "Ill-health."

"But, Ernest—"

The young man disappeared, leaving in his place a middle-aged man who was on the verge of losing his temper. "Are you going to inform me that there is nothing wrong with me but late nights and too much wine? Because I warn you, Tha, I am in no mood to listen to that little homily just this minute."

Tabitha considered half a dozen replies, some conciliatory and some caustic, and at last suggested that perhaps Lord Rune would like some tea. Lord Rune acknowledged this suggestion with a faint inclination of the head. Tabitha rang the bell, and Ernest moved restlessly over to the settee. He had always maintained that the chairs, with their carved lotus leaves and gilded sphinxes, had a harmful effect on his spine and his spirits. "Good God, Tabitha, how long are you going to live with this damned Egyptian rubbish? It makes me peevish every time I call."

Tabitha had discussed her taste in furniture with her brother before and was not about to discuss it again. "Your plan," she reminded him. "Oh, Dirge"—to a Roman-nosed parlor-maid—"Lord Rune and I will have tea. And please send up enough for the girls, who I expect will want to join us."

Dirge nodded disapprovingly and swept out.

"You were saying," reminded Tabitha, "something about ill-health."

"Yes." Lord Rune stretched out on the settee, placing his heels on the angular arm-rests. "Well. It is well known that women admire strong and sinewy men, men who exult in vigorous labor and who daily bathe their limbs in wholesome sweat. Now I"—he cast a mischievous look at his sister—"am not like that."

"No," agreed his sister, with a good deal of feeling.

Perhaps Lord Rune did not care for so swift an agreement, but he went on. "I am a poor stick," he said, in failing tones. "I have head-aches, and my stomach is always in a state of unrest. I require frequent bleedings, and weekly purgings—"

"Ernest!" Tabitha struggled between the need to reprove him, and the desire to laugh. "You can *not* tell a young girl about your purgings! Even Lucy, who is not as delicate as my girls—which is hardly surprising, what with the vultures and the tracts—"

The door opened, and Lord Rune's nieces tripped in, followed by their mamma's protégée.

"Oh," cried Grace, with a very creditable affectation of surprise, "Uncle Ernest is here! How charming!"

The two Theale girls advanced and deposited identical chaste pecks upon Lord Rune's cheeks. Miss Saint-Clair, who wore a freshly pressed gown and an expression of acute self-consciousness, sat down on the edge of the chair nearest the door.

"Are you quite well, Uncle?" Cassy asked anxiously, running her blue eyes over Lord Rune's supine form.

Ernest pulled himself up into a sitting position. "I am tolerably well," he responded, without enthusiasm.

"Alas," said Tabitha, "your uncle is seldom quite well, Cassandra."

Cassy stared at her mother with mild surprise. She did not recall ever having heard her mother say *alas* before. "Oh, dear," she murmured. "I am very sorry."

"He seemed quite well at the Gratham's musicale," inserted Grace, daringly. "He was well enough to admire Lucy's singing."

Lord Rune sought for a deflating remark, thought of one, and caught Miss Saint-Clair's eye. Her expression of agonized embarrassment was so heartfelt that he could not utter it. "I am sure that everyone must admire Miss Saint-Clair's singing," he said formally, and then felt guilty as the girl's face lit up.

Grace, pleased with herself at having extracted a compliment from him, leaned forward and smiled. "Have you come to hear her sing today?" she asked, nodding encouragingly in order to prompt his response.

Lord Rune looked away from Lucy's face. "No,

not today," he demurred, in languid tones. "I have the head-ache."

Grace frowned at this unsporting rejoinder, and then brightened as Dirge entered with the tea-tray. A chest like a small sarcophagus was drawn into the center of the room, and the girls drew up their chairs around it. Ernest, seeing the relish with which Miss Saint-Clair consumed buttered toast, was reassured. Either she was not so besotted as he had feared or young girls in the throes of love did not lose their appetites.

She had evidently dressed just prior to coming downstairs, for her gown was suspiciously unrumpled and her hair, knotted at the back of her head, was very neat. The simple coiffure suited her much better than Celestine's handiwork had done, and the rose-pink print became her rather nicely. Ernest could almost suspect her of having a modicum of taste. He tried to imagine what she would look like in a plain bodice, one without ribbons and frills, and then choked. In his disinterested desire to improve Miss Saint-Clair's turn-out, he had stared much too long at her bosom, and she was aware of this and mortified.

"Uncle," Cassy said urgently, holding a tray of biscuits up to his cravat.

Lord Rune remembered his manners, and his role, and closed his eyes faintly. "Not biscuits," he said, "not at this hour."

"Your uncle's digestion is not good," Tabitha informed her daughters. She remembered the many times she had spoken disrespectfully of her brother's digestion and improvised, "He has not been well since he returned from Budapest. Budapest," she continued, warming to her theme, "is very bad for the digestion.

The climate is not salubrious, and the food is indigestible."

"What a horrid place it must be," remarked Grace, without immoderate sympathy. "I am sure you are much happier in London, aren't you, Uncle?"

"Indeed," agreed Lord Rune, taking a sip of tea.

"It must be very disagreeable to be ill in a foreign country," submitted the tender-hearted Cassy. "One would feel so very lonely."

Grace shot an approving smile at her sister. "In London," she told her uncle firmly, "you will not be lonely."

Ernest began to think that his sister's reference to sharks was akin to euphemism.

"Only think," continued Grace, "here in London you have relations to console you and give you tea. You must come to visit us, and Lucy will sing for you, and soon you will be feeling just the thing. Isn't it queer, Cassy?" she opened her round eyes very wide. "Before this week, Uncle Ernest scarcely knew us, and we scarcely knew him. I doubt he could even have told us apart. Now, however—"

Lord Rune did not wait to hear his niece's prediction of a new state of affairs. "I could tell you apart," he protested. "Cassy is the one—"

Tabitha shifted in her chair, and Lord Rune grinned at her, sensing her discomfiture. "Cassy is the one with hair like moonlight," he said, "and Grace is the one with hair like sunlight."

The sisters surveyed each other, much struck with this description. Cassy blushed, her pink nose making her look more rabbity than ever.

"How pretty!" approved Grace. "How would you describe Lucy's hair, Uncle?"

Once again Ernest's attention was focused on Miss Saint-Clair, who had left off eating buttered toast and begun on the biscuits. His eyes met hers, and he mutely begged her pardon.

"Black as a crow's wing?" he hazarded. "Black as soot? I'm afraid I have overtaxed myself, and Miss Saint-Clair must be content with commonplaces." He sighed deeply, and tried to look as old and tired as possible. "I am too old for gallantry."

His nieces would not permit this. Miss Saint-Clair, whom he had feared to wound, did not look wounded at all. She leaned forward and selected another biscuit, which she nibbled in an abstracted manner.

"I am sure that forty is not old," Cassy was saying persuasively, and Lord Rune forgot himself and snapped.

"I am thirty-five."

Cassy turned crimson, Grace giggled rather nervously, and Lucy selected another biscuit. Lord Rune felt a touch of remorse; he had snapped at Cassy, the shy one in the family. "I daresay I look much older," he added, gently. "I am so often ill, you see, and I don't sleep well." He turned to Miss Saint-Clair, to see how she was receiving this information, which was, after all, being offered for her benefit.

She did not look repelled. Nor did she look sympathetic. There was a tiny line between her brows, as if something puzzled her.

"I have a great susceptibility to bilious attacks." He spoke the words directly to her, but her expression did not change. "Last night, for example, I found myself in considerable distress." Cassy and Grace looked a little disgusted but Miss Saint-Clair continued to chew. "I am often compelled to awaken my valet and have him prepare me a stomach draught. And sometimes that does not help. Even after drinking it, I continue to feel queasy."

"Your uncle's stomach has always been delicate," said Tabitha.

Lucy poured herself another cup of tea and added two lumps of sugar to it. "I wonder if the oysters at the Grathams were quite fresh," she remarked. She took a sip of tea, and put down the cup. "I rather fancied they had a peculiar taste."

Something in her voice compelled Lord Rune to look at her again. The perplexed look that he had glimpsed in her eyes was gone and so was her air of self-consciousness. She bore his regard with composure.

"Oysters are very trying," announced Lord Rune, trying to sound pettish and succeeding.

"Really, you should be more careful," Miss Saint-Clair reproved him. "One of Papa's parishioners had oyster stew one summer day, and it made him turn quite yellow. And"—she widened her eyes impressively—"he was dead as mutton within the month."

The placidity with which this anecdote was uttered did nothing to appease Mrs. Theale. *"Lucy,"* she said repressively.

Lucy lowered her eyelids again, demurely, but without shame. "I beg your pardon, Godmamma, if my conversation is coarse, but it really will not do for Lord Rune to go on eating oysters that he suspects are not fresh. I am persuaded that you would not wish me to be over nice when damage to your brother's health might be the result."

Tabitha did not answer. Lord Rune, fascinated by the turn the conversation was taking, tried another tack. "I am also susceptible to a putrid sore throat," he announced, with the faint air of pride that invalids often display. "You, with your fine singing-voice, would naturally fear a putrid sore throat."

Lucy brushed her fingertips together in order to detach any biscuit crumbs that might cling to her hands. "Not fear, exactly," she answered meditatively, "because I am never ill, but I will own that a putrid sore throat sounds very disagreeable." She looked up and smiled at him, the radiant smile that she had given him at the musicale. "Do you have sensitive skin, as well? My grandmamma was prone to boils."

"Boils?" echoed Ernest.

"Her skin was wont"—Lucy took the last biscuit, broke it in two, and conferred half upon him—"to erupt. She eventually found that a paste of comfrey and castor oil proved effective where calomel had not. I could easily find out the recipe, if you like."

Her dark eyes were brimming with laughter, and Ernest realized, with a shock of glee, that she was laughing at him. He eyed the corners of her mouth, and saw them trembling, and felt a corresponding quiver about his own. "Thank you, no," he declined, just managing to keep his countenance. "I am not at all susceptible to boils."

"Warts, I believe, are very trying," Lucy said tremulously.

"I believe they are," said Ernest. "But I do not suffer from warts."

"I am so glad," said Miss Saint-Clair, simply.

A sound not unlike a cough forced itself out of Lord Rune, and his shoulders began to shake. A giggle from Lucy seemed to settle the matter, and Tabitha blinked with surprise as her brother and her god-daughter gave way to peals and peals of laughter. Cassy and

Grace turned to their Mamma, seeking enlightenment, and Tabitha could not give it; she had no idea what had occasioned such an outburst. "Ernest," she said help-lessly, and frowned at him even as his mirth subsided. "Ernest," she repeated. Why, after vowing that he would not flirt with Miss Saint-Clair, was he smiling at her with such treacherous delight? Tabitha looked at Lucy's happy face and felt tempted to box her brother's ears. *"Lucy,"* she snapped, and Lucy's smile wavered and disappeared.

"Have I not told you that a lady does not guffaw in that unseemly manner?"

Confused, Lucy shook her head and then nodded.

"Especially," went on Tabitha, all the more se-verely because she disliked having to rebuke her god-daughter so publicly, "when the rest of the company has no idea what is so amusing."

Grace opened her mouth to ask what was so amus-ing, thought better of it, and was silent.

"As for you, Ernest," Tabitha said crisply, "I think we have heard quite enough about your aches and ail-ments, and I beg you will talk of something else."

There was a highly uncomfortable silence. Lord Rune looked furious, Lucy was almost in tears, and Mrs. Theale, having finished her admonitions, could think of nothing to say. At last Cassy cleared her throat and spoke timidly.

"Do you still collect porcelain, Uncle?"

"Yes," answered Lord Rune stiffly, and then soft-ened at the sight of his niece's face. "You must come over and see my collection some afternoon. I have one or two new pieces that are very fine."

"Uncle Ernest has some beautiful china-ware," Cassy told Lucy. "Some of it is very old."

"Oh," said Lucy, meekly.

There was another silence.

Lord Rune rose. "I believe I have outworn my welcome," he declared. He bowed, managing to communicate perfect courtesy and utter contempt in one easy movement.

"Ernest—" began Tabitha.

"Uncle—" began Grace.

"Please—" whispered Cassy.

Lord Rune bowed again, this time to his nieces.

"I am sure you are always welcome here," Cassy faltered.

"Yes," agreed Grace, "and you are so seldom in London. It would be a pity if you didn't come again."

They looked at him pleadingly; two blue-eyed, vulnerable, dainty little sharks.

"I will surely come again," Lord Rune told them. "If I am not too ill." He spoke the last words over his shoulder and left the room without looking back.

4

"*He will* never *come again,*" wailed Lucy, as she pulled hairpins and artificial pansies out of her hair.

A week had passed—a week that had included two concerts, a musicale, and an evening at Almack's. Lord Rune had attended none of these gatherings. Nor had he called. The three young ladies of the Theale residence pondered this fact as the lady of the house dozed across the hall. Gowns and shawls, fans and flowers were discarded as the girls sprawled across Cassy's bed and attacked the problem.

"I'm sure he will," Cassy said helplessly.

"He has a disgust of me because I laughed at his illnesses." Lucy had spent the week brooding over Lord Rune's last visit and had grown more pessimistic with each day that passed. "And because I look so repulsive."

"You don't, Lucy." Only that morning Grace had

compared Lucy's round arms with her own slender ones and marveled at the difference in size, but she spoke resolutely, determined to lay stress on her friend's best features. "You've got the longest eyelashes and the smallest feet of any of us—oh, don't cry! It was Mamma who angered him, not you! Cassy, tell her it was Mamma."

Cassy put her arms around her friend, which made her wail more loudly than ever. "It was, Lucy. Mamma was quite rude to him, and I don't wonder he was miffed. But he said he would come again, and I'm sure he will."

Lucy raised a tearful face from Cassy's shoulder. "But it was Godmamma who first made him meet me," she argued. "Why would she send him away? And how could she, if he didn't want to go?"

This was unanswerable. The two sisters regarded each other with consternation over Lucy's lachrymose form. Grace was the first to rally. "Well, but what do you care, Lucy?" she demanded, in bracing tones. "At Thursday's musicale Lady Therrington said you had the finest soprano voice in London. And you stood up three times at Almack's, and Baron Baumfalk—"

A louder wail drowned out this last observation, and Lucy choked, between laughter and tears. Cassy shook her head. "I don't think you ought to have mentioned Baron Baumfalk," she told her sister and was belied by the snort of laughter from her afflicted friend.

"That old pig," Lucy said elegantly. "He had something horrid dribbled down his coat tonight, and he kept prosing on about Cherubini. Cherubini!" she repeated, scathingly, and Cassy cautioned, "Shhh!"

"Well, but, a suitor is a suitor," insisted Grace, in a whisper. "And he's not so very much older than Uncle

Ernest. He just looks older because he's so fat and bald—" But the combination of laughter and scorn that had revived Lucy dissolved at this logic, and she began to cry again.

"I was so sure he would come tonight!" Lucy gave a last yank at her hair, and the dark locks fell unevenly around her red face, giving her the look of a mad-woman. "I spent the last of my money from home on new slippers and that ivory fan—" She rubbed her eyes with the back of her wrist and sniffed. "I suppose it was only my singing he liked, after all," she concluded. "But no one else ever—" She did not finish her sentence, but her eyes filled with tears and she gazed into space.

"We could go and visit him," Cassy suggested hesi-tantly.

Grace stopped playing with the ribbons on her night-cap and reached over to grab her sister's wrist. "We could!" she exclaimed. "Lucy, stop crying and lis-ten. We could go and call on him!"

Lucy blinked at her.

"We could," Grace repeated. "You heard him say that we should come and look at his porcelain."

"He said Cassy—" Lucy began.

"He said *you*," Grace corrected. "And *you* could mean all of us. In fact, I think I saw him look over in your direction when he said it. Don't you, Cass?"

Lucy could not help smiling at this bit of improvi-sation. "He did not," she contradicted, picking up a pillow and hugging it to her breast.

"He may have done," Cassy said, fair-mindedly. "But Grace is right. I suppose we could visit him. After all, there can be nothing improper in visiting our uncle."

"In fact, it's very dutiful of us." Grace lay back against the pillows, well pleased by her metamorphosis into an affectionate niece. "I'd as soon look at Uncle Ernest's china as visit Aunt Edith any day."

"But," Lucy faltered, "Godmamma—"

"Mmmn," said Grace, profoundly.

There was silence as the three gave their attention to this problem. Cassy went to the chest of drawers and took out a little box of sweets. With some difficulty, she peeled three toffees off the bottom of the box and passed them round. After a moment or two of meditative sucking, Grace produced a solution.

"We needn't tell Mamma," she decided. "We can go to the library—Mamma seldom accompanies us to the library—and call on Uncle on the way home."

"But he's not on the way home," Lucy objected. "He's in the other direction. And won't your Mamma send Twitterboots?"—referring to the footman.

"What if she does?" Grace asked. "Twitterboots won't fuss."

"We'll have to tell Mamma afterwards," Cassy reminded her, "because Twitterboots will."

"She might be angry," Lucy pointed out. "Ever since Lord Rune called, she's been saying how tiresome he is."

Grace flopped over and stretched across the bed, snatching up the box of sweets. "These are getting dreadfully old," she complained. "We have to get some more." She popped another in her mouth and chewed thoughtfully. "I don't think she'll be very angry," she said, around the toffee. "After all, we're only visiting our uncle."

Thus it was that Lord Rune, in the process of recovering from last night's dissipations, was informed that the

Misses Theale and Miss Saint-Clair had called to see him.

"Sharks," muttered Ernest.

"I beg your pardon, sir?"

"Never mind," Ernest sighed. "Send Pudder to me. I am going to get up."

Flitworm drew back the bed-clothes with an air of profound respect. "Mr. Pettibone thought as how you might not like to be disturbed," he said breathlessly, "but I remembered, sir, how upset you were when your sister called and Mr. Pettibone did not treat her with sufficient ceremony. I felt sure, sir, that you would want to see the young ladies. I am," Flitworm said apologetically, "myself a family man, sir. In theory," he added hastily. "In theory only. My duties have not allowed me time to seek conjugal felicity, but I have the highest regard—"

"Pudder," repeated Lord Rune. "I want to see Pudder."

Flitworm tiptoed over to the window and patted the closed shutters, as if to reward them for shading his master's eyes. "Yes, sir," he approved. "A very fine valet, your Mr. Pudder. It is a privilege to work with such a man. If you will excuse me, sir, I will just run along and try to find him."

"An excellent idea."

"Thank you, sir. I am not quite certain where he is, since you usually rise somewhat later in the day, but I am sure that he is doing his duty. Not like some, sir, if you take my meaning. There are some who take advantage of—of a lack of supervision, if I may put it so boldly—in order to pursue their own pleasures. I would not for the world trouble you with details—"

"Good," said Ernest. "Do not."

"No, indeed, sir. Now, if you don't mind, sir, I will just go and fetch Pudder, and we will have you ready to receive visitors in a trice. There is"—Flitworm clasped his hands, and looked down at the Persian carpet with abject humility—"there is just one thing I would venture to suggest, if I might be so bold—"

"You may be bold if you are brief."

"Thank you, sir." Flitworm took a step closer to his master and then stepped back again. When he spoke again, it was in a whisper. "Cook," he hissed, "does not seem to be in just now. I could"—he raised his eyes heavenward—"I *could* try to get the young ladies some tea. It is not my place, precisely, to help with the kitchen-work, but I have never been a high stickler. There is such a thing as an emergency. There is also a second possibility, which I hesitate to bring to your attention, sir, but that might serve."

Lord Rune did not respond. He was rubbing the back of his neck, and his eyes were tightly shut.

"It is this," continued Flitworm, in a nervous whisper. "The young ladies, sir, mentioned that they wished to see your porcelain collection. They said this to me," he explained, evidently fearing that his master would accuse him of eavesdropping, "and I thought, perhaps, that I might show them into the porcelain room so that they could look at the china while you dress."

Lord Rune stopped rubbing his neck and regarded his footman with surprise. "That's a damned good notion," he said. "It'll cut down on the time I have to spend with them, and it'll remove you from my bedroom."

Flitworm bowed, deeply moved by this expression of his master's esteem. "Thank you, sir," he said, "you are very good, sir. I am very happy to serve you in any way I can. There are some masters, sir, who would not thank me for my initiative, but you—"

"Flitworm," Lord Rune reproved him, "you are keeping the young ladies waiting."

A look of horror passed over the footman's face. "Yes, sir," he breathed. "I will send Pudder right away, sir."

With solemn dispatch, he tiptoed out of the room.

For three-quarters of an hour, the Misses Theale and Miss Saint-Clair were left alone in the porcelain room.

For Cassy, who had just borrowed *The Mysteries of Udolpho,* it was very tolerable. For Grace, who was not bookish and who glanced over the porcelain in five minutes, it was tedious beyond bearing. She flung herself down on a Grecian chair and yawned.

Lucy did not share her ennui. To examine the rooms where Lord Rune lived, to look at the objects he loved and admired, could not but give her pleasure. She explored the glass cases lingeringly, dreamily, savoring the curved and shining surfaces as if they were snippets of music. There were Venetian goblets, decorated with fine lacework, and glass from ancient Rome, catching the light with an almost sinister sheen. There was porcelain from Sèvres and Capodimonte, an oxblood vase as tall as an umbrella, and a Greek amphora. Lucy smiled at a capering Arlecchino and frowned at a medieval platter depicting the Last Supper. Then she proceeded to the next glass case.

For some time she stood and gazed into it. The bowl inside was not large, it was not even entirely symmetrical. It was a little smaller than a saucer, mildly curved and thin. In color it was a muted grey-green, the color of the sea in bad weather. In the center of the bowl was a line-drawing of a fish.

Lucy stared at it. She could not define what she liked about it, but she felt, beyond doubt, that it was the most perfect thing in the room. She wanted, very much, to touch it. Without thinking, her fingers brushed the latch of the case, opened it, and took out the bowl. It was very light, and she cupped her hands around it tenderly. So intent was she on the wonder in her hands that Lord Rune entered the room without attracting her attention.

"Good God," ejaculated Lord Rune, "don't drop it!"

Lucy spun around, startled. Her grasp on the bowl neither tightened nor relaxed. "I'm sorry, I'll put it back in the case," she said.

She suited the action to the word, and turned back to Lord Rune. She was surprised how little shame or fear she felt. If Lord Rune had greeted her gallantly she would have been overcome with shyness, for he had grown more desirable with every day of his absence. As it was, he had begun by being rude and she hadn't deserved it. He was in the wrong. The thought gave her a peculiar sense of confidence.

Lord Rune ran his fingers through his hair, aware that two pair of blue eyes were regarding him reproachfully. "I beg your pardon, Miss Saint-Clair," he said at last. "I don't usually greet my guests by shouting at them."

"It doesn't matter," replied Lucy, tranquilly. "I don't blame you for wanting to protect your things. That bowl is very beautiful."

Lord Rune looked at her quizzically. "Do you think so?"

"Yes," answered Lucy. "I think it's the best thing in the room."

She spoke so positively that Lord Rune was intrigued. "So do I," he answered, It took him a moment or two to remember his duties as a host. Then he turned to his nieces. "This is an unexpected pleasure," he said gravely and bowed.

The faint irony in his voice was lost upon them. They beamed at him, enchanted by the circumstance that had inspired their friend to praise his favorite bit of china. Grace rose from her chair to contemplate the remarkable bowl.

"It's eleven hundred years old," Lord Rune told them. "And, as you can see, not made on a wheel. It's Tang Dynasty. Chinese," he added, seeing that this last meant nothing to them.

"It's pretty," said Grace, uncertainly.

Lord Rune looked down at her and laughed. "Hypocrite," he mocked her. "You don't think it's pretty at all."

Grace grew pink under his scrutiny and lowered her eyelashes, feeling her uncle's charm for the first time. "It's so muddy-looking," she protested demurely. "It doesn't even look clean."

"It is perfectly clean." Lord Rune assured her. "In fact, I always wish I could taste it. It looks salty to me, as if it would please the tongue." He looked sideways at Lucy, and asked, gravely: "Am I shocking you, Miss Saint-Clair?"

"No," answered Lucy. "Tongues are quite unexceptionable."

"I like that shepherdess," Cassy volunteered diffi-

dently. "I remember when I was little I always wanted
to play with it, and you wouldn't let me."

Lord Rune opened the door of the case, and placed
the figure into her nervous hands. "You are a true
Briton," he told her. "This was made in England, in
Chelsea, about forty years before you were born. If you
like, you may play with it now."

Cassy admired it as quickly and as thoroughly as
she could and passed it on to her sister.

With some amusement, Lord Rune realized that he
was enjoying himself. It had been some time since he
shared his collection with anyone, or, indeed, examined
it himself. He guided the three around the room, answering questions that pleased him none the less for
their naïveté, and inquiring after the girls' preferences so
doggedly that they gave up trying to please him and told
him what they thought. Even Grace, who had yawned
over all porcelain an hour earlier, developed several in-
cendiary opinions of her own, and Cassy delighted her
uncle by telling him that the bare-breasted Venus (after
a painting by Boucher) was really very graceful, although, of course, improper.

As for Miss Saint-Clair, nothing could have ex-
ceeded her willingness to express herself. Her responses
were immediate and her accounts of them were, to say
the least, dogmatic. If Mrs. Theale had seen her god-
child as she maligned the medieval platter, eyes spar-
kling, eye-brows threatening, she would have been
horrified. Lord Rune was not horrified at all. However
delicate his digestive system was, his sensibilities were
elastic; he could tolerate, and even enjoy, feminine
vigor. It amused him to realize that Miss Saint-Clair,
who had atrocious taste in clothes, had remarkable taste

in porcelain. By which he meant taste that corresponded with his own.

When all the glass cases had been thoroughly explored, Flitworm appeared and apologized profusely for intruding. In a low voice, as if he were speaking of something obscene, he informed his master that Cook was back and that there would be tea if Lord Rune desired it. Lord Rune, reading hunger in three pairs of eyes, said that he did desire it and invited his company to stay. Once out of the porcelain room, the three young ladies underwent a change. They became conventional; they uttered banalities about the Season, the weather, and Lord Rune's health. Miss Saint-Clair sat on the edge of a chair and was tongue-tied.

If the time in the porcelain room had passed quickly, the hour of tea-time passed very slowly indeed. Lord Rune was glad when his company went away.

5

The Theale sisters were victorious. They had bearded their uncle in his lair and emerged full of tea and crumpets. They had faced their Mamma, prepared to brave her displeasure, and found her docile. Yes, Twitterboots had said that they called on dear Ernest. Had they enjoyed themselves? How very kind their uncle was! She hoped they had remembered their manners.

So stunned were Cassy and Grace by this show of affability that they could hardly stammer out an affirmative answer. Nor were they alert enought to parry a suggestion that Aunt Edith should be the next relation to enjoy their company. Before they were fully aware of it, they had agreed to visit her the very next day. Mrs. Theale, smiling at her daughters indulgently, was well pleased. She had wondered how to reconcile herself with her brother; she had begun to fear that an apology would be necessary. She turned her smile on Lucy, whose eyes were dark with suspicion, and remarked that perhaps Lucy would like to visit Aunt Edith too.

Lucy agreed, aware of the love that misery is said to bear for companionship, and the next day was spent making the penitential call. Aunt Edith sat in a chilly room and served tepid tea, reciting a litany of slights received and virtue unrewarded. Her servants were slothful; her friends neglected her. Her maid persisted in dressing her hair in a style that did not become her. The new rector of St. Andrew's church had made pastoral calls on her friends, but had omitted to visit her. She had few visitors, in fact, and she was very lonely. It was certainly a change to see her nieces! They must come and see her again, very soon. Perhaps they could come every week?

With unwonted cunning, the Theale girls evaded this last question and sidled out of their aunt's parlor, sick with guilt but determined to escape. A drive home past the shop windows, and a half-hour of uncontrolled giggling did much to revive their spirits, and when they arrived home they found a letter from their uncle.

It was an invitation to ride with him in Hyde Park the following morning. He would meet them at ten o'clock and would supply them with mounts, as Mrs. Theale did not keep saddle horses in London. Afterward, he would bring them home and hear Miss Saint-Clair sing again, if she would be so kind.

The response to these proposals was ecstatic. The three girls charged upstairs to try on their riding habits. Lucy, who did not own a habit, hoped to squeeze into one belonging to Cassy or Grace. Mrs. Theale heard wails of despair issuing from her daughter's bedroom and mounted the steps with a consequential air. She informed three half-dressed damsels that she had an old habit that could be altered to fit Lucy and was rewarded with smiles and hugs and little shrieks of rapture.

The next morning dawned fair. Tabitha, surveying her daughters and god-daughter, was proud of them. The severe lines of the riding habits emphasized her daughters' slender waists, and their faces were eager and merry. Even Lucy, she noticed with surprise, was looking rather handsome. The somber blue of the riding habit flattered her generous curves, and her hat was set at a dashing, if improbable, angle.

She was, unbeknownst to her aunt, feeling rather scared. Neither she nor Grace were horse-women; at home she rode a donkey, and the length of her rides were determined entirely by the animal's caprice. She had often set out mounted and returned on foot, and she hoped that Lord Rune would not overestimate her equestrian skills. Mrs. Theale could have reassured her on this point; Ernest never overestimated anyone's skill at riding, except his own. He met them at Hyde Park astride a huge liver chestnut, which was prancing and blowing in a way that made Lucy distinctly nervous.

Cassy reached out and stroked the brute fearlessly. "How handsome he is!" she observed. "What is his name?"

"Flambeau," Lord Rune answered her. He nodded toward the groom, who stood with three horses in hand. "The grey is Cygnet; she's yours. The little bay is for Grace; his name is Mercury. The tall black—Dragonfly"—he pointed briefly with his whip—"is for Miss Saint-Clair."

He had meant to tease Lucy about Dragonfly, who was fully sixteen hands tall, but the chestnut took the movement of the whip very hard, and Lord Rune's attention was diverted. It was left to Grotwhistle, Lord

Rune's groom, to mount the girls, and it fell to him to grin at Lucy and remark, "No fear, young lady! He's an actor, that Dragonfly, but there's no harm in him!"

Lucy devoutly hoped that this was so. She felt as if she were perched on the balcony of a third-story window rather than on a horse, and the movement of the horse made her think that the balcony might be preferable. She took up the reins, and with them, surreptitiously, a lock of Dragonfly's black mane. Dragonfly tossed his shapely head and moved forward restlessly. Lucy raised her chin and arched her back, trying to look competent.

Lord Rune drew up beside her. "Stirrups adjusted?" he asked.

Lucy nodded uncertainly. Grotwhistle had adjusted her stirrup; he would probably know the correct length better than she would. "She's a beautiful mare," she acknowledged, with what she hoped was an appreciative smile.

Lord Rune returned her smile, but with irony. "Gelding, Miss Saint-Clair," he corrected, gently. "She is a beautiful gelding."

"Oh." Lucy looked down at the silky black hair between her gloves and felt ill-used; how was she to know? One couldn't, if one was a lady, bend over and stare between a horse's hind legs. The tension in her face was not lost upon Lord Rune. "It always surprises me how people assume that a mare is a lady's mount," he said. "I myself have always found mares temperamental."

Lucy looked up, encouraged. "Have you? At home, my"—she hesitated—"donkey is a mare, and she's very difficult. In fact," she confided, "she usually tosses me."

"Donkeys are very clever, I believe."

"Daffodil is," Lucy agreed, with strong feeling. "She's sweet, when you're not riding her, but when you are, she waits until you're daydreaming and then she shies. She doesn't have to have anything to shy *at*," she explained bitterly, "she's not particular in the least. She just shies, and that's the end of me, because"—Lucy looked at him imploringly, begging him to understand —"I have no seat."

"I see."

Lucy's eyes narrowed, trying to discover if this was a statement of understanding or a less than flattering comment upon her present posture. She was not fated to find out; Grace, who had made Grotwhistle adjust her stirrup three times and finally reverted to her original choice, drew up beside them. Lord Rune looked around for his other niece, who was walking Cygnet back and forth. "Shall we be off?" he asked, giving Cassy an approving glance.

"Yes," Grace assented, "and let's trot!"

"Let's not," mumbled Lucy, but Grace had already moved ahead of her, and Dragonfly was quickening his stride hopefully. Lucy tightened the reins and gave him a polite, unpressing nudge with her heel. He broke into a trot, with a toss of his head that made her stomach lurch.

Lucy straightened her back and took a hold on her courage. The trot was not too bad. Dragonfly's stride was very long, and smooth; it was a good deal easier to maintain her seat than it was aboard the treacherous Daffodil. For the first time since she beheld Lord Rune that day she became aware of her surroundings. The air was very fresh, and the sky was clear. Around her everything had a vivid and polished look, as if the scene had been painted in bright enamels. The sunlight brushed the horses' flanks, the moist ground, the new green leaves. Everything was in motion, and everything looked smaller than usual, as if she lived in an elegant and miniature world.

It occurred to her to wonder if Dragonfly would stop if she asked him to, and she tugged at the reins surreptitiously. Dragonfly halted at once, his magnificent neck arching showily.

"You darling," Lucy murmered and nudged him into a walk again. She was beginning to enjoy herself. She raised her head and pressed her elbows close to her sides, determined to aid Dragonfly in his pretensions.

Lord Rune, who had been watching Grace bounce up and down on Mercury, chose that moment to look at her and was pleased. He had thought she would show to advantage in the saddle. He drew up beside her, aware that the black horse and the chestnut together were a gorgeous sight. "Feeling better, Miss Saint-Clair?"

Lucy nodded decidedly. "Oh, yes! He's lovely! Do you know, I wasn't quite comfortable just at first, but now I feel splendid."

"You look splendid."

"Thank you," Lucy replied, so dubiously that Ernest's grin broadened.

"You do, you know. For one thing, Dragonfly is showing you off. He's full of humbug; a four-year-old child could ride him, but he capers like a regular fire-eater and makes you look as bold as Boadicea."

"Oh," said Lucy, crestfallen. She had not believed his compliment but she did not like it being transferred to her horse.

Lord Rune seemed to understand. "For another thing, though you haven't any seat, you do have a straight back and quiet hands and you hold your elbows in. Look at Grace." Lord Rune jerked his head to the side, where Grace and Cassy were trotting along. Cassy sat her horse with composure, her figure erect and almost still. Grace flopped forward over the horse's neck, her spine curved, her arms akimbo. She seemed to be enjoying herself a good deal.

Lucy was not to be betrayed into disloyalty. "Cassy rides very well," was her only answer. "She loves all animals. Sometimes she lets the mice out of the mousetraps, although Godmamma mustn't know."

She did not watch Lord Rune's face as he digested this information, for Dragonfly suddenly snorted, his ears pricked forward. Lucy had let go of the mane, but she took hold of it again.

Ernest spoke soothingly. "Humbug, Miss Saint-Clair, humbug."

"Do you think so? Daffodil—"

"But Dragonfly is not Daffodil. He's pretending that dead branch is a crocodile, but he doesn't believe it. Just tell him to stop pretending, and he'll settle down and do as you ask."

Lucy giggled. "Dragonfly," she said, authoritatively, "that is not a crocodile. Walk on."

Dragonfly obeyed, walking on with just a slight suggestion of a prance. Lucy relaxed, enjoying the buoyancy of his movements. Ahead of her two ladies on sorrel mares walked sedately. Neither horse had the good looks or the presence of Dragonfly.

Grace turned round and trotted back to them, her eyes aglow. "I cantered!" she cried, breathlessly. "Did you see me? I couldn't remember just how to tell him to canter, but I clucked to him and he did! And Lucy, it's ever so much easier than trotting!"

"Is it?" asked Lucy. Daffodil often used a canter as a prelude to a peculiar, twisting kind of shy.

"Yes, and you must canter too," Grace declared. "Here comes Cassy; we can all canter. We'll be intrepid. Cassy, Lucy wants to canter."

Cassy inspected her younger sister critically. "Shorten your rein, Gracie, it's hanging in a loop on one side." She turned to her uncle. "Such fine horses, Uncle Ernest! We haven't had so pleasant an outing in some time."

"I am delighted to hear it." He cast a teasing glance at Lucy. "But I must not keep you from your canter. Run along and I will watch."

He saw Lucy set her chin, her eyebrows reminding him of the *David* of Michelangelo. Then Flambeau realized that three of his stable-mates were going to canter and that he was not, and Lord Rune was obliged to convince his horse that so unjust a circumstance could endure.

When he next looked up he saw that the three girls were cantering together, Lucy in the lead. It had not taken her long to discover that Dragonfly's canter was even smoother than his trot, and she was posing shamelessly, her back arched, her profile uptilted. Her hat flew off, and Lord Rune had a moment of fear that Mercury or Cygnet would shy at it. They did not, and their master congratulated himself on his choice of mounts.

Flambeau was champing at the bit, and at last Lord Rune indulged him, allowing the great horse to lengthen his stride. The park was becoming crowded. Lord Rune had planned this outing in order to exhibit his new protégée, and it was time to do so. He pulled up beside Lucy's hat, dismounted, dusted it off, and rode after her. With a flourish he returned it and teased her as she pinned it back on. Her cheeks were red with excitement.

He spent the next half-hour hacking with her, introducing her to a number of people who had already met her and forgotten her. Exhilaration became her; with great vigor she agreed that the weather was charming, and she laughed at any pleasantry that was proffered. He was amused to see one or two gentlemen looking at her admiringly; Miss Saint-Clair looked good on a horse, when that horse was Dragonfly.

He was riding beside her and wondering whether to tell her so, when he saw a bee light on Dragonfly's flank. There was a split second when he wondered what to do about it. Then the bee stung. Dragonfly bolted.

Lucy's clasp on the mane became convulsive. She had not seen the bee, and she was entirely unprepared for this rush of speed, but Daffodil, who had done little else to benefit her as an equestrienne, had endowed her with quick reflexes. Her knee squeezed the crutch of the sidesaddle; the ball of her foot pressed against the stirrup. Around her the miniature world had become a whirlwind; trees and grass and horses and riders became a single, insubstantial streak.

It was Flambeau, not Lord Rune, who made the decision to fly to the rescue, but Lord Rune concurred. It was unlikely that Dragonfly would find the sound of pursuing hoofbeats soothing or that Lord Rune would be able to catch up with the black horse. Nevertheless, he was responsible for his sister's god-child, and he had to do something. He galloped after the runaway, aware in the back of his mind that he and Lucy were creating a highly dramatic tableau.

The tableau ended over the crest of a hill. Lucy had let go of the mane long enough to tug at the reins. It was a frantic tug, more of a yank than a tug, and Dragonfly was unused to yanks. He stopped with a suddenness that precipitated Lucy onto the ground.

Lord Rune drew rein, seeing with horror the empty saddle and the crumbled figure on the ground. Then, as he watched with his heart in his throat, the figure rose.

Lord Rune dismounted and ran to Lucy. Her riding habit was torn, and she was crying, great breathless sobs that frightened him. Dragonfly stood trembling, with the reins over one ear. He sensed that he had done something wrong.

"Lucy, are you hurt?"

Lucy continued to sob. Through her sobs she gasped out something incoherent, ending with, "—breathe—."

"Oh," Lord Rune said, comprehendingly. "Have you knocked the wind out of your lungs? That's the most miserable feeling in the world."

Lucy jerked her head up and down in assent and accepted his handkerchief. Dragonfly stopped examining his conscience, tossed his head so that the reins fell forward, and began to graze.

"I'm not h-hurt, really," gasped Lucy, wiping her face with a grass-stained glove while her clean glove protected his handkerchief. "But I—n-never fell off—anything so big—Daffodil—"

"Daffodil is little," Lord Rune said, to save her the trouble. "Are you sure you haven't broken anything? Your ankles—?"

"Yes." Lucy sniffed, shuddered, and stopped crying. "I didn't fall on my feet; I fell—" She looked down at the ground. "I just fell," she said. "And my riding habit is torn and everyone saw," she added, her eyes filling with tears again.

Lord Rune considered putting an arm around her and decided against it. "Yes, everyone did see," he agreed. "It was very picturesque. You kept your head up, you know, and your hair came down, and you rode like a gypsy. In fact," he assured her, "for those brief moments, you had a seat. Quite a good one."

Lucy reached up and touched her hair self-consciously. "Really?" she asked, beginning to smile through her tears.

"You have my word as a gentleman."

Lucy's smile persisted. One cheek was smudged, and her hair was very wild. It was a remarkably effective smile.

Lord Rune turned away from her and went after Dragonfly, who had forgotten bees and humanity and was tearing away at the grass. "The fall itself," he remarked, after a moment, "was probably more harrowing than picturesque. I did not witness it, and neither"— he scanned the landscape briefly—"did anyone else of social consequence."

"Well, of course," said Lucy, "you would be glad of that."

Lord Rune turned to stare at her. She had spoken without irony; it was the possible implication of what she said that startled him. He wondered if Tabitha had said anything to her about his sponsorship. No; she would not be so stupid. And yet—

"Will you give me your cravat?" asked Lucy.

"My cravat?" repeated Lord Rune, disoriented.

"Yes, for a sash." She was holding the torn edges of her skirt between her fists. "I can't ride and hold this."

Lord Rune was a man of fashion; his cravat was dear to his heart. Nevertheless, Lucy's suggestion was a practical one. He loosened the folds that had cost Pud-

der so much labor and gave it to her. She turned her
back, modestly, and tied it about her waist.

"Very dashing," Lord Rune approved, dismissing
his thoughts about Tabitha. "Are you nervous about
riding back? You needn't be, you know. Dragonfly
bolted because a bee stung him; he won't do it again."

"No," said Lucy, but without conviction. The
smile that had transformed her face had disappeared.
Lord Rune did not reassure her again. Once again, he
went in search of her hat and watched her pin it on.
Then he clasped his hands together and caught her boot,
throwing her into the saddle.

"Ready?"

"Almost." Lucy scowled down at Dragonfly's ears
as she adjusted her reins. "No—wait—I've lost my stirrup."

Lord Rune reached under the train of the riding
habit and helped her to find it, keeping his eyes discreetly on her hands. Her fingers were entangled in the
mane, and they shook. "Miss Saint-Clair—" he said.

"Yes?"

"Will you allow me to take you driving tomorrow
morning?"

The reins tightened suddenly between the gloved
fingers. Lord Rune, looking up, saw the scowl replaced
first with a look of astonishment and then with joy.

"Oh, yes!" Lucy said. "I should like that above
anything!"

Lord Rune nodded, his own countenance blank.
He had no idea what had impelled him to ask her, and
her candor embarrassed him. "Good," he uttered after a
moment. "Good."

He patted Dragonfly on the neck and went to remount Flambeau, his mind vaguely unsettled. His sister had asked him to polish and refine Miss Saint-Clair; what if her gaucherie were more contagious than his sophistication?

6

Lucy had never paid much attention to clothes. At home, she was the family seamstress, and the work of constructing gowns for four women had led her to concur with her Mamma's opinion that vanity was a fruit of the Fall. With all her heart she sought to convince two finery-hungry sisters that simplicity was more desirable than ornament, and she turned a deaf ear to their pleas for frilled hems, embroidered petticoats, and petal-shaped sleeves. She arrived at her godmother's house wearing gowns as plainly cut as those of Dirge the parlor-maid, and Mrs. Theale's first concern had been to persuade her to exchange them for something more fashionable.

To these persuasions Lucy yielded at once. Indeed, Mrs. Theale's first and indelible impression was that Lucy was a very grateful and biddable girl. She was not a bit affronted by her godmother's suggestion that what was proper in Yorkshire would not do in London, and with charming docility she agreed to confine her sewing to fancywork. Her first visit to the dress-maker left her breathless; the knowledge that she might wear as many ruffles as she liked, without having to hem and gather them herself, went to her head. She cast a covetous eye over Angelica's wardrobe, which was embroidered, flounced, and beribboned, and hopefully ordered the same.

The result was unhappy. The dainty, intricate gowns that flattered the Theale girls looked absurd on Lucy, and she was objective enough to perceive the difference. Nor could she fail to realize that Angelica and Lizzy, Cassy and Grace were all prettier than she. It was daunting to know this, and still more daunting to watch the wispy gowns grow tight as Lucy grew stouter. The Seasons passed. Lucy renounced the fruit of the Fall, and concentrated on her music.

Now, however, there was Lord Rune: more desirable than Lucy had thought any man outside the pages of a novel could be. And because of this, Lucy's clothes were intolerable. Intolerable! She could not imagine how she had ever worn them.

Cassy and Grace were sympathetic. They were quick to apprehend the relationship between the desirability of a man and the adequacy of a wardrobe. Nor would they listen to their friend when she became embarrassed by her reawakened vanity and muttered that it didn't matter. Of course it mattered! Of course Lord Rune cared how she looked! Why, Lord Rune was in love with Lucy! He was! Had not Lucy and Lord Rune chosen the very same bowl for their favorite! (And such an ugly thing, too, Grace added candidly.) Was this not evidence of a perfect accord of sensibilities, an absolute harmony of minds? And did not such harmonies—for what had been singular had become plural—lead, inevitably, to the altar?

Lucy demurred. In her private heart she hoped that the shared admiration of the Tang bowl was a promising omen, but she had doubts. Her doubts led her to put forth the possibility that a man and a woman might esteem the same bowl without joining together in holy matrimony.

Had she no heart? cried Cassy and Grace. Had she no sensibility? She was cynical, and it was perfectly horrid to be cynical. And besides, they reminded her, Lord Rune had kissed her hand. It was their strongest argument, this kissing-of-the-hand, and they had wielded it quite often enough to believe in it. Their conviction almost persuaded Lucy, who longed above all things to be persuaded. But, she argued, Lord Rune had agreed to pretend to admire her in order to oblige his sister. Might he not kiss her hand in order to display an admiration he did not feel?

No, answered Cassy and Grace, in unison. Admiration was one thing, osculation was another. One could admire without kissing. Kissing was clearly optional and therefore an indication of Lord Rune's true feelings. And besides, they chorused, he had asked Lucy driving. He was going to see her twice within forty-eight hours, which was surely indicative of the warmth of his sentiments.

Yes, sighed Lucy, but she would look a perfect fright when he saw her, and all of Lord Rune's admiration—whatever the quantity might be—would turn to indifference.

The Theale girls understood this logic, but they believed such a calamity might be averted. Cassy would lend her fringed parasol, and Grace offered her lavender gloves. Lucy could wear the lavender striped gown that made her look taller—No, Lucy said, she couldn't. It was dreadfully tight across the front, and she couldn't move her arms in it. What pressing need, demanded Grace impatiently, had she to move her arms? Lord Rune would be driving. As for the wrinkles across the bodice—well, they would be covered by Lucy's grey spencer, which was a little warm for spring but very becoming.

Lucy nodded cautiously. Yes. The grey and the lavender would be pretty together. As for the spencer being warm, that would not signify, since it did not look warm. Her bonnet, however, would not do. Nothing could exceed its shabbiness, and how she could have tolerated so large a poke she could not imagine. With the poke bulging out above, and her bosom bulging out below, she would look like the letter B. No man could wish to drive out with the letter B.

This statement reduced the Theale girls to silence. They could not contradict it. Cassy offered to lend her new cottage bonnet. Lucy was moved by her friend's generosity and refused it. Cassy repeated her offer. Lucy again refused, this time pointing out that a celestial blue bonnet would not become a lavender dress. Cassy subsided.

It was Grace who thought of retrimming an Angoulême bonnet of Lizzy's—a little out of fashion now, but very flattering—and Lucy herself who sat up half the night to perform this delicate operation. She polished her own shoes, having forgotten to ask Twitterboots, sorted a pile of stockings in order to choose the most immaculate, and dreamed all night that she was riding naked on a great black horse. The Angoulême bonnet had fallen off; it hung by the ribbons down her back.

The following day it rained.

Lord Rune sent Flitworm over with a note that said he was indisposed and would call when he was better. It fell to Mrs. Theale to break the news to the three girls. Grace cried that it was the most provoking thing imaginable, and Cassy looked grave. Lucy tossed her head and said it did not signify.

This last response, which might have been expected to reassure Mrs. Theale, did nothing of the kind. Experience had taught her that subterfuge of any kind was a symptom to be dreaded. She asked Lucy, who was looking very heavy-eyed, if she suffered any ill effects from her fall. Lucy shook her head.

The week that followed was a melancholy one. The rain continued. Lord Rune did not write. Lucy alternated between silent brooding and an air of resolute good-humor. Cassy and Grace took to refurbishing their gowns—an activity that their Mamma deplored.

They were in the final stage of this activity (the first three stages were Industry, Destruction, and Tears, and the final stage was Supplication for New Gowns to Replace Ruined Ones) when Mr. Bloomsbury came to town. He had been in Devonshire for the last month, and Cassy had not expected him until May. The melancholy in the house lifted. Cassy floated upstairs and down with a beatific smile on her face. Lucy and Grace fussed over her hair, solicited her confidences, and teased her without mercy.

Outside the Theale house, the rain stopped. Flitworm braved the muddy streets to deliver another message. Lord Rune had recovered from his indisposition and wished to remind Miss Saint-Clair of the proposed drive. The very next day a perch-phaeton, drawn by two white horses, stopped before the Theale house. Lucy, who had been watching from the window, grabbed the fringed parasol and shouted a goodbye to her godmother. She dodged past the parlor-maid, who was bringing her mistress a cup of chocolate, and ran down the marble steps.

Lord Rune greeted her with some surprise. "Good day, Miss Saint-Clair. You are remarkably prompt."

Lucy chose to acknowledge this as if she were sure that it was a compliment. "Thank you," she gasped. She had been afraid that Lord Rune would step inside and tell her it was too warm to wear the spencer. "I didn't want to keep the horses standing."

"You're very courteous," Lord Rune said graciously. "May I help you to ascend?"

Lucy murmered assent, somewhat flustered by the suavity of Lord Rune's manner. How slender and aristocratic he looked, after the brawny Mr. Bloomsbury! It was felicity to touch his hand. Then it struck her that her own hand might seem damp, even through the borrowed glove, and she hastened to disengage her fingers. "What handsome horses!" she said, somewhat breathlessly.

"Thank you."

Lucy folded her hands in her lap and arranged a lacy handkerchief between her fingers. The bodice of the lavender gown was certainly very tight. She cast a sidelong glance at Lord Rune. He wore a dark green frock coat with silver buttons and a waistcoat of pale grey. His Hessian boots gleamed as if they were made of black lacquer, and his linen was so white that it intimidated her. She could not think of a thing to say.

Lord Rune glanced sideways and diagnosed her state of mind very accurately. Evidently a week's absence had not alienated her. It occurred to him that he was not sure whether he was glad or sorry that her infatuation continued and then he scoffed at himself. Of course he was sorry. He liked her far too well to sacrifice her peace of mind to his vanity. He saw her torturing the exquisite little handkerchief and took pity on her. "Aren't you going to ask after my health?" he asked encouragingly.

"Oh!" Lucy looked at him, stricken. "I am so sorry! Are you quite recovered? We were dreadfully sorry to hear you were ill."

Ernest's eyes narrowed in amusement. "Do you really expect me to believe that?"

Lucy's contrition turned to confusion, and then to belligerence. "Why shouldn't you?" she asked, squinting at him as the carriage turned towards the sun.

"Why should I?" countered Lord Rune, deliberately provocative. "A young lady who callously spoke of my warts and boils—"

"I wasn't callous," interrupted Lucy, hotly. "I merely inquired—"

"To have inquired was callous," retorted Lord Rune, in lofty tones. "It implied that I looked like the sort of person who would have them."

Lucy drew a deep breath, defying the bodice of the lavender gown. "I implied nothing of the kind," she answered, militantly. "And if I had, it would have been no more than you deserved. You would prose on and on about every malady you could conceive of, half of which I daresay you never contracted."

"I have contracted them all," Lord Rune said, forcefully. "And after you mentioned boils, I became possessed of the notion that I would contract them too. I assure you, Miss Saint-Clair, my peace of mind was utterly cut up. I have taken to sleeping with a lit candle beside my bed, so that I can examine myself when I begin to erupt."

Miss Saint-Clair seemed impressed by this testimony. Her eyes glowed and her shyness had deserted her. "And do you?" she asked.

"Do I what?"

"Do you erupt?"

Ernest shook his head. "It pains me to disappoint you, Miss Saint-Clair, but thus far I do not."

"I am not disappointed," answered Miss Saint-Clair, in dulcet tones.

Lord Rune eyed her sardonically. "Do not seek to deceive me," he warned her. "I know very well that you will not be satisfied until I am as leprous as a Harlequin. Until that time, however, you may console yourself. I have just overthrown a very unpleasant cold—a poor proxy, but mine own."

Lucy looked sympathetic even as she laughed. "I'm so sorry," she said. "We all were. You mustn't think, Lord Rune, that I would be amused by any real illness you might suffer."

It was Ernest's turn to fall silent. It was one thing to fence with Miss Saint-Clair in jest; it was another thing to parry her sincerity. "Any real illness?" he echoed, after a minute pause. "Ever since that afternoon at my sister's—"

He stopped abruptly. Innocently, Lucy raised her eyes and waited for him to finish. "Ever since that afternoon," he continued, "I have been puzzling over your levity at my expense. What made you so certain, Miss Saint-Clair, that the illnesses that I spoke of were not real?"

Lucy looked him full in the face. "They weren't, were they?"

Lord Rune hesitated. "I am something of a *malade imaginaire*," he answered evasively. "Have you by any chance read Molière?"

"Yes," answered Lucy, surprising him. "I like French. Only—" she regarded him steadily, "—you haven't answered my question."

Lord Rune had no intention of answering her question. "I am rather like Monsieur Molière's unfortunate hero," he said. "My illnesses—and I do have them, Miss Saint-Clair—have a recreational quality. They give me something to think about. They add suspense to an otherwise insipid existence. Imagine, if you will, the life of a rich and spoiled gentleman—a gentleman like myself. What I desire I obtain. What would weary me I avoid. I go from city to city and everywhere I go, I meet other rich gentlemen—and ladies—like myself. They are bored and I am amusing. They treat me like a prince and they bore me to death. I drink port with the men, write sonnets to the ladies, fight an occasional duel, and dress magnificently. It is stupendously dull, and after a while my constitution rebels against it. Then I become ill."

He finished with a small and ironic flourish. He had no idea what had induced him to go on so long.

"Perhaps it's the port," suggested Miss Saint-Clair.

"I beg your pardon?"

"The port," repeated Miss Saint-Clair. "Perhaps drinking port makes you ill, and feeling ill makes you bored."

Her placidity nettled him. "Did Tabitha tell you I drink too much?" he demanded harshly.

"No," answered Lucy. "Do you?"

It was an outrageous question, and Lord Rune did not hesitate to answer it outrageously. "Yes," he snapped. He sounded as churlish as he felt. "Yes, I drink too much."

He half expected her to comment on this acknowledgement, but she did not. She was silent for so long that he wondered if his tone of voice had wounded her or if she realized the shamefulness of her own conduct. He stole a look at her and saw that she was neither embarrassed nor offended. The lace handkerchief lay between her fingers unmolested. A faint line between the ferocious brows indicated that she was thoughtful, no more.

Her serenity, which had exasperated him just a moment ago, now struck him as being a wonderful and luxurious thing. He was not going to have to atone for speaking the truth. He had spoken it, and she had not felt it incumbent upon her either to soothe or to scold. He felt pleasantly light and curiously naked. He reached out and brushed the feather on the Angoulême bonnet.

"You have a white plume," he said, smiling at her as if he had made a remarkable discovery.

"Yes," said Lucy, dizzily. Lord Rune withdrew his hand.

They entered the park. The horses' hooves, which had clattered against the cobblestones, were muffled by the damp earth. They struck the ground with a soft thud, disengaging themselves with a gentle sucking sound. The sunlight was very bright and the air was moist and fragrant. The wind scattered dappled shadows over the grass and caressed Lucy's plume.

Lord Rune urged the horses into a trot. "You haven't answered my question, Miss Saint-Clair. Why were you so suspicious of my infirmities?"

Lucy paused before she spoke, considering. "I don't know. I didn't know then, either, but I was quite certain that you and Godmamma were hoaxing us." She looked up at him and spoke impulsively. "Lord Rune, why were you hoaxing us?"

Her gaze was penetrating and also trusting, as if she had no doubt that Lord Rune would explain the mystery to her. Such was the power of this unquestioning faith that Ernest opened his mouth to begin. Then he remembered: the reason why he had stressed his ill-health was because he hoped to alienate Miss Saint-Clair's affections. He could not tell her that. No young lady, however strong-minded, should have to hear that the man she adored wished to change her love to disgust. He sought for an alternative explanation and could think of none. He scanned the park hastily, in search of any distraction that could put an end to her questions, and seized on a familiar face. Without thinking, he called out "Jenny!" and turned his horses toward a well-known carriage.

It was a very dashing carriage, a high-perch phaeton upholstered in peach-colored silk. The original upholstery had been cream-colored, as Lord Rune had good reason to know: he had paid for it. Seated against the soft cushions was a small, rather plump damsel, with auburn curls, a fetching smile, and a modish gown one shade darker than the upholstery. Lord Rune admired the gown, and then realized that he was about to commit a gross impropriety. He pulled up his horses, handling the reins with less than his usual skill.

The lady in peach did not notice. She had always

been short-sighted, and her attention was claimed by a curricle in her path. Lucy, observing her companion's sudden rigidity, was moved to lay a hand on his arm. "Lord Rune! Lord Rune, are you quite well?"

Lord Rune nodded dumbly. Fascinated, he watched his former mistress pass the curricle with only an inch to spare. Lucy leaned closer to him, and whispered to his shoulder, "Lord Rune, if you don't want to meet the lady—"

What her advice would have been Lord Rune was never to know. The peach-upholstered phaeton drew up alongside his own, and Jenny hailed him with a flash of dimples. His head cleared. He liked Jenny. He had always liked Jenny, and no vicar's daughter was going to force him to cut her. He inclined his head in lieu of a bow and managed a shaky smile.

"Ernest, my dear!" He was aware that Lucy was taking in every detail of the other woman's appearance, from the low-necked gown to the tiny laugh-lines around the beautiful eyes. "Dear, disgraceful Lord Rune! Where have you been this age?"

"Budapest." He took a deep breath and turned to Lucy. "Miss Saint-Clair, this is an old friend of mine, Jenny . . . Jade. And Jenny, this is Lucy Saint-Clair, who is god-daughter to my sister."

He emphasized the last word, and Jenny, who had extended her hand in a friendly manner, snatched it back and looked perplexed.

Lucy looked from one to the other and then extended her own hand. "How do you do, Miss Jade?"

Jenny shot a tentative glance at Ernest and then took the proffered hand, clasping it as if she expected it to explode.

"*Jade* is such a pretty name," Lucy said shyly.

"Your eyes are almost jade-colored." She squeezed the kid-clad hand and then relinquished it. "I'm very happy to meet you."

Jenny eyed her suspiciously. Her eyes went from the missish gown to the outmoded bonnet. Last of all she consulted Lucy's face, and suddenly she laughed.

"And I'm glad to meet you, Miss Saint-Clair," she answered heartily, "which is not say we're likely to meet again. Ernest"—She jerked her head at Lucy, significantly—"this isn't the thing."

"I know it," Lord Rune admitted. He leaned forward and touched her glove, very lightly. "It's been a long time, Jenny."

The tenderness in the gesture made Miss Jade shake her head at him. "That's enough, Ernest," she rebuked him, and she winked at Lucy. "A pleasure, Miss Saint-Clair," she said, and drew the whip lightly across the horse's back. The mare broke into a trot, and she drove away, curls bouncing and head held high.

Lord Rune watched her until she disappeared past a clump of trees and then selected a road leading in the opposite direction. He did not doubt that a very unpleasant scene was about to take place. Nor could he make light of Miss Saint-Clair's right to be angry; he had just insulted her unspeakably. He headed for a secluded path and hoped she would not cry.

"I don't blame you a bit, you know," Lucy pronounced.

He stared at her. She was not in tears. She was not blushing. Her sang-froid was utterly unruffled.

"It would have been very rude not to have spoken to Miss Jade, once you had recognized her," Lucy went on, "especially if your friendship had been a close one."

She had the delicacy to look down at her lap. "I gather your friendship was a close one?"

Lord Rune did not answer at once. He wondered how anyone could be so naive and then decided that no one could be. He answered, between his teeth, "Yes, it was a close one, Miss Saint-Clair, and if you must ask impertinent questions, I beg you will not do so with an innocent air. I find it both tiresome and fatuous."

"That isn't very polite," flashed Miss Saint-Clair.

Lord Rune felt a sudden hysterical desire to laugh.

"After all," Miss Saint-Clair went on indignantly, "I was only commending your sense of honor."

The desire to laugh left him. He must have misheard her. "My . . . sense of honor?"

Lucy nodded. "About recognizing Miss Jade. Because—I am not going to mince words—she is your"— she stopped, not wanting to mince words but not knowing the right word to use. She finally settled on an Old Testament term—"your concubine, isn't she?"

"Was," corrected Ernest, numbly.

"Was," repeated Lucy, brightening. "Godmamma tries to keep Cassy and Grace and me from knowing about such things, but of course, it isn't possible to ignore them altogether. All gentlemen have concubines, but they lie about it, and I have sometimes thought that their lies are as bad as their harlotries. Most gentlemen would have pretended not to know your Miss Jade, or made up some taradiddle about mistaking her for someone else. *That* I would deplore. Hypocrisy of any kind is repugnant to me," she concluded, giving the lace handkerchief a vicious little wrench to emphasize her words.

"Miss Saint-Clair"—Lord Rune stared forward, unwilling to look at her—"I cannot allow you to cherish a higher opinion of me than I deserve. If I had recognized Miss Jade in time, I wouldn't have introduced you to her. It was discourteous to you and uncomfortable for her, and if I had had greater presence of mind, I would have behaved as 'most gentlemen' do."

"There, do you see?" Lucy said eagerly. "You might have accepted my compliments, and instead you have explained that you were not at all honorable, but only clumsy. I think your candor does you great credit, Lord Rune."

The hysterical desire to laugh had returned full force. Lord Rune passed a hand over his face. Clearly Miss Saint-Clair was determined to admire him, and admire him she would, however many sophistries she might have to employ. He could not resist saying, "Candor is evidently a quality you prize, Miss Saint-Clair. It seems to outweigh my intemperance, my profligacy, and my lack of savoir-faire."

"You don't usually lack savoir-faire," Miss Saint-Clair said kindly.

"No. Only in your company."

Miss Saint-Clair bestowed a glowing smile upon him. "Is that true?"

He did not know how to answer her. He had not intended to pay her compliments, but she seemed to be able to extract them from contumely. "Miss Saint-Clair, can you get blood out of a turnip?"

"No," answered Lucy, wide-eyed.

"You relieve my mind."

The black brows knit, trying to make some sense out of this last interchange. After a moment or two they rose. "Lord Rune—"

"Yes?"

"Perhaps"—her voice was not quite steady—"perhaps my candor has given you a disgust of me?"

It was an excellent opportunity to deliver a set-down, but Lord Rune could not avail himself of it. "Not at all," he replied. "Your candor gives your conversation a good deal of novelty. My only complaint is that you seem to have decided that I am superior to 'most gentlemen' without having any evidence to that effect. My dear Miss Saint-Clair, 'most gentlemen' would not introduce you to their concubines. Many gentlemen—if you will believe me—do not have concubines to introduce."

The white plume lopped sideways as she tilted her head to look at him. "I don't believe you," she said. "There are temptations, you know." Lord Rune, who did know, almost groaned at the turn the conversation was taking. "It only wants a little imagination to think how it must be . . . to be a man, I mean, and surrounded by temptations and without a chaperone. If one were impulsive, it would be very trying indeed. One might resist temptation nine times out of ten, but there would always be that tenth time, and after a while one would not be pure. Why, think of Francesca and Paolo!" She raised her eyes to his, much struck by the comparison. "Think of them! They had no intention—they had no idea that they were falling in love, until they read about Lancelot kissing Guenevere in a book. And then—" She waved her hands expressively, and quoted, " *'Quel giorno più no vi leggemo avante!'* "

Lord Rune had not read Dante for many years, but his Italian was very good. " 'That day we did not read any further' " he translated, the implication dawning on him as he spoke.

"That's right," approved Miss Saint-Clair. " 'That day we'—" Her voice died off. "It sounds better in Italian. I can't think why."

"I can," said Lord Rune.

Lucy paid no attention to this last remark. "The other thing you might consider," she informed him, "—and which might make you feel much better—is that carnal sinners are only in the second circle of the infernal world, which tells us that Dante considered it a lesser sin. Indeed, if we are to depend on Dante Alighieri, there are many, many vices more reprehensible than the carnal ones."

"Pray do not enumerate them." Lord Rune held up a beseeching hand. "My sensibilities have suffered enough shocks for one day. Miss Saint-Clair, how on earth did you come to read Dante in the original Italian?"

"It was in the library. The vicar before Papa was a great scholar, and he had both the English and the Italian." Lucy shrugged. "So when our governess taught us Italian—and I needed it for singing—I picked up the Dante and tried to puzzle it out. I couldn't have managed if the English hadn't been at hand," she admitted, "but the sound of it is beautiful, even if one doesn't understand. I learned some of my favorite parts by heart."

"Such as Francesca da Rimini." Lord Rune raised his eyebrows quizzically. "You are very lucky, do you know that? Most young ladies are not allowed such literature."

"No, I don't suppose they are." Lucy wrapped the handkerchief around her thumb like a bandage, and then unwrapped it. "That's why it's so hard to be a young lady, sometimes," she explained. "I've read too much. I don't have delicacy of mind. Sometimes I think that if I had been brought up like Cassy—with improving books, and chaperones, and aromatic salts—I might have delicacy of mind, but at other times I'm not sure. I *liked* reading about Francesca, and the Wife of Bath, and Pamela."

Lord Rune startled her with a burst of laughter. "I'll warrant you did. No, don't look at me like that; I'm not maligning you. It would hardly be fitting if I did, since I am not pure myself."

"But you're a man," Lucy pointed out. "Men don't have to be pure. It must be very convenient," she added wistfully.

"It is."

She shook her head. "And you're not even ashamed," she mused. "Mr. Bloomsbury is in London, and Cassy blushes every time we mention his name, because she has delicacy of mind. But men—men commit harlotries, and they aren't embarrassed in the least. It's men who ought to have chaperones."

"It's men," corrected Ernest, "who ought to have aromatic salts."

His face was perfectly serious, but Lucy was seized with a fit of giggles. "Are you pretending that I shock you?" she asked.

"No. I'm not pretending at all. You don't happen to have a vinaigrette in your reticule, do you? I am feeling rather faint."

This sally delighted Miss Saint-Clair so much that she almost choked. "Perhaps you could have a collection of smelling bottles," she suggested, when she had gained control over herself. "Like Mr. Abelard's collection of chicken-skin fans."

Lord Rune raised his eyebrows. Mr. Abelard's chicken-skin fans were decorated with nymphs and shepherds in a number of compromising positions, and Mr. Abelard showed them only to his intimate friends.

"Don't tell me you've seen Ceddie Abelard's fans!" he ejaculated.

Lucy gave him a mischievous smile. "No. I've only heard about them."

"Even that . . ." He wondered what she had heard and decided he would rather not ask. "Where on earth did you hear about them?"

"Almack's."

"*Almack's!*"

Lucy shook her head at him. "For a man of the world, you seem very naive," she said. "All sorts of gossip can be heard at Almack's. I know about Lady Curry's losses at the gaming table, and Elinor Fitzhugh's secret engagement to the Marquis of Clouet, and that Laurence Feather fought a duel in Green Park Thursday last."

"Was he wounded?"

"Not a scratch. Also," Lucy boasted, "I know that Jack Seddingham spent four hundred guineas on a new hunter that isn't worth forty, and that the Countess of Lethington sometimes goes down into her own kitchen, and cooks. Although why that should be considered so shocking I have no idea."

Lord Rune did not seek to enlighten her. "Miss Saint-Clair, who tells you such things?"

Lucy smiled at him a little sadly. "I have been a wall-flower for four years."

A moment's meditation was enough to persuade Lord Rune that this was not the non sequitur that it seemed to be. "I see," he said. "You sit near the older women—"

Lucy interrupted him. "I don't eavesdrop," she defended herself. "I don't, truly. But so many of them are deaf, and after my first Season, they didn't *see* me anymore. They're quite used to me, and they don't think of me as a young girl. I'm invisible, really."

Lord Rune inclined his head. Yes. A plain girl with no dowry could easily become invisible at Almack's. And an invisible woman—"Miss Saint-Clair!" he said urgently.

"Yes?"

"I am going to give a masquerade."

Lucy digested this passively. "Well, and why should you not?" said she. "Godmamma does not like them, but I daresay that a private one—"

"Hush," Lord Rune commanded. "Don't distract me. I'm planning."

Lucy hushed. The handkerchief wound through her fingers and then back again. She folded it into tiny squares and then into triangles. When she looked up again, Lord Rune was smiling.

"You are about to become a gypsy," he told her, "and you are going to tell fortunes at my party."

7

If Mrs. Theale, that bastion of family propriety, had ever disliked masquerades, the news that her brother was planning to host one enabled her to forget it. It had been years since Ernest opened his house to the London ton, and the intelligence that he was about to do so gave rise to a flutter of excitement. Invitations were shuffled like playing cards, Tabitha's parlor was besieged with callers, and the Misses Theale, always popular, received so much attention that Grace began to fancy herself a siren.

Tabitha welcomed the callers, squelched her youngest daughter as best she could, and fought a spirited battle with her sister Edith over the honor of serving as Lord Rune's hostess. The outcome of the battle was never in question, as Lord Rune detested his maiden sister, and poor Edith left the Theale house in high dudgeon. Her only comfort lay in the fact that she had unburdened herself; at last she had told Tabitha the truth about herself and her ill-bred daughters.

The ill-bred ones listened to their mamma's account of the battle with great vivacity. They defended their mamma against the absent Edith with a volley of slurs and ended by hoping that their aunt would hold a grudge. It was not the first time the Howard sisters had quarreled, and the ensuing grudge-time was much to be desired. Aunt would not call; it would be absurd, even disloyal, to call on her. It was an ill wind that blew no man good, Grace observed sagely, and Tabitha did not reproach her. Tabitha, in fact, was in no mood to censure anyone. She had contrived to deliver a few stinging remarks of her own during the battle, and the thought of them refreshed her. Also she was pleased—very pleased—that Ernest was going to pay his debt to society.

"It will doubtless be very expensive," she told her daughters, "for your uncle, you know, will have everything of the best. The wines alone—and the supper and the musicians and the flowers . . . It will all add up. He will have to lay out a good deal of money." She ran her eyes over the Egyptian frieze that encircled her drawing-room and performed a few swift calculations, none of which seemed to ruffle her sense of well-being. "Of course, there will be no need to hire plate, for he will have it sent up from Westmorland. Our family has never hired plate. I only hope dear Ernest will know whom to invite! It has been so long since he bestirred himself, and he had such a reputation at one time—I daresay some people will come just to see the house and wonder what he paid for things!" She added, with unusual mildness: "People are so vulgar!"

"I thought talking about money was vulgar," said Grace, daringly.

"It is vulgar," Tabitha replied, with unusual affability, "but it is human nature, after all, and nothing could be more vulgar, my dear, than for a child to criticize her mamma." She saw her daughters exchange appreciative glances, and assumed her most dignified air. "I must remember to tell Ernest to have the chandelier cleaned! It is quite magnificent—Venetian glass and very old—and if those dreadful servants smash it, they ought to be hanged, every one of them! Ernest must compel them to *clean,*"Tabitha declared, passionately. "He must. Why, all of London will be there! If—" But the consequences of all London dancing beneath a dusty chandelier were too dreadful to contemplate, and Tabitha fell into a brown study. When at last she spoke, it was with such resolution that Cassy and Grace were impressed.

"It will have to be borne upon him," she said, and her daughters nodded. "He has been very tractable as of late. On the whole, you girls have done him good."

Which led Cassy and Grace suggesting that it was Lucy's duty to convince Lord Rune to clean his house.

Lucy demurred. It was hard for her to think of her hero as the unwitting victim of lazy servants and harder still to believe that she should criticize him. She had not noticed anything amiss in Lord Rune's house; it was sacred ground, where he had shown her his procelain and given her tea. She listened, troubled, as Grace dwelt on the problem of the dusty chandelier, and she agreed that it would be a sad thing if London were to disparage Lord Rune for his servants' faults, but farther than this she would not go.

She was destined to change her mind. The next day,

Cassy was inspired to visit Hookham's library, and association of ideas demanded that afterward the girls call on Lord Rune. Pettibone answered the door after a prolonged wait. One side of his face was creased and red, as if he had been sleeping with his head against his sleeve, and his eyes were bloodshot. He herded the girls into the drawing room, and left them without a word.

Lucy looked about the room. Lord Rune prized his porcelain room, and it was the cleanest in his house. This room was but seldom used and even more seldom cleaned. A folded newspaper had slipped behind the Turkish settee and lay with one corner exposed. The shutters were drawn, and a half-empty tankard of ale decorated the mantel. Lucy turned to Cassy and said, dubiously, "Perhaps we oughtn't to have come."

"It isn't really early," Cassy said, "and he could have said Uncle wasn't at home."

Grace wrinkled her nose. "It smells bad in here," she complained. "Vinegary, like spilled wine." She went to the window and opened the shutters. "There! That's better!"

It was really a little worse. The spring sunlight shone mercilessly on dusty woodwork and carelessly polished furniture. Lucy, intent on opening a second window, saw four dead flies lying on the grimy sill. "Godmamma was right," she stated. "I don't believe his servants do any work at all." She aligned a painting on the wall and swooped down on the newspaper. "March," she read aloud. "March, and now it's April. Why, this could be a beautiful room—it is a beautiful room—and instead it's"—she pronounced the adjective with dark satisfaction—"It's squalid."

The door closed behind Lord Rune. "What's squalid?" he asked.

Lucy turned to face him. He was, as ever, immaculately dressed, but there were dark circles under his eyes, and the vitality that had characterized him during their drive together was gone. "What's the matter?" she asked, as if they were the only two people in the room.

"Nothing." He smiled as he shook his head, but wearily; he had drunk too much the night before and then been unable to sleep. His head ached, and he was not at all certain that he wished to entertain visitors. From the look on Lucy's face he divined that she was speculating on what might be wrong with him, and in order to distract her he repeated, "What's squalid?"

Lucy averted her eyes. Cassy was blushing, and Grace emitted a faint squeak. Lord Rune's eyebrows rose maliciously. "Do I scent a mystery? Really, you must tell me, Miss Saint-Clair! I am a little dull this morning, and I count upon you to amuse me."

Lucy looked at Cassy and then at Grace. Both were studying their hands, which lay demurely clasped upon their sprig muslin laps. Clearly, neither of them were going to be any help. She took a deep breath. She had, after all, discussed Francesca de Rimini with Lord Rune, and surely bad housekeeping was less shocking than the sin of lust.

"I was regretting that this room is not very clean," she told him.

Lord Rune's gaze, weary, but intelligent, swept over the room. His nieces were mortified; their cheeks were pink, and their eyes were downcast. He smiled, greatly to the girls' relief, and somewhat to his own. Unconsciously he had planned to have a bad day; he had forgotten that he had a sense of humor.

"I often regret it myself," he said. "Please sit down, Miss Saint-Clair. I am sorry that you must seat yourself in the midst of squalor, but you must pardon me; I am a bachelor, and I live in a bachelor establishment."

He took a handkerchief from his pocket, and deliberately dusted the seat of a rosewood chair. Lucy, who had heaved a sigh of relief at his smile, frowned at the handkerchief. "I don't see—" she began, and then stopped. "I mean, thank you," she finished, and sat down.

"You don't see—?"

Lucy cast a despairing glance at Casey, who grimaced hideously at her and then bestowed a fixed smile on her uncle. "We are so looking forward to your masquerade," she said.

"We are," agreed Grace, rapidly. "I shall be Juliet."

"I am going as the goddess Diana," volunteered Cassy.

"That will be charming," approved their uncle, "but I fear we have interrupted Miss Saint-Clair's dissertation on my housekeeping. She had just said 'I don't see' and I confess that I am in a state of painful suspense as to what she was going to say."

Lucy, nettled, did not hesitate. "I don't see why bachelors can't be clean," she answered and thrust the newspaper into her host's hands. "March," she said, briskly.

"March?" echoed Lord Rune, at sea. "My dear Miss Saint-Clair, I realize that you are a spirited young lady, and I admire your spirit, but I am not going to march about my drawingroom at two o'clock in the afternoon. It isn't the thing."

Lucy glowered at him. "The date on the newspaper," she explained. "It was lying on the floor and must have done so for weeks. And there are four dead flies on your windowsill. One would be excessive. Flies die in the autumn. Obviously no one has cared to dust for simply months and months"—she saw Cassy and Grace looking at her with horror, but swept on—"I suppose it's indelicate of me to talk about dead flies, and indeed, I am very sorry, but it is also indelicate to have dead flies —and you have them."

"Indeed I have," agreed Lord Rune, with his most enchanting smile. "Mice, too, I shouldn't wonder."

Lucy would not smile back. "It isn't funny," she reprimanded him. "Of course," she added, after another glance at Lord Rune's spellbound nieces, "I hold your servants entirely to blame."

"I don't," answered Lord Rune.

Lucy knit her brows. "Why not?"

"Because they're only aping their betters," answered Lord Rune blandly, "or rather, they have no 'better' to ape, and so they emulate me. The master is idle and so is the man. Who am I to play the hypocrite and prose on about industry and sobriety?"

Lucy's brows drew still closer together. "You are their employer," she answered, "and it isn't proper for them to be idle."

Lord Rune leaned forward in his chair. "Why, Miss Saint-Clair, you have a puritanical streak. Your father would be delighted."

References to Lucy's parents seldom had a good effect on her. This time was no exception. "It isn't proper for you to be idle, either," she asserted, eliciting a little gasp from Cassy.

Lord Rune's faint smile broadened to a grin. "It isn't, is it? Of course"—he leaned indolently against the back of his chair—"you are never idle."

Lucy bit her lip. She was not at all sure how to respond. The truth was that at Mrs. Theale's home she had very litte work to do. She embroidered, read aloud, and amused herself. At the vicarage there had always been work at hand—dusting and dress-making and visiting the poor. She did not miss any of these activities. "I work on my music," she said lamely.

"She does," Grace defended her. "She practices for hours and sings the same thing over and over. And she never misses a single day."

"And she does my hair," chimed in Cassy, "and when we're in the country she arranges the flowers and walks the dogs."

"Estimable," said Lord Rune. "I had no idea that you were such a paragon of industry."

He spoke lightly, but the words stung. Lucy scowled down at her own sprig muslin lap, seeing the blue print blur into a solid color. She did not know whether to be ashamed or angry; she was, of course, both. Her behavior had been indefensible; his sarcasm was intolerable. Lord Rune watched her face for a moment and then rose. He took a step closer to her, remembered the presence of his nieces, and cleared his throat.

"I meant it, you know," he said. "You could not sing so effortlessly if you had not worked hard on your music, and your energy is such as must awaken admiration."

Lucy looked up, realized that she had tears in her eyes, and hurriedly looked down again. Lord Rune sought for a somewhat lighter tone.

"I suppose that you could scold my servants with a clear conscience."

Lucy raised her head, her lips curving in response to the smile in his eyes. "Indeed I could," she said. "Nothing could give me greater pleasure."

A sudden demonic temptation flashed through Lord Rune's head, and instead of resisting it, he reached for the bell-cord. "No host could deny a guest so trifling a wish," he said, and rang the bell.

Three pairs of eyes stared aghast as Pettibone opened the door. "Yes, milor'?"

"I should like to see the servants," Lord Rune commanded. "Except Cook—and Pudder."

Pettibone regarded his master expressionlessly. It was not the custom for servants to mingle with the master's guests. "All of 'em?" he asked, at last. "The knife-boy too?"

"Certainly the knife-boy," assented Lord Rune. "No doubt he is dull and Miss Saint-Clair will sharpen him against the grindstone of her tongue."

Lucy rose, unable to believe her ears. "Lord Rune—"

Pettibone gaped at the assembled company, wondered if his stomach draught, which certainly smelled like gin, had addled his wits, and decided that it would be folly to argue. "Very good," he answered mechanically, and left the room. Lucy stared at the closed door, and then spun around to confront her demented host.

"Lord Rune, Lord Rune," she repeated breathlessly, "you must have misunderstood—you must be teasing me. You cannot mean—I *cannot* scold your servants."

"Certainly you can," contradicted Lord Rune. "You will enjoy yourself hugely, and so will I."

"But—" She put out a tentative hand to touch his arm and then stopped, raising her hand to her lips. She could think of nothing to say.

"It really wouldn't be right," Cassy pointed out, "and—" She shook her head, at a loss for words.

"And they won't listen," Grace argued, "because Lucy isn't the master—or the mistress," she corrected herself, and looked vaguely pleased. "If you were to marry someone, *she* could scold the servants for you," she went on, so archly that Cassy covered her face with her hands and Lucy groaned.

"Oh, Grace, do, hush," Lucy begged. "I am sure you are jesting, Lord Rune, and that you will speak to the servants yourself—but I *can*not, I can*not*—"

The door opened. With unwonted swiftness Pettibone had assembled Lord Rune's staff, and they filed into the room, glancing at Lucy and the Theale girls as if they were dangerous animals.

They were an ill-assorted lot. Directly behind Pettibone stood Flitworm, who was tidy but who looked terrified, and behind him the knife-boy rubbed his nose against the palm of his hand. The second footman, Cheezum, was sucking a toothpick. Two gentlemen-in-waiting, Grubb and Fishbine, were dressed in contrasting livery: Fishbine was vain and wore livery that would have been suitable for a ball: Grubb was far from sober and constantly slovenly. A tough-looking female in a stained apron, who was evidently Lord Rune's housekeeper, stood with her arms crossed over her chest. She was Mrs. Grubb and she had been keeping her son company over a bottle of port. By nature she was gentle and resigned to her lot in life, but port made her bellicose. Last of all, Lord Rune's cook, an enormous Russian, blocked the doorway and surveyed the entire company with a hopeful smile. He had not been summoned, but he had come; and a strong aroma of freshly chopped onions came with him.

Lucy stopped in mid-sentence. Lord Rune's staff was a modest one for a man of his fortune, but it seemed

very large to her, and all of its members looked villain-
ous. Even the blameless Flitworm, she felt, had a mania-
cal look in his eye, and the bloated Grubbs positively
frightened her. She opened her mouth to speak and no
sound came out.

Then Cheezum scratched his stomach.

It is a peculiarity of the male sex that stomach-
scratching is often accompanied by a facial expression
of profound stupidity. Cheezum was not intellectual by
nature, and the stupidity of his expression was unusual
—was almost preternatural. The coarseness of his gesture and the vacuousness of his countenance were too
much for Miss Saint-Clair. She immediately lost her
temper.

"Have you no shame?" she rapped out.

Cheezum started guiltily, his hand still circling his
abdomen. Mrs. Grubb put her hands on her hips. Lord
Rune inclined his head towards Lucy in the slightest of
bows. "Miss Saint-Clair has something to say to you."

Lucy's temper, a little daunted by Mrs. Grubb,
flared higher.

"I haven't," she contradicted, "but I will, because
your master is too lazy to speak for himself. I daresay
you will not be surprised—not very surprised—if I tell
you, without mincing words, that the state of this house
is disgraceful."

The knife-boy sniffed. Lucy scowled at him, and he
subsided, putting his hands behind his back. Submission, even so small a submission, encouraged her, and
she squared her shoulders and went on.

"I know that housework is not interesting," she
said, "because at home, I keep house, and it's very tedious doing the same things over and over, with no time
in between to forget how tedious they are. I know that it

is dull work, but it is work that you agreed to do, and work that you take money for doing, and it is my opinion"—she fixed her eyes on Cheezum, daring him to scratch again—"that you ought to do it."

Flitworm bowed slightly. "That's very well-spoken, Miss," he said, "and as a matter of fact, I myself have thought—"

"You oughtn't just to think," Lucy interrupted mercilessly, "you ought to *do* something. Look at this room!" She went to the mantel and took up the tankard of ale, flourishing it so that it splashed over her wrist. "How long has this been here?"

The heavy-eyed Grubb roused himself. "Thursday, that would be," he replied, after some cogitation. "Gen'r'ly speaking, there's not much ale drunk in this house, but Thursday last his Lordship—"

"Yes, I dare say, but there is no need for ale to remain from Thursday, or newspapers from March, or dead flies from October," flashed back Lucy. "This might be one of the most beautiful houses in London, and instead—"

Mrs. Grubb took her hands off her hips and crossed them over her breast again. "What dead flies?" she demanded, in stentorian tones. "Where are they?"

"There are a great many dead flies on the window-sills," Lucy answered icily, "and how you—how anyone —can fail to see them is a thing I cannot comprehend."

Once again, Flitworm interrupted her. "Indeed, Miss," he said, "I have indeed noticed them, and I've said again and again, Miss, that they were the wrong thing for a gentleman's house, but—"

"Do not toad-eat," Lucy answered, sternly. "If you saw them and did not get rid of them, then you are doubly guilty."

So saying, she pulled out her handkerchief and went to the windows, sweeping the sills and crushing the dead flies up into the square of white lace. The servants watched her. No one spoke. Cassy and Grace were too appalled, and Lord Rune had turned away, evidently wishing to conceal his face.

Lucy turned back at last, the handkerchief in her hand. "Take this," she directed Flitworm, and he did not dare refuse. She braced herself to resume her discourse and to face the hostile faces before her without flinching, only to see—or did she imagine it?—that they had grown substantially less hostile.

She did not imagine it. The conscientious Flitworm, the pious Flitworm, the gruesomely neat and regular Flitworm, was the aversion of the staff. The Russian, who could not understand enough English to know exactly what was going on, still grasped that Flitworm had been squelched, and he beamed at Lucy and waved his chopping knife in an amiable fashion. Lucy, thus applauded, became still more eloquent.

"I began by asking if you were dead to shame," she said, "and I shall finish by asking if you are dead to pride. Before you there is work that can be done well and with dignity, or done badly and shame you and your master. You are the caretakers of beautiful things, of a house that might be admired by all London, and you must remember this and bestir yourselves. It will not be easy to restore it to decency after it has been squalid for so long, but we are not beasts, born to lie about in rumpled linen and drink and scrat—and waste time. We are meant to strive," Lucy declaimed, unconsciously beginning to imitate the Reverend Saint-Clair's most impassioned delivery, "and climb upward—and be steadfast, and unmovable, for our labor is not in vain."

She cast a solicitous eye over her audience, to see if they appreciated how well the words of St. Paul applied to their situation, and saw that she had lost them. A stifled sound, half-whimper and half-gasp, came from their master. Lucy set her chin. Evidently Lord Rune was diverted by her discourse. She would put an end to that.

"I said that it will not be easy to restore the house to order," she said, "and for that reason, Lord Rune will raise your salaries, by"—she hesitated, and then said vindictively—"By one third."

The attention of her audience no longer wandered.

"You will receive better salaries," Lucy proclaimed, "and, as well, your master will endeavor to be more attentive to your work and your needs. He realizes that he has been shiftless, and it is a source of no small dissatisfaction to him. However, he is not beyond reparation. From now on he will try to prove a better master. This also means"—she bent her most threatening glance on Cheezum—"that he will know when you do not attend to your work, and those of you who do not will be discharged. Without references."

She acknowledged the Russian's wave of the chopping-knife with a stiff nod. "That is all," she concluded. "You may go."

They went. As one, they turned toward the door, Mrs. Grubb even dropping an involuntary curtsy. The doors were maneuvered shut with exquisite uniformity, and the nearly bald head of the genuflecting Pettibone vanished from sight.

Lucy, staring after it, was surprised to find herself trembling. Her heart raced, and she made an indefinite gesture with her hands.

"You will beggar me, you know," observed Lord Rune.

He did not sound angry. Lucy risked a glance at him and saw that he merely looked reproachful.

"No," she hazarded, "I don't think I will."

She spoke cautiously, but she met his eyes quite steadily, so steadily, in fact, that Lord Rune was aware of a twinge of discomfort. He was reminded that the coat he was wearing would have paid Pettibone's annual salary many times over. He felt a little defensive and wondered why; he was an easy master and not ungenerous.

"They were not ill-paid, you know."

Lucy looked startled. "Oh, no! I'm sure they were not!" she said, and Lord Rune was surprised at the depths of his relief; her good opinion could mean nothing to him.

"At home, our servants are always behaving badly, and I have sometimes wondered if perhaps they wanted more money. We've never tried giving them any—Papa says that too much money is very bad for people of that class"—she unclenched her fingers, and spread her hands, appealing to his understanding—"but I have sometimes thought that a little extra would—would make them—would inspire them—I thought—"

"You thought you would like to make the experiment," Lord Rune prompted her. "With my capital, of course."

Lucy bit her lip. "You are laughing at me," she accused, and lowered her eyes in case he wasn't.

"Yes," agreed Ernest. "There are some things, Miss Saint-Clair, that are magnificent and comic at the same time."

For a moment their eyes met; dark eyes and green

eyes, as Lucy's smile widened and Ernest's altered. Then something—perhaps only an intake of breath—made Ernest remember that they were not alone and that he was not in love.

"We have shocked the sharks," he said.

"I beg your pardon?"

Ernest turned to his nieces and sketched a mockery of a bow. "You are very quiet."

Grace, who had been looking forward to saying that she had never been more shocked in her life, thought better of it. Cassy, who had been even more shocked than Grace, opened her mouth and shocked herself. "We're hungry," she said plaintively, as if Lord Rune were Mamma and she and Grace ten years younger.

"Yes," Grace agreed, attempting the pout she had been practicing before the mirror. "We want our tea."

Lord Rune gaped at them. Then the laughter that he had controlled for the past half-hour overtook him, and he roared so loudly that the servants stopped gossiping in the kitchen and stared at the ceiling, certain that their master had gone mad.

8

Three days later, Lord Rune rose at the unwonted hour of nine o'clock, supervised the unwrap-
ping of the Howard chandelier, and assured a
lachrymose Mrs. Grubb that the task of dusting the
ceiling moldings could be left to Flitworm and Fishbine.
He cast an astonished glance over the newly waxed
staircase, complimented Grubb on the purity of his
linen, and sidestepped Flitworm, who was desirous of
prolonged intercourse. These lordly duties fulfilled, he
donned a driving coat and set off in the rain for Old
Bond Street.

The dressmaking establishment of Sybil Rant was a
respectable brick building with a small plate glass window to the right of the door. Lord Rune, who had fi-
nanced its purchase, had recommended a larger
window, but Sybil Rant, who contemplated the window
tax with irreconcilable loathing, had informed him that

one window was enough for her. Ernest, giving the window a brief inspection, was inclined to think that Sybil had been right, for display was not her strong suit. The window showed a length of watered silk, a brisé fan, and a fashionably dressed doll with a fierce immobility of countenance. None of these specimens hinted to the spectator that the unfestive Miss Rant was, in fact, the finest dressmaker in London.

It had been Lord Rune's association with concubines—as the vicar's Lucy called them—that first led him to Sybil Rant, and his admiration for her artistry had survived a dozen more amorous liaisons. When fire destroyed her former shop, Lord Rune lent her the money to rebuild. He had not expected to be repaid. In this he did Miss Rant an injustice; she was parsimonious but not dishonest and she could find no satisfaction in money that belonged by rights to another. Her payments were meticulously regular, and over the years something like affection had grown between patron and protégée. To be sure, the affection was indirectly expressed: Lord Rune took pleasure in provoking Miss Rant, and she responded with growls and sniffs, grudging every courtesy that was due him.

It was early in the day for shopping when Lord Rune grasped the knob of Sybil Rant's shop, and the rain had discouraged customers. Sybil sat alone in the showroom, with a heavy ledger before her. She stared blankly at her benefactor and then donned a pair of spectacles, which magnified her pale eyes to unearthly size. For a moment she blinked at him from behind the glass.

Sybil Rant was forty or fifty years old. She had a broad, freckled face, intelligent grey eyes, and colorless hair, which she dressed in two thin plaits, crossing them over her head in a neat, though countrified manner. Her gown, which was made of some lusterless fabric, hung loosely over contours so thoroughly concealed as to seem ghostly. She wore a brooch of very fine moonstones, and her manner, when she spoke, was as devoid of allure as it was of affectation.

"You're a stranger," she greeted Lord Rune. Her voice was very deep and rather flat. She never hurried her words.

Ernest removed his dripping coat.

"No fire, Sybil?"

"It's April."

Lord Rune shook his head. "There's such a thing as an excess of economy, you know."

Sybil Rant rose. "There's such a thing as extravagance, too, and I want no part of it." She bent her spectacled glance on his coat and ventured, "I suppose you've come to talk."

"If it's quite convenient, yes, I have."

Sybil relieved him of his coat and led him into the back hall. "You've come at worse times." She hung the coat on a fragile-looking peg and sighed. "Come along."

So encouraged, Lord Rune followed her up the stairs and into a workroom, where half a dozen women labored in the rainy light. Their voices, which had sounded fluent and lighthearted from the stairwell, hushed as Sybil entered the room, and they assumed uniform expressions of devout concentration.

"One of you had best go downstairs and mind the shop," Sybil announced, and the tallest of the women laid down her scissors and left the room. Ernest, watching the exodus with amusement, made a show of counting the remaining women.

"Six women under you, Sybil?"

"Seven. One's ill." Sybil paused before a young woman who was toiling over a bodice of bottle-green silk. "There's some things as can't be ironed right, Phoebe."

The hapless Phoebe froze.

"If there were an honest bone in your body, you'd rip that out and start afresh." Sybil tapped her finger against a minute pucker, and then passed by, leading Lord Rune up another flight of stairs. "These girls get worse every year," she went on, without troubling to lower her voice. "If they're not bone-lazy, they don't have the wits they were born with. I have to tell them everything." She opened the door of her office and jerked her head to invite him in.

It was a dark and funereal little room, in which Sybil's saturnine taste had indulged itself to the fullest. Tall, graceful windows had been hidden by draperies of puce velvet, and the furniture was walnut—carved, dark, and massive. Both the sofa and the armchairs had great claw-and-ball feet, which had tripped Lord Rune more than once before now. Above the mantelpiece was a painting of a sinking ship; one of the survivors swam toward the viewer with one arm upraised in permanent and hopeless entreaty. Three clocks and four hour-glasses—Sybil had a fondness for time-pieces—had the chilling effect of a memento mori.

Lord Rune, who always pretended that he found the office delightful, rubbed his hands together and seated himself in the cruelest of the chairs. "Lord, it's good to see you again!"

Sybil Rant took off her spectacles and cleaned them with her handkerchief. "What d'you want, Rune?"

Ernest leaned back against the lumpy upholstery.

"Deucedly comfortable," he commented. "I believe you're glad to see me, Sybil. Why, your face is wreathed in smiles."

Sybil regarded him impassively. "What d'you want, Rune?"

"I want a gypsy costume."

Sybil sniffed and took a seat on the sofa, stepping over the claw-and-ball with the caution of long practice. "Won't suit you."

"It isn't for me. It's for a lady."

"Where's the lady?"

There was a pugnacious quality about the question that put Lord Rune on the defensive, even as he relished crossing swords with his old opponent. "You wrong me, Sybil. The lady in question is indeed a lady—a vicar's daughter, in fact, and will visit you under the protection of my sister." He drummed his fingers against the arm of his chair. "I've been wanting to send her to you for some time but I wanted to talk to you first."

Sybil, seeing that he hesitated, waited a polite moment before administering a goad. "I have work to do," she threatened.

Lord Rune, combating rudeness with rudeness, retorted, "It can wait." He saw the dressmaker open her mouth in protestation, and temporized. "For a moment. I'm going to send you three new clients, Sybil—clients of perfect respectability and substantial capital. My two nieces, Miss Theale and Miss Grace Theale, and my sister's god-child, Miss Saint-Clair. They will be needing costumes for a masquerade that I am giving."

Sybil regarded him unenthusiastically. "May the seventh," she supplied, somewhat to his surprise. "One of my clients was in yesterday. Fancies herself as the goddess Pomona. 'What's she?' I asked, and she told me it was a goddess of fruit. She wants a toga with garlands of berries all over it." She fixed her eyes on the painting of the doomed ship, and shook her head. "Lady Selina Marling. As shapeless a young woman as you can find in a twelvemonth. It's almost more than I can manage to give her a shape in ordinary clothes, but you must needs give a masquerade, and she must needs tell me to deck her out in fruit. As for me, I've debts to pay and my living to earn, and so I said, 'Very well, Lady Marling, fruit you have asked for, and fruit you shall have.' Although how I shall contrive to make it become her, I'm sure I don't know."

"Yours is a fate to be pitied."

Sybil sniffed. "Much you know about it."

Lord Rune, instead of retaliating, found himself in agreement with her. "That's true," he said, with an air of mild surprise. "None of the ladies of my acquaintance have ever entreated me to deck them out in fruit. Although, as you remember, Celia Coventry's passion for ostrich plumes expressed itself in a number of unusual—"

Sybil's mouth twisted. "That's enough," she said. "What's brought you here, Rune? Don't tell me you want a gypsy costume; I don't have one, and I'm not likely to make one until I've measured your vicar's daughter and made up my mind what will become her."

Lord Rune nodded emphatically. "Exactly so," he approved. "I particularly want Miss Saint-Clair's costume to become her. In fact, you must surpass yourself, Sybil. Miss Saint-Clair is the ultimate cause of this damnable masquerade, and for once in her life she has to look presentable. More than presentable," he said, challengingly. "She is going to tell fortunes, and I intend for her to be the cynosure of all neighboring eyes, as dear old Milton would put it. Her costume must be markedly original and decidely picturesque. Furthermore, I should like you to encourage her to order a whole new wardrobe—her clothes are quite impossibly wrong. You will turn pale with rage at the sight of them. Of course, she has no money"—the expression on Sybil's face was daunting in the extreme, but Lord Rune continued—"but my sister will pay for her costume. I shall pay for the others—my nieces'. I have become remarkably avuncular of late."

Sybil, who was not quite certain what *avuncular* meant, said, "Have you?" in a voice of awe-inspiring grimness.

Lord Rune stiffened a little. "Yes, I have," he asserted. "My sister—Mrs. Benedict Theale—persuaded me to interest myself in my nieces—and in her goddaughter. Lucy—Miss Saint-Clair—is in her fourth Season. She has not had the good fortune to attract an eligible *parti*, and I agreed—as a sort of a wager"— Ernest became suddenly absorbed in the cuff of his topboot—"to bring her into fashion."

"I suppose," Sybil interposed, "you're talking about the chit you introduced to Jenny."

Lord Rune lost all interest in the top-boot and gaped instead at Sybil Rant, who enjoyed his stupefaction far more than her dour countenance expressed. The confrontation lasted only a moment. Ernest recovered by quirking an eyebrow and shoving his hands deep in his pockets.

"So you've seen Jenny, have you?"

"She was in yesterday."

"I thought that flame-colored gown had your look about it. I congratulate you."

Sybil grunted, but a ghost of a smile touched her

lips and would not be wholly banished. "She looks well enough." For a very brief moment, she gazed ahead, her pale eyes glimmering with some secret pleasure, and then she turned back to Lord Rune, directing so piercing a glance at him that he crossed his legs and pressed his spine deeper into the unyielding upholstery.

"It's a pretty piece of business, Rune, introducing a bread-and-butter miss to a bit of muslin. What possessed you?"

Lord Rune dug his hands deeper into his pockets. "Gossip don't become you, Sybil."

Sybil sniffed, a quiet sound, but one that resounded with frustration. The "girls" one floor below, who saw their mistress as a basilisk and a sphinx, would have rejoiced at the sound, finding in it evidence that Miss Rant was curious and consequently human. Lord Rune, a hard-hearted man, allowed his lips to curl into a smile and did not answer.

After a short pause, Sybil volunteered, "Jenny liked the look of the girl. Says she shook hands and spoke very prettily."

"She did."

Lord Rune's tone of voice was blandness itself. In spite of that, a look of satisfaction of intelligence gleaned and treasured, flashed across the dressmaker's face.

"So you're buying clothes for her."

Ernest shook his head. "That's just it. I can't. And Tha— well, that's the damnable thing, Sybil. My sister Tabitha has absolutely no eye, and she's spent a deal of money on Lucy already. She won't be eager to spend more—and the girl needs a whole new turn-out. Naturally, I mustn't seem to have anything to do with it." He smiled ruefully, remembering the scene in the park, and quoted, " 'It isn't the thing.' "

Sybil's countenance, never very mobile, seemed to have petrified. "So. The girl is to have new clothes, and she's not going to pay for them. Neither is your sister going to pay for them. Neither are you going to pay for them." She drew a deep breath, and Lord Rune held up a hand, mutely trying to stem the oration that was bound to follow.

"I suppose you think this is a charitable institution, my Lord Rune, and that I make clothes to amuse myself between dress-balls and Venetian fêtes, but it isn't, and I don't. I have my living to earn and my business to see to, and the only charity I subscribe to is a penny in the plate on Sunday, and I begrudge that." She saw that Lord Rune looked restive, and she raised her voice in order to prevent his interrupting her. "It may or may not interest you to know that silk and muslin have gone up, but they have, and you may not think, my Lord, that I have to pay those girls anything, but I do. It's more than they're worth, but there it is; you can't find a decent girl nowadays and you have to pamper the fools that you do find. And last winter the front window was broken by a snowball." The eyes behind the thick spectacles were accusing. "So there was the cost of the glass gone from my pocket, and if you think a spool of thread costs what it did ten years ago, you're mistaken. Not to mention the pins and needles those girls waste every day—although if I've told them once, I've told them a hundred—"

"Sybil, for God's sake!" Lord Rune's voice wavered between annoyance and amusement. "If you talk that way to your girls, they have my heart-felt sympathy —no, don't look at me like that; you'll turn me to stone!

And don't fancy yourself ill-used, either! You know perfectly well you're being a dead bore and no one's asking you for a farthing!"

So brutal a rejoinder might have intimidated many women; it might have been expected, at least, to have distracted Miss Rant from the issue that concerned her. Sybil was not, however, easily bullied. "Who's going to pay for these clothes?" she demanded.

"I am."

Sybil smiled sourly, happy to have the opportunity to contradict him. "I thought you said you couldn't," she complained. "If this Miss Saint-Clair is a lady, she won't stand for it, and neither will your sister."

"They won't know anything about it." Ernest's voice was strained; his patience, never abundant, was running thin. "That's what I've been explaining to you. That's what you're going to manage for me."

A guttural sound issued from Sybil's throat, a sound not unlike the hooting of an owl. The youngest of the apprentices, upon first hearing a similar sound, had begun by offering Miss Rant a glass of water and finished by pounding very tentatively between Miss Rant's bony shoulder blades. Lord Rune had heard the sound before and had no difficulty in classifying it as a laugh. He waited patiently until it had stopped—it never continued for very long.

"It will really be very simple. I have recommended you to my sister as a skilled dress-maker who is in need of respectable clients. She will bring Miss Saint-Clair— and the nieces who have compelled me to turn avuncular—to the shop for costumes. Miss Saint-Clair's face and form will make a deep impression on you, and you will explain to her that her present clothes are unsuitable. That should not present the slightest difficulty—

they are repellent. You will propose that she buy more becoming ones, she—or my sister—will indicate that she has no money to buy them, and you will sulk a little. That, at any rate, should come naturally. Finally, you will offer to create a new wardrobe at a price so ridiculously low that my sister, God bless her, will be unable to resist it. The actual cost will, of course, be passed on to me—and I need hardly remind you that I am a very wealthy man." He spoke the last words meaningfully, as if he expected Sybil to remark upon the advantages implicit in his proposal. He was destined to be disappointed; Sybil considered gratitude servile and never admitted to being at an advantage.

"I don't want to," Sybil said.

Lord Rune, hearing the obstinacy of her voice, was inspired to lose his temper. He rose from the tormenting chair as if he could bear it no longer. "Dammit, Sybil—"

"For one thing," Sybil Rant stated, "I'm not good at pretending."

Her voice was flat, imperturbable. Lord Rune gazed at her, the lines of his face rigid, and then, unwillingly, grinned. Sybil spoke the absolute truth; she was not good at pretending. If she had had a modicum of tact she might have been the most successful dressmaker in London, as well as the most skillful. Instead, she was ruthless, riding roughshod over her patrons' most cherished vanities, refusing outright to make a gown in a style or color that would not suit its wearer, clinging to her own, uneuphonious name in a London full of Célestes and Thérèses and Madeleines. That Sybil's intolerance for pretense was the weakest point in Lord Rune's strategy he knew very well. He spoke coaxingly, even caressingly.

"Oh, come now, Sybil! It will not be so very difficult as all that! Just tell the girl—she's the dark-haired one, by the by—that her clothes are a nightmare and that a different sort of gown would be the making of her! Tell her that you're hoping to attract more customers among the haut ton. Tell her that you are pining to design a new sort of gown and that you need a striking sort of beauty to set it off, and—"

"But she ain't a striking beauty," protested Sybil.

Lord Rune had been sufficiently caught up in his strategy as to be somewhat startled by this objection. "I beg your pardon?"

"She ain't a striking beauty," Sybil repeated, with an air of much-tried patience that made him want to swear at her again. "Jenny says she's only fair-to-middling."

Lord Rune drew a deep breath.

"And I *have* customers among your ton," Sybil added, belligerently. "They don't pay their bills—half of 'em. Why, that ferret-faced Countess of Aberneath was in last week, wanting a new gown, and I was obliged to speak to her. I said, 'If you've come to pay your bills, that's one thing, but not one penny will I advance, not if I was to die for it.' She didn't know what to say to that. And then—"

Lord Rune silenced her by the simple expedient of kicking a footstool across the room. It banged against the double doors, causing a crash loud enough to cause the "girls" below to cast up their eyes, rapt with curiosity. He forebore to clutch his foot, which hurt very much, and addressed Miss Rant with a gentle dignity that was particularly winning.

"You will oblige me in this matter," he said, almost deferentially, "because I loaned you money when bankruptcy stared you in the face." His smile broadened, growing almost saintly in its benevolence. "It isn't in your line, I'll grant you that, but you will do it, you obstinate old gorgon, and I daresay you'll do it as well as you do everything else."

Sybil looked at the overturned footstool. "You're an ugly customer, to throw that up to me after all these years." There was not the slightest trace of resentment in her voice.

"Am I not?" Lord Rune lifted Sybil's hand to his lips. "You'll have to revile me for it some time—not now, for the vulgarity of a clock informs me that half an hour has passed—quite long enough for a social call." He bowed. "Your most obedient, ma'am."

Sybil regarded her hand gloomily, as if she had spilled something on it. "You can see yourself downstairs."

Lord Rune bowed again, even more gracefully than before. Sybil Rant went to the mantel, and examined one of the hour-glasses in order to ignore him more thoroughly. "You might as well put that footstool back as you go out," she commanded, "and don't bang the shop door unless you want to pay for new glass."

She had the satisfaction of hearing a muffled chuckle as he descended the stairs, and she put down the hour-glass with a gleam in her eye. "Interesting," she commented, to no one in particular. "Interesting."

9

It was seven-thirty in the evening of the seventh of May, and Mrs. Grubb was lighting the candles for Lord Rune's masquerade.

She performed her task with the reverence of an acolyte, watching each wick darken and curl until the flames grew tall and steady. They were scented candles, purchased at great expense from Shire Street, and the silver and porcelain sconces that held them had been rubbed so ruthlessly that no atom of dust, no smear of tarnish, sullied their perfection. One by one the flames flared, and gradually the rooms filled with light.

They were rooms transformed; so much so that Mrs. Grubb was a little in awe of them. The last two weeks had been hectic and laborious for Lord Rune's servants. Before Lucy, their days had been long, aimless, and idle; now they were swift, purposeful, and exhausting. Floors had been waxed and polished; furniture had been rubbed to a lacquer-like sheen. The ornamental plasterwork had been sponged until it looked as innocently white and glossy as whipped cream. The windows had been scrubbed until they glinted like jewels; the windowsills had been swept free of the carnage that had so disgusted Miss Saint-Clair, and the draperies had been taken down and brushed. The fastidious Fishbine had actually split his breeches standing on a ladder to redrape them, and Cruddup, the knife-boy, had shown unwonted zeal for beating the carpets.

Tonight, most of the carpets were rolled up and stored upstairs. The downstairs rooms were emptied for dancing, with only a few pieces of furniture arranged against the walls. Orange trees and blooming gardenias softened the austerities of the stripped rooms and filled them with fragrance. The grand staircase was festooned with ivy and white ribbons and the alcove in the large drawing-room was transformed into an arbor for the musicians. Mrs. Grubb, catching a glimpse of the arbor in the gilded mirror, turned to look at herself against a background of green foliage.

Lord Rune, at the urging of the potent and dreadful Miss Saint-Clair, had ordered new liveries for his servants, and Mrs. Grubb had a new dress. It was pale grey, with a thin silver stripe running through it and a frill of fine lace at the throat. The possession of it had actually motivated Mrs. Grubb to risk the dangers of pneumonia and wash her hair. Now the taper in her hand cast a benevolent glow over her lace cap and white curls, and Mrs. Grubb gazed at herself with something like astonishment.

A drop of hot wax fell on her hand and recalled her to her task. With a faint sigh, she turned away from her reflection and went into the green saloon, which had been transformed into a gaming-room. Four tables, in-laid with squares of ebony and ivory, stood ready, each with a fresh pack of cards directly in the center. Mrs. Grubb lit the candles, removed a drooping petal from a bouquet of white peonies, and passed into the reception room.

Here a hundred glasses, each of heavy lead crystal, glittered as the light was kindled; here, too, were great mounds of shattered ice, each with bowls of fruit nested within. Their colors were intense, stained-glass colors: purple blackberries, crimson raspberries, the frosted green of gooseberries and hothouse grapes. There were blood oranges cut in wheels and a magnificent cake, frosted in white and lashed with spun caramel. Blue and white Ming bowls were heaped with ices, champagne gold and strawberry pink. A layered trifle and a platter of swan-shaped meringues flanked an epergne full of sugar-violets and candied rose petals. On a nearby side-board an ornate silver trough sheltered more ice and bottle after bottle of champagne.

Downstairs, Grigori the cook toiled over the mid-night supper. The activity of the last weeks and the sense of festivity in the air had incited him to an orgy of cooking. For the past week, he had fascinated the rest of the staff with his descriptions of a Russian banquet, and he worked so violently and spent money so lavishly, that only Pudder, who remembered Lord Rune's salad days, could pretend to be unimpressed. The atmosphere in the kitchen was volcanic; hot, pungent, and volatile. In a haze of heat and smoke, Grigori stirred sauces and murmured Slavic phrases under his breath; they might have been curses or incantations. Around him a multi-tude of odors seethed and competed: garlic, wine, cav-iar, lemon, cranberries, and cabbage. A suckling pig

hissed and sizzled over the fire; salt fish swam in a bowl
of sour cream. A dish of chicken and asparagus was
tenderly garnished with dill and rosemary; a sirloin of
beef cooled in a lake of blood and burgundy. Saffron
bread rose high, only to be punched down by the Russian's huge hands, and thin pancakes were flipped and
tossed and sprinkled with honey. The pile of dirty dishes
beside the sink grew so tall that Cruddup and Cheezum,
who were to wash them, avoided looking in that direction and sought solace in a bottle of champagne.

At midnight, the dining-room doors would open
and the candles would be lit with ceremony. The wicks
were linked together by threads soaked in flammable
liquid, and a single flame would ignite all twenty-four
simultaneously. It was a conceit of Grigori's, which he
had once seen and never forgotten. Flitworm, who was
to light the first candle, was decidedly nervous about it.

The table was set, the linen immaculate. Mrs.
Grubb, seeing that all was in order, locked the door and
proceeded into the little saloon. This had been adapted
to make a dressing-room for the ladies and afforded her
another chance to admire her new dress. Mirrors, col-
lected from all over the house, lined one wall. A Sèvres
tray held dress-pins, and hair-pins, and a gilt oddments
tray proffered a hospitable assortment of almonds and
chocolate creams. Mrs. Grubb selected one of the latter,
rearranged the rest, and took the liberty of sprinkling
her handkerchief with Hungary water. By the light of
six candles she adjusted the lace frill one last time,
touched her handkerchief to her lips so that no trace of
chocolate remained, and slipped off to await the first
guests.

*   *   *

They were, predictably, the Theale family and Miss Saint-Clair. Lord Rune, hearing that they had come, told his valet that his hair would do very well as it was and tried to wave aside the curling iron that was being brandished before him. In vain; Pudder had his reputation to think of, and his lordship should not attend a party looking like a savage. A series of ministrations followed: Lord Rune's hands must be massaged with lotion; the merits of an onyx and ruby ring must be disputed; the black velvet doublet—Lord Rune was dressed as Hamlet—must be given a final inspection for hanging threads. It was fully ten minutes before Lord Rune lost his patience, swore, and announced that nothing would induce him to apply a scented pomade to his brown curls. He left the dressing-room with an air as thunderous as any the melancholy Dane had ever assumed and set off to examine his protégée's costume.

He had not far to look. Miss Saint-Clair, in a state of considerable trepidation about her appearance, had left the rest of the company and stood in the musicians' alcove, examining herself in the mirror that had earlier reflected Mrs. Grubb. Lord Rune, coming across her a moment or two before he expected to, stopped short and stared.

He had asked Sybil Rant for a gypsy costume; he had not expected his request to be obeyed so realistically. He had had a vague idea of bright and gaudy fabrics, transformed by Sybil's hand into something romantic and picturesque. He was somewhat shocked to see that Miss Saint-Clair, instead of looking her usual dowdy and respectable self, looked like a positive vagabond. She wore a loose gauze blouse, a black laced corset, and a tattered grey skirt, faintly spangled, over a crimson petticoat.

For one appalling moment, he could have cursed Sybil; in that moment, Miss Saint-Clair glimpsed him in the mirror and turned. The torn fabric of the skirt swung and glimmered; the spangles caught the light, and a glimpse of petticoat shone, as iridescent and fleeting as the plumage of a bird. He began to see the subtlety of Sybil's idea; the blouse looked worn, almost dingy, but its subdued pink-grey made Lucy's shoulders and bosom look rosy, opalescent. He was compelled to note that Lucy's shoulders were superb, that her bosom was impressive, and that her waist—in comparison to wide shoulders and cascading skirts—was gracefully, even engagingly, curved.

His inspection was leisurely; Lucy's face, which had begun by looking hopeful and a little sheepish, darkened, and she lowered her eyes to the black ribbons that laced the corset.

"Miss Saint-Clair—"

She looked up, patently eager for his good opinion, and the practiced gallantry never left his lips. He looked past her, at the reflection of her bare shoulders, and stated, almost brusquely, "Sybil is a genius."

Lucy's face fell; it was not the compliment she coveted. "She's very clever. I don't mean me—" She shook her head, and stepped back, the thin fabric rustling. "I don't really know if I like this costume or not; I think I present a—a very singular appearance." She smiled shakily. "Of course, it is a masquerade, and even Godmamma says I have nothing to blush for—Miss Rant draped this blouse herself, and although I dare say it looks very careless, it can't slip off my shoulders. Miss Rant promised me it wouldn't. She's very good at fitting things. Cassy and Grace look so very pretty! You must see them!" She bent her head and played with a rent in the spangled overskirt. "My petticoat is shot silk—sometimes red and sometimes silver. I can't think why Miss Rant put it underneath the grey—"

She stopped again, and her mouth twisted. "I suppose I am nervous," she said, in a voice that trembled. "I'm not at all sure that anyone will ask me to tell fortunes, and I didn't expect to present such a—a singular appearance."

Lord Rune, casting aside his good resolutions, took a step closer to her and caught hold of her hands. He was aware that Tabitha and the others must be waiting in the morning room and might come in search of him, but it could not be helped. Clearly his fortune-teller was in need of distraction and reassurance. He stroked the back of her hands with his thumbs, and calculated what would be best to say. His fertile imagination did not fail him, and he murmured:

> "A sweet disorder in the dress
> Kindles in clothes a wantonness:
> A lawn about the shoulders thrown
> Into a fine distraction:
> An erring lace, which here and there
> Enthrals the crimson stomacher:
> A cuff neglectful, and thereby
> Ribbands to flow confusedly—
>
> A winning wave, deserving note,
> In the tempestuous petticoat:
> A careless shoe-string, in whose tie
> I see a wild civility:
> Do more bewitch me than when art
> Is too precise in every part."

He had the satisfaction of watching Lucy's face brighten, even as she averted her eyes and ducked her head. Her curls fell forward, shadowing her face, and he completed the poem—and his iniquity—by disengaging one hand and brushing them back. "Does that answer your question, Miss Saint-Clair?"

Lucy, more pleasurably flustered than she had ever been in her life, shook her head. "Yes—that is—I don't know. Did I ask a question?"

"I think you did."

Lucy pressed her cheek against his hand, and gazed down at the overskirt, running the torn edge between her thumb and forefinger. "I don't remember. Your poem was so very—I don't recall ever having read it. Is it Jonson?"

"Robert Herrick."

Very tentatively, Lucy curled her fingers around his. "I don't think we had Robert Herrick in the vicarage library."

"No?" Lord Rune relaxed against the wall, almost unaware that the clasp of their hands had tightened. "I must find you a copy. He was a priest, as well as a poet, so"—his lips quivered—"there can be no objection."

Lucy shook her head so energetically that her curls swung. "None at all," she concurred. A tinge of color had come into her face. "I daresay it might be considered an improving book. Indeed, I hope that the tone of my mind is sufficiently nice to apprehend it."

Lord Rune made a half-hearted attempt to keep his countenance and failed. "The tone of your mind—" A wave of laughter overwhelmed him, and he lifted Miss Saint-Clair's hand to his lips. The sight of her face— merry, eager, mischievous—swam before his eyes. Without thinking, he pressed the fleshy part of her hand against his mouth; his lips parted, and he caught her flesh between his teeth.

Lucy was scandalized. She snatched back her hand, and gasped, "What are you *doing?*"

"Oh, good God!" said Ernest. He felt his own color rise, and added guiltily, "I beg your pardon, Miss Saint-Clair."

Miss Saint-Clair looked down at her unmarked hand, and back at him. "You bit me!" she accused him. "Like a dog!"

Lord Rune's features contorted themselves in an attempt to look sober and finally relaxed into a shame-faced grin. "My dear Miss Saint-Clair—don't look at me like that, or I shall laugh—I—I have insulted you unspeakably—quite reprehensibly—and you are very right to be shocked. I beg you to forgive me."

Lucy turned her hand over, studying it in a stupe-fied manner. "I don't think it was as bad as all that," she said uncertainly, "because, you know, you didn't hurt me in the least. Still, it was a very peculiar thing to do. Whatever made you do it?"

Once again, Lord Rune tried to look meek. "It was a temptation," he explained, and the shamefaced grin broke out anew. "There are temptations, you know. Why, think of Francesca da Rimini. She—"

Lucy, caught between laughter and wrath, shushed him. "Do be quiet! I ought never to have talked about Francesca to you. I daresay Godmamma would say it was not the thing. Besides, it is not at all to the point." She cast a sidelong look at him and drew a deep breath. "Even Francesca da Rimini wasn't a *cannibal!*"

Lord Rune, hearing the militant note in her voice, knew himself forgiven. He opened his mouth to defend himself, and remembered just in time that love-bites were not something that he ought to discuss, even in jest. Nor did Miss Saint-Clair look particularly receptive; a thoughtful look came over her face, and her eyes gleamed.

"Of course, one might compare you to Count Ugolino, who ate his children. He was in the ninth circle of the infernal world."

"The ninth circle! My dear Miss Saint-Clair, have mercy!" Lord Rune lifted his hands imploringly. "I don't mind being classed with Francesca, in the second, but I will not be consigned to the ninth!"

Lucy giggled, even as she admired the silver lace at his lordships' wrists. "I didn't consign you. I merely remarked on the similarity between your behavior and Count Ugolino's. It's not my fault if—"

She stopped, looking past him, and he looked beyond her, into the glass. His sister had come into the room and stood watching them. For a split second, Lord Rune experienced a profound sense of disorientation, of embarrassment. Then he shrugged. However keen-eyed Tabitha might be, there was nothing for her to see. He turned to salute her, bowing deeply, and the strangeness that he felt was forgotten.

10

Grace was perfectly happy.

Philosophers are fond of saying that the state of perfect happiness is elusive. Few mortals ever grasp it; fewer still sustain it longer than a moment. Grace had remained in the ticklish state for nearly three hours. Her renaissance gown of flame-colored taffeta, with its bronze-slashed sleeves and pointed waist, was a fascinating garment, and the rustle of her skirts was sweeter than music. She had stood up for every dance and had danced particularly well. A certain young viscount who had haunted her dreams since the beginning of the season, partnered her twice. To be sure, he was not so mysterious, so compelling, as she had thought he would be, but Grace, rational in her felicity, did not quibble. If he was not so handsome as she had thought, his smile was engaging; if his witticisms were strained, no one could doubt his willingness to please. It would be a brilliant match, and Mamma—glimpsed through the shifting mosaic of dancers—was looking excessively pleased.

If Grace relished the bliss of gratified vanity, Cassy, no less fortunate, reveled in the rarefied circumstance of requited love. Her Arthur—dressed as his royal name-sake—stood close beside her, quite unconscious of how the breadth of his shoulders stirred her secret heart. They were not dancing, and this, too, was joy. Cassy, who danced passably with Grace or Lucy, suffered agonies in the arms of a strange young man. No wall-flower was ever more humiliated than Cassy, trapped in the toils of the waltz, her feet at strife with her partner's shoes, her lips too stiff with misery to shape an apology. Early in their acquaintance, Mr. Bloomsbury had explained that he was a very poor dancer, little guessing how his beloved's heart kindled at the disclosure. Only the simplest of dances could lure him onto the floor, and once there he danced cautiously, deliberately, counting under his breath in a way that Cassy found both soothing and endearing. He never distracted her with conversation or appalled her by varying his steps, and he turned a deaf ear to her self-deprecation. "All my fault," he would say, and no protestation on Cassy's part could make him believe otherwise.

Arthur often told himself that he would have loved Cassy if she had been the most avid dancer in London, but it was decidedly convenient that she was not. He felt guilty about this; one's fiancée ought not, perhaps, to be convenient—but his gratitude outweighed his guilt. Arthur was comely and virile, his muscles were formidable, his seat on a horse was heroic—but he was not agile. He was aware that he danced gracelessly; worse still, the combination of anxiety and swift movement made him puff. He hoped that Cassy would not notice until she was his wife. A wife might be kind enough to overlook a little puffing, and it was the sort of thing that was less hideous in a husband than in a lover. He cast a sidelong look at her to make sure she was enjoying herself, saw her lips close over a spoonful of strawberry ice, and felt his chest swell with adoration. Cassy, swallowing, met his eyes and immediately looked away.

The genius of Sybil Rant, which had chosen a severe, square-necked gown for Grace's Juliet and clothed Lucy in tatters and spangles, had been gentle with Cassy. Her Diana tunic was blue and silver, modestly and exquisitely draped. The flowing lines flattered the girlish slightness of her figure, and the soft colors suited her fair coloring. Arthur, inferring his bride-to-be's costume from the broad hints dropped by her sister, had given her a crescent of diamonds to wear in her flaxen hair. The sight of the crescent—and the memory of how rapturously it had been received—emboldened him. He spoke in the apologetic tone that characterized all his compliments.

"If you had been in Troy, Paris would have given that apple to you, and there would have been no Trojan war."

The poetry of this sentiment rendered Cassy speechless. She looked down at her ice, making little dents in the glittering mound with her spoon, and whispered, "Thank you." The erudite Miss Saint-Clair would have pointed out that the golden apple had been bestowed at Mount Ida and that the goddess Diana not coveted it, but Cassy had no inconvenient knowledge of mythology to interfere with her pleasure. Also, she had a good deal of sense; no more than Grace did she quibble. She drew a circle in her ice and turned a decorative shade of pink. Arthur, that most excellent of British kings, turned his attention to the dancers. His pleasure was as acute as hers and his sensibilities were as nice. Compliments should be delivered, and accepted, in profile. The two of them gazed at the harlequin scene before them, enjoying both their intimacy and their privacy.

"There are three Robin Hoods here tonight," Cassy remarked presently. "I think the short one is Laurence Feather."

"Perhaps," agreed Mr. Bloomsbury placidly. He had removed his helmet long ago; it was very heavy and made the tip of his nose turn red. He nodded toward a couple before them. "There's Grace—Miss Theale, I mean."

Cassy smiled and fanned herself with her silver half-mask. "You must call her Grace, of course. You will be her brother very soon." Any reference to the coming wedding flustered her, and she fanned herself more rapidly, unconsciously imitating her mother. "What a little romp she is! It's partly the dress, you know; she likes to feel the skirts flutter." Privately she thought her sister was fluttering to very good effect; she had finished her two dances with the viscount and had begun a quadrille with the viscount's best friend. Cassy scanned the crowd for a glimpse of Lucy and failed to find her. Her uncle stood by the main staircase, where a knot of people had gathered, and as she gazed at them, they burst into laughter. Cassy strained forward; a closer look showed her what she had missed before. Lucy stood on the staircase, a step or two higher than the people around her, and her dark head rose above the crowd.

Cassy plucked at her fiancé's sleeve. "Arthur," she said, "that's Lucy."

Arthur, who had been wondering what perversion of the human mind had led to the invention of the quadrille, looked puzzled. "What's Lucy?"

"Those people." Cassy nodded. "They're all gathered around Lucy, and she's making a speech."

Arthur followed her glance. As he was taller than his fiancée, he could see more; there was, indeed, a crowd gathered around Miss Saint-Clair, and it was listening to her. The shortest Robin Hood had pressed between a balding Julius Caesar and a doughty Henry VIII and stood with his hand outstretched. "She's reading palms," Arthur reported, and Cassy looked shocked.

"She can't read palms. She's the daughter of a clergyman."

Arthur did not argue. Wordlessly, he offered his arm to his beloved and guided her through the crowd. The quadrille ended; and the silence following the music enabled them to hear Lucy's words with very little difficulty.

She was wearing the jet-trimmed mask that Sybil Rant had devised for her, but there was no doubting her identity. The fantastic dress, the wilderness of curls, the clear, carrying voice were unmistakable. It was also unmistakable that she was enjoying herself. Her lips curved with mischief, her color was high, and her movements were supple.

"The lady that you love," she was saying, "is giddy and golden-haired and frivolous—and false."

There was a ripple of laughter among the masculine part of the crowd. Laurence Feather, the red-cloaked Robin Hood, had a well-known weakness for "prime articles," and was famous for fickleness and generosity. His latest mistress was a somewhat meritricious blonde, whose virtue was as light as her protector's surname.

"You have fought two—no, three duels," Lucy went on, "and will dare another before the leaves fall. And yet you will die in bed"—she tilted Mr. Feather's sturdy hand to read it better,—"of gout, and too much Madeira."

This time the laughter was general—Mr. Feather's fondness for eating, drinking, and combat being common knowledge. In vain did Mr. Feather solicit a different fortune; the gypsy ignored him and turned her attention to the next client.

"You are too proud," she began daringly, and the crowd around her tensed. His Grace of Sisleigh had not removed his mask, but his erect carriage and partly-bald head was enough to reveal him to his intimates. "You are not unjust, but your temper is passionate. Your heart was broken when you were young."

The tension in the crowd deepened. It was well known that the Duchess of Sisleigh had died in childbirth and that His Grace had not remarried. What was not known was whether the Duke had suffered greatly or if the attentions he was paying an impecunious young widow were likely to lead to marriage. His friends did not dare to ask him; he was a reserved man. It was not unlikely that he would lose his temper; his carriage, always lofty, had stiffened. The fortuneteller went on as if unaware of the risk she was taking.

"There is happiness within your reach, if you are not too proud to take it. There is one who loves you in secret. And"—her voice grew deeper, almost stern—"there is more to admire in you than rank, though you do not suspect it. Do not be so humble. And do not be so proud." She rapped the palm briskly with her finger-tips and then turned to the next hand.

"You must be wary of quadrupeds," she began, and the owner of the hand burst out laughing.

"There's little divination in that, Gypsy! Anyone can tell the scars of a dog-bite!"

Lucy traced the marks, nodding her head wisely. "So they can. But I said quadrupeds, not just dogs. That flea-bitten grey from Tattersall's—" She coughed, re-membering her role, and when she spoke again, her voice bore the trace of a foreign accent, signally hetero-geneous in kind. "I see a pale horse, who is dangerous for you. And I see a gaming-table, and a bottle of wine, and they, too, are dangerous. And there is a biped, with auburn hair—"

Once again a chorus of laughter covered the ques-tioner's protests. The fingers of the outstretched hand tightened, and poor Mr. Seddingham demanded, "Is she dangerous, too?"

Lucy patted the scarred hand comfortingly.

"She means you no harm—I am the seventh daugh-ter of a seventh daughter, and I can tell you that. It may even be that she loves you with all her heart—but that I cannot say. It would be better if you went to her and asked her what you've long been asking yourself. And when you go"—She gave the pause its full measure—"do not ride the pale horse! Now, who will be next?"

A very young girl, dressed as a shepherdess, edged forward and held out her hand. It shook slightly and the fingers were cold. The gypsy paused, as if summoning her uncanny powers; Cassy suspected, correctly, that she was wondering what to say.

"You wish to ask me about a matter of the heart," she said at last, and the young girl gasped at this omniscience. Instead of agreeing, however, she turned red and murmured something about her mamma.

"Yes, you wish to ask me about a matter of the heart," the Gypsy insisted, "but"—relenting—"perhaps not your heart. I think you want to know about a young man—there is a young man, perhaps a brother, or a cousin—who is in love, and you wish to find out—"

"Oh, yes!" breathed the shepherdess.

"You wish to find out"—Lucy lingered over her choice—"if he truly loves."

The shepherdess nodded, her cheeks growing rosier still.

"The young man"—the gypsy sounded as if she were stalling a little—"is handsome, and young. Perhaps he is very young?"

The shepherdess murmured something about the young man being older than she was, but not very much. The Gypsy drew a deep, satisfying breath. " 'Who can look into the seeds of time, and say which grain will grow and which will not?' "

"I don't know," answered the shepherdess, looking nonplused. "I don't understand you."

Lucy laughed and chafed the little cold hand protectively. "Never mind," she said. "Young men—like your brother, or your cousin—are hard to predict. That is all I meant." She was silent for a moment, evidently searching for her accent. When she spoke again, she had regained it.

"There are some things that cannot be foretold," she said, "and the fate of a fickle young heart is one. Only time can answer some questions, time, and trial, and waiting." She saw the disappointment on the flushed young face, and went on. "Come now! Are you so unselfish that you care only for the fortunes of your friends? Let me tell you your own."

The hand tried to curl shut, but Lucy ran a finger over the lines of the palm.

"I see a wedding in a fine country house," she said, "and the bride with white roses in her hair. I see a fine young man, who loves her, and three—no four—children. And I see long life, and a letter from across the seas—and a secret, guarded safe for a long, long time. And that," she said firmly, for the shepherdess was smiling again, "is all I see."

She glossed over the girl's thanks and turned to select her next client. A man in a dark red domino stood before her with one hand outstretched. The man was a stranger, and his hand was an unusual one; strong, shapely, with long, tapering fingers and a deeply etched palm. It looked like a sensitive hand, and she took a gamble. "This is the hand of a poet."

Laurence Feather snorted. "Gordy? There's a joke! He's a brusing rider and a devil of a fellow with his fists, but he's no poet!"

Lucy winced behind her mask. Sir Errol Gordion was an intimate of Laurence Feather's; a country squire, a distinguished marksman, and a notable Corinthian. His pursuits were exclusively and aggressively masculine; she had heard of him, but never met him. He never entered the doors of Almack's, and hostesses lavished invitations on him in vain. She felt an impulse to recant, but obstinacy would not let her. "No," she said, "this is the hand of a poet. He may ride and shoot as much as he likes, but he cannot deceive me. He has a poet's heart in his breast."

The hard, well-shaped hand suddenly squeezed hers.

"I don't know who you are," Sir Errol stated, in his soft Devonshire voice, "and I'm dashed if I know how you know it, but you've spoken the truth. I've written verses—rubbishy stuff, most of it, about the forest and the Grey Wethers, and I've never told anyone about 'em. I've burned 'em—most of 'em—so that no one would know what a moonsap I am." His mouth relaxed into a smile, and Lucy smiled back, liking him. "I'm glad you didn't prophesy my death."

There was a brief moment of quiet; then the crowd surged forward, more eager than ever to hear the gypsy's words. There was a sea of outstretched hands—gloved hands, jeweled hands, rough and dainty, withered and unlined. Lucy, a little overwhelmed, backed up another step. Her good luck was beginning to frighten her, and she was afraid that her invention would fail.

A hand cuffed in silver lace outdistanced the others and caught hold of her wrist. With relief Lucy recognized the black velvet sleeve and the little ruby ring. Her face burst into a smile, and she squeezed the proffered hand tightly.

"Most gypsies have a passion for dancing," Lord Rune remarked, "and there is just one more waltz before the unmasking. Will you allow me, Madam Soothsayer?"

The dark head nodded vehemently, and the crowd shifted. Lucy scampered down the steps, her spangled skirts billowing, and Lord Rune, grinning in a very un-Hamlet-like fashion, led her onto the floor.

11

Not the least of Lucy's talents, insofar as Cassy and Grace considered them, was an ability to manipulate the closed-air stove in the basement of the Theale townhouse. Both of the Theale girls were genteelly ignorant of the domestic arts and were apt to pity Lucy's vicarage upbringing. The intelligence that their friend knew how to turn a dress, clean a fish, and paper a wall left them speechless with compassion. In one particular, however, their pity gave way to admiration: Lucy could cook. Midnight feasts, which had long been chilly affairs, were now banquets, with Lucy presiding.

Lord Rune's masquerade lasted until the small hours of the morning, but a weary Mrs. Theale led her charges away shortly after the midnight supper. Lucy— vibrating with excitement and hungry as well—conceived of the idea of a nocturnal feast in the carriage and managed silently to convey it to Cassy and Grace. A half-hour was allotted for Mrs. Theale to fall asleep (ten minutes would have sufficed, had the girls but known it) and Cassy was dispatched to listen for the sound of snoring outside her mother's door. Returning triumphant, she found Lucy and Grace had gathered the necessary shawls, robes, and candlesticks, and the three made their way downstairs.

It was a stifled, rather than a silent procession. Grace giggled softly but persistently; the sound—as Cassy somewhat irritably told her—was like a kettle boiling over. Lucy, as the eldest, felt it was her duty to "shush" the younger girl, and her shushing, like all her vocalizations, carried. Luckily, Mrs. Theale was a sound sleeper and did not waken even when Lucy paused at the entrance to the kitchen and stamped a slippered rhythm against the whitewashed floor.

Cassy gripped her friend's wrist warningly. "Must you?"

"Yes," Lucy whispered back. "It frightens the mice."

Grace, on whom the effect of Miss Saint-Clair's tom-tom had been convulsive, took her shawl out of her mouth long enough to say, "Mice?"

"Well, there *are* mice," Lucy told her apologetically. "I expect I've frightened them away, though. Come along." She led the way into the kitchen and lit the kitchen candles. Grace inspected the base-boards, holding her candlestick at a precarious angle, and Cassy began to collect teacups, saucers, and spoons. The clink of china and the growing light made the room seem less mysterious. The girls relaxed and began to speak aloud.

"I don't see any mice," Grace said. "When did you see mice?"

"Last time." Lucy knelt before the stove, opening

drafts and stirring ashes in a masterful manner. "You had a cold—Cass and I wanted chocolate—five or six of them charged out, in a sort of wing-formation, and galloped toward my feet. They were big brutes, too, more like rats than mice."

Grace looked at her suspiciously. "You're teasing."

"Yes, she is." Cassy opened a canister of tea and began to heap spoonfuls into the cups. "There was only one, and it was a little one, too, but it made Lucy squeal."

"I was surprised," Lucy defended herself. "Cassy, do see if there's anything in the pantry. I'm hungry."

Cassy obeyed, taking a candle and venturing fearlessly around the corner. "What sort of hungry?"

"Every sort," Lucy answered fervently. "I hardly tasted a bite tonight; people kept thrusting their palms in front of me. Is there any cold goose? And toast, of course—there must be bread and butter."

"There is," Cassy re-emerged with a loaf in her arms. "There isn't very much, but you can have most of it. I'm not hungry, and I daresay Grace isn't either."

Grace looked up from her mouse-hunt. "It's all very well for you," she said plaintively, "you're engaged, and Mamma doesn't mind if you eat. Lucy and I wore those tight waists and hardly ate a morsel."

"You had two helpings of trifle," Cassy contradicted her. "I saw you."

Grace offered no protest. She settled herself in the cook's pet wing-chair and hugged her knees to her chest. "I didn't really want two helpings of trifle," she explained, "but Viscount Sexton brought me the first one and I thanked him very civilly, and then he brought a second. It made me laugh—I think he was trying to make me laugh—I can't think why." She looked shyly at her sister and said, "He's very amusing."

There was a minute pause. Cassy put down her teaspoon. Lucy, who had been nibbling a crust of bread, swallowed. They perceived that Grace's statement was really an appeal, and they hastened to respond to it.

"I think he's handsome," said Cassy.

"So do I," agreed Lucy.

Grace drew an ecstatic breath. "Do you? He is rather too thin, of course, and that Scaramouche costume made him look silly, but he doesn't look at all silly in his usual clothes. And his hair curls naturally—I suppose I am goosish—but I have a partiality for curly hair." She hazarded, "I think he's handsome, too."

He will probably get broader as he gets older," Lucy said comfortably. "Gentlemen do."

"His hair is beautiful," Cassy said, "and he seems quite taken with you."

Grace ducked her head, trying to look maidenly, and was hindered by a grin of satisfaction. "He does, doesn't he? He danced with me twice, and asked if we ever went to Almack's, and I said we often did on Wednesdays, and he said perhaps he would see me there. He doesn't like Almack's at all—he says it's a dead bore—and I said so too—and I said that they serve horrid cakes there, and that made him laugh. And then he said he might be there this Wednesday—and I thought perhaps he meant he would come in order to see me. Do you suppose—"

She fixed pleading eyes on her sister, who said kindly, "Of course he did!"

"He will certainly come," Lucy agreed, emphasizing her certainty with a flourish of the bread-knife, "and ask you to dance."

Grace hunched her shoulders and stretched her nightgown over her knees in an agony of delight. "I don't suppose he will, really. I daresay he will not. But if he should—Cassy, do you think I should wear my white, or the pink with the shell trimming?"

"The pink," Cassy answered immediately.

"And my pearls," added Lucy.

"You looked ever so pretty this evening," Cassy assured her sister. "I could tell that Arthur thought so."

"I daresay everyone thought so," confirmed Lucy.

Grace cuddled her knees. "I do like that costume," she admitted. "I think Sybil Rant is much cleverer than Madame Aurore. Even Mamma admits that Cassy has never worn anything that suits her so well as that Diana-dress, and Lucy—! When you danced, and those skirts floated, and changed color, it was beautiful! Truly!"

"You danced very gracefully," Cassy agreed, "especially with Uncle."

Lucy, realizing that the conversation had shifted to focus upon her affairs, found herself unable to meet her friends' eyes. "Our steps seem to suit," she said softly, and knelt before the stove to hide her face.

"I know," breathed Cassy, waxing sentimental in turn. "It's just the same with . . . Arthur."

She seemed inclined to fall into a reverie, but Grace, reminded of a grievance, frowned on her. "Yes, but you and Arthur don't only dance," she retorted. "You wander off into little alcoves and kiss."

"Grace!" Cassy's voice was so indignant that both girls shushed her. "How dare you! I—we—do *not!*"

"You do," Grace countered, ruthless. "Not to-night, perhaps, at the masquerade, but yesterday afternoon, when he gave you the crescent for your hair." She rose from her chair, and began to stride back and forth, striking a teaspoon against her palm to punctuate her speech. "Mamma and I came in from Hookham's, and the two of you were standing an arm's length apart, and his cravat was rumpled, and you were blushing. And you've never said a single word to me! You always promised you would tell me what it was like."

Cassy's face was so suffused with blushes that Lucy took pity on her. She indicated the darkest corner of the kitchen, and warned, "Mice!"

Grace squeaked and seated herself on the table, peering around the floor with such consternation that her sister was seized with a fit of giggles. "You—" She glared at Lucy, who joined Cassy in her mirth, and was unable to find sufficiently insulting words to continue. She was obliged to fall back on a childhood refrain, and hissed, "Lucy is a goosie!"

Lucy ignored this bit of invective, and applied herself to the task of rescuing the toast, which was beginning to char. "Does anybody mind if the toast is black?"

"I don't," answered Grace.

"Neither do I," said Cassy.

This decided, harmony was restored. Cassy buttered, Lucy poured tea, and Grace resumed her seat in the wing-chair, waiting graciously for the others to serve her. Conversation languished, milk and sugar and jam were passed in amiable silence. Excitement had provided all three girls with appetites, and Lucy, in particular, disposed of her toast with unladylike rapidity. "Wasn't there any goose in the pantry?"

Cassy licked the jam-spoon. "There was, but it smelled odd."

Lucy shrugged and set off for the pantry. "I suppose it's all right, really." She returned with a platter on which reposed a somewhat battered-looking carcass, a wedge of cheese, and an onion. The last made Cassy stare.

"You're not going to eat that onion, are you?"

Lucy possessed herself of a carving knife and began to carve chunks of flesh off the goose carcass. "Why shouldn't I?"

"Your breath! Tomorrow you'll have morning callers! You can't breathe onion all over them!"

Grace stuck the handle of her spoon in the jam-pot and dug out a morsel of apricot. "Cheese is bad, too," she informed Lucy. "Mamma never gives us cheese before a party."

Lucy laughed, hoisting herself up on the oak table and swinging her feet. "Gypsies don't have to have sweet breath. Gypsies can eat whatever they like, and accuse Dukes of being too top-lofty, and dance the waltz, and drink champagne instead of silly ratafia."

Cassy's eyes were wide. "Did you really drink champagne?"

Lucy sniffed to check the progress of the toast and slid off the table. "I did indeed. Mr. Feather proposed a toast in my honor—and I said it wasn't fair, because I had no glass. And someone gave me one—I think it was Sir Errol Gordion—and we drank"—she cast down her eyelashes in a parody of modesty—"to the future, and its fair clairvoyant."

The Theale girls exchanged glances. Mrs. Theale was an indulgent parent; her daughters had abundant pin-money, read novels without fear of reprisal, and were even allowed (had they but known it) to raid the pantry in the middle of the night. They were not, however, permitted to drink wine in company. Mrs. Theale was adamant upon this point. Once, in her schoolroom days, she had enjoyed rather too much Christmas punch and disgraced herself by flirting violently with an impertinent footman. Mrs. Theale's daughters had never heard this story, but they often heard their mamma say that too much wine caused many a young lady to make a fool of herself. They asked, nearly in unison, "Does Mamma know?"

Lucy had the grace to look contrite. "I don't think so. I only had half a glass, because people kept asking me to read their palms." She hesitated. "I'm not quite certain that Godmamma liked it that I was telling fortunes, but I shan't do so any more. Lord Rune said I must refuse—and I don't want to read any more palms."

"Lucy—" Cassy's brow was knit with worry, and she lowered her voice. "Lucy, did you *plan* to tell fortunes at the party?"

Lucy nodded.

"Did Uncle—"

Lucy nodded again and busied herself with the toast. "It was your uncle's idea," she explained, buttering so vigorously that the bread crumbled. "He says that I have a—a decided talent for improvisation, and he thought it would amuse people if I pretended to tell their fortunes. I didn't really think that anyone would ask me, but Lord Rune said it was the obvious thing to say, and that people can be relied upon to say the obvious thing. And he was right. Within the first half-hour, three people asked me—in a bantering sort of way, you know—if I could see into the future. I didn't answer them—I couldn't at first—but then I did, and it was so easy! I had no idea how easy it would be! Why, people believed every word I said—and no one seemed to notice that half of what I saw in their palms was common sense—and the other half was common gossip!"

"Weren't you embarrassed?" Cassy sounded awed.

"Behind the mask? No." Lucy laid down her butter-knife and began to divide the toast among the plates. "It was a little frightening as the evening went on, though. People were so avid, and so many of the things I made up turned out to be true. Like Sir Errol Gordion writing poetry—that was fortuitous—and Derringham saying he was planning a trip to the continent after I foretold a journey over water. That was lucky, too. And then, I didn't really know that Crimshaw had a violent temper. I only imagined it, because he is such a patient, bloodless sort of man." She licked a dab of butter off her palm. "Although, now that I think on it, I accused a great many people of having hot tempers, and not one of them denied it. I suppose London is full of Apaches."

The Theale girls accepted their second helpings of toast with mixed emotions. Nothing in their upbringing predisposed them to regard their friend's conduct as unexceptionable. Grace was the first to speak. "Then you just said whatever came into your head?"

Lucy nodded, her mouth full.

"But Lucy—" Cassy floundered, "I heard one man say you have the sight."

Lucy gave a great, close-mouthed guffaw of laughter, choking so violently that Grace proffered her tea. "Stuff," she replied, when she was able to speak. "I haven't even any sensibility—or at least, a great deal less than most people." She saw that Cassy looked troubled, and said soothingly, "It was only for a night, and it's over. I won't tell any more fortunes—indeed, your uncle says I mustn't—and everyone saw me unmask. They know I'm not really a gypsy, and it will all be forgotten in the morning."

Cassy looked unconvinced, but Grace's eyes sparkled. "I thought it was wonderful," she declared. "And I don't think it will all be forgotten. I think you will have morning callers, and afternoon callers—and that Uncle himself will call and congratulate you on your success."

Cassy brightened at the last words. "He may very well," she agreed, "and it's true, Lucy, that he was much diverted. And if he approved, what you did cannot be so very shocking, after all."

She did not sound as certain of herself as she might have wished, but whatever qualms she had were lost on Lucy. She had returned to the goose-carcass and was stripping the breastbone with her fingers, a dreamy look in her eyes. "Cassy," she said, "what is it like?"

Cassy blinked at her over her teacup. "What is what like?"

"Kissing." Lucy avoided her friend's gaze and fixed her eyes on the blue platter. "How does it feel?"

Cassy hesitated, torn between acute embarrassment and her sense of pride in being the only one who had kissed a man. "I don't know," she fluttered. "I can't tell."

Grace put down her teacup with a clink. "You do know," she said accusingly. "Don't you tell me, Cassandra Theale, that you've never kissed Mr. Bloomsbury, because you have, and I know you have." She pouted, not even troubling to make her pout charming. "I think you're horrid not to tell."

Cassy opened her mouth to defend herself, but Lucy spoke first. "I once saw a village girl kiss the sexton," she volunteered. "And it wasn't a quick thing, not at all. It went on for a long time, and I couldn't see what was taking so long. What I want to know"—she wrenched a string of skin off the goose—"is whether one just presses the lips together or whether one moves them around, like chewing."

Grace nodded approvingly. "Yes, that's just it," she agreed. "And another thing: is it wet? Aunt Edith is always wet when she kisses me, and I want to scrub my face with my handkerchief—although of course I don't, because Mamma would be affronted. If it's wet—" she said judiciously, "I'm not sure I want to do it. But then" —she scrutinized her sister—"you do it. And I don't believe you dislike it, either."

Cassy, smiling tremulously, shook her head. "I don't," she admitted, "but I can't tell you—I don't know how to tell you how it's done."

Lucy spoke patiently. "Do you press or do you slide?" she demanded, clearly determined to reduce the matter to its essentials.

"Neither. Both. I—I can't explain." Cassy lowered her eyes to her empty plate, blushing at her own temerity. "It's . . . warm . . . and . . . it makes one feel queer and . . . shaky . . . and . . . greedy. It really is almost *rude*. And yet it isn't horrid."

Grace lowered her voice to a whisper. "Is it wet?"

Cassy's color deepened. "Not—not most of the time. But when it is, it—it's rather exciting. And really it isn't horrid."

"Ugh." Grace wrinkled her nose. "I think it must be."

"Oh, I don't know," Lucy said, trying to sound impartial. Her voice was rather gruff. "I don't think it sounds so very bad. If one—liked a gentleman, one might be willing."

The wistfulness in her voice made Cassy reach out and squeeze her hand. "I'm sure that Uncle—I mean, I daresay it will not be very long before you find out for yourself," she said, and Lucy sighed deeply and reached for the cold goose.

12

The night of Lord Rune's masquerade was a night for prophecy. Not only was Cassy correct in predicting that Lucy would soon penetrate the mystery of osculation, but both girls had been right to expect a rain of callers. That rain—at first a welcome shower—was to become a downpour, but Mrs. Theale, the remote cause of the monsoon, did not suspect it.

Mrs. Theale was perhaps to be pitied. It was she who first summoned her brother's powers; it was she who initiated Lucy's success. She had not foreseen that this success would be a *succès fou,* that it would be, in fact, a *succès de scandale.* She was faced with a dilemma not uncommon in the darker fairy tales; she had asked for aid, received it, and was now threatened by it.

Not that she suspected. She left her brother's masquerade in a spirit of drowsy contentment, only a little dubious about the propriety of fortune-telling. She informed her maid that the masquerade had been most diverting and that she would sleep late the next morning.

She was destined to be denied this pleasure. Early the next morning she was awakened by shrieks of girlish rapture. An inquiry as to the cause brought her the news that a parcel had arrived from Old Bond Street. From this, Tabitha deduced rightly that Lucy's gowns had come and that they were superlatively handsome. She resigned herself to the fact that she would not fall back to sleep and rang for the breakfast tray.

It was a short-sighted thing to do. No sooner did her daughters learn that she was awake than they crowded into her bedroom in night-caps and high spirits, eager to share their excitement over Lucy's new wardrobe. They bounced on the bed and sat on Tabitha's feet. Their voices rang with jubilation; they were still blithe and bright-eyed from the night before. Tabitha, the most affectionate of parents, could not help thinking they were rather horrible.

Nor was Miss Saint-Clair a restful spectacle. As usual, she had lost her night-cap among the bed-clothes, and her hair stuck out at all angles. Her feet were bare, her breath smelled of onion, and she peacocked before her god-mother in a ball-gown of amethyst satin.

Tabitha gaped. She often wore amethyst herself; it was a matron's color; it was worn even by widows of many years' standing. It was a respectable color—but it was seldom worn by young girls. Miss Rant, who had been blunt to the point of insulting, had said that Lucy should abandon the pale pinks and blues the Theale girls wore. "There's no use pretending she's fresh out of the schoolroom if she's in her fourth Season," she pronounced, "and she looks a good deal older than one-

and-twenty. Mutton dressed as lamb—that's what your ton will be saying behind their hands, and that's no credit to either of us."

Tabitha, quick to see the stricken look in her god-child's eyes, refrained from telling Miss Rant what she thought of that lady's manners. Instead, she exerted herself to distract poor Lucy from Miss Rant's ruthless judgment, with the result—she marveled at it—that her god-child now stood before her in a state of outlandish splendor.

There were six gowns in Sybil Rant's parcel, and none of them were free from the taint of singularity. To begin with, they were all longer in the bodice and wider in the skirt than the customary mode. Miss Rant had stated unequivocally that in five years the natural waistline would be in fashion: Miss Saint-Clair might as well be among the first to encourage its downward descent. Tabitha, fearing that a detailed analysis of her god-child's figure would follow, made haste to agree. It was then that Miss Rant astonished the company with an offer of unprecedented kindness: If Miss Saint-Clair would demonstrate what Miss Rant foresaw as the coming mode, Miss Rant would provide her with half a dozen gowns at a very low price.

Tabitha had accepted, taking into account her own purse, Miss Rant's skill, and Lucy's beseeching eyes. Now she was uncertain whether to be grateful or not. On one hand, her god-child had never looked so dashing; on the other, she was not sure that a dowerless girl and a vicar's daughter ought to look dashing.

She was given no time for speculation. Her daughters, much struck with their friend's transformation, poured forth their joy with a volubility that made her want to pull the pillow over her head. Lucy, basking in her friends' admiration, dashed out of the room, only to reappear in an emerald-green walking dress, with tassels, lace ruff, and mancherons.

Tabitha blinked. Maternal instinct told her that this dress ought to be called into question, but she could not think why. It was not unusual for a gown to affect a military air; it was even considered patriotic to wear such a gown. The color was unexceptionable, and the trimmings were as elegant as they were jaunty. What bothered Tabitha—and she did not realize it—was that the dress emphasized Lucy's robust curves. Tabitha had always thought it was a pity that Lucy had curves. She had several curves herself, and she knew them for uncomfortable things that interfered with the pleasures of the table; one was always trying to diminish them, or disguise them, or—painfully—to constrict them. The prevailing fashion was unkind to curves, and the prevailing aesthetic considered them vulgar. Sybil Rant, instead of being discreet about Lucy's, had drawn attention to them with the mannish trappings of military uniform. The result was as provocative as it was subtly humorous.

Tabitha did not know what to say. Before her, Lucy pirouetted, showing off a generous flare of skirt. Shrilly, Cassy drew her mother's attention to the niceness of the lace, while Grace bounced up and down and begged for an identical gown for herself.

She was saved from replying by Celestine, who entered with the breakfast tray. The smell of chocolate and warm bread did much to restore her; she was mistress of herself once more. She ordered her daughters off the bed, silenced Grace, and defended her food against Cassy's marauding fingers with a smart slap. She threatened Lucy with a variety of severe illnesses, all caused by insufficient footwear, and finished by asserting that she did not want to see anyone—or anything—until after breakfast.

Murmuring against this last austerity, the three girls quitted the room. Tabitha drew a deep breath and set about replenishing her strength—and her curves—with bread and chocolate. The room was very peaceful. She buttered a roll and spread blackberry jam on top of the butter. The butter melted, forming pale rivers through the red-purple of the jam, and the warm sweetness of both overflowed onto her palm. She began to feel optimistic. Perhaps Sybil Rant's gowns looked eccentric because they were modeled by a girl with bare feet and riotous hair. Or perhaps—she sipped her chocolate—society might overlook a little eccentricity. Society had, after all, overlooked Lucy for the past three years; it would be very strange if it began to notice her now.

Alas for Mrs. Theale! Her instincts, usually so keen, were blunted by butter and blackberry jam. Already Lucy's circumstances had altered and London tongues were at work. The wheel of fortune had turned; Lucy Saint-Clair, the dowdy and dowerless, was about to become the fashion, and her eccentricities, like her curves, could no longer be concealed.

Lord Rune was delighted.

He called at his sister's house the next day, armed with the verses of Robert Herrick and the sheet music for Lucy's newest aria. His sister informed him complacently that Lucy was out driving with Sir Errol Gordon. Always subtle, Grace lost no time in pointing out that the enormous bouquet in the canopic urn was a tribute from Laurence Feather and that Lucy had received six invitations that morning.

Lord Rune, hugely amused, leaned back in his Egyptian chair without even remembering to wince. His nieces diverted him for the next half-hour with speculations about Lucy's new-found success and descriptions of her gowns. Their Mamma tried to restrain them; nothing, she said, could be less interesting to a gentleman than the details of a lady's toilette! Lord Rune gave her a smile from beneath half-closed eyes and contradicted her. On the contrary, he said. He had always been fascinated by the fine points of feminine dress and was by no means as ignorant on the subject as his nieces might suppose.

Tabitha, rendered speechless by the possibility that he might enlarge upon this theme, yanked the bell-cord and called for tea. Lord Rune listened lazily as his nieces prattled on. He realized, vaguely, that he had grown fond of them; they were very agreeable girls. His eyes went to the sphinx-clock on the mantle; he wanted to see Lucy. He wondered how she felt about her sudden popularity and if she would delight, as he did, in the absurdity in it. Lured by a sham gypsy, London, fickle, worldly London, had taken to its bosom a vicar's daughter with more wit than beauty and no money at all. It was improbable; it was delicious.

He finished his tea and placed the cup on the small sarcophagus, only half-listening to Grace's speculations as to whether the Duke of Sisleigh would offer for Millicent Gray. Bibble, the butler, entered and proclaimed that Mr. Laurence Feather had called.

It was then that Ernest realized that he was waiting, actually waiting for the sought-after Miss Saint-Clair to return from her drive.

It was an unwelcome revelation; Lord Rune, for reasons that he did not understand, found it repellent. He felt startled, and somehow ill-used; he wondered if there was anyone he could blame. Then he shook himself, figuratively speaking, and wondered what was the matter with him. He decided that Mr. Feather was the matter; he had not come to exchange banalities with a callow young puppy like Laurence Feather.

He picked up his tea-cup, saw that it was empty, and put it down again with a somewhat disjointed reference to a business engagement. He was halfway home before he remembered that he had left the verses of Robert Herrick on the sofa. He hoped that Tabitha would not read them.

Tabitha, as it turned out, did not. Tabitha liked novels, but she had no use for poetry. She disliked it so much that she privately considered its readers guilty of literary hypocrisy. That her god-child—usually such a simple, unaffected girl!—enjoyed it was beyond her comprehension. She found the book on the sofa, saw from the margins that it was verse, and asked her daughters if it belonged to them. Lucy, divining by intuition what the book must be, claimed it as her own, and Tabitha asked no more questions.

Tabitha was pleased with Lucy. She had feared that sudden distinction might overwhelm her godchild, causing her to turn either vainglorious or bashful, but Lucy surprised her by regarding the fruits of her new-found popularity with a nice mixture of irony and detachment.

It was rather irregular for a damsel so favored to appear detached. The ton was more used to its favorites appearing—or attempting to appear—coyly naive or loftily blasé. A lady who listened to compliments with bemused interest and who neither blushed nor preened herself was a novelty, and novelty was at a premium. Lucy's singing, so long ignored, was suddenly in demand, and her exquisitely eccentric clothes met with nothing but approbation. Her mannerisms—from her vehement speech to her rather astonishing laugh—were celebrated, and in a few instances copied.

Lucy was gratified but not deceived. For the last three years society had served to remind her that she lacked beauty, birth, and fortune; she had hungered after attention and been denied it. Initially hurt, she had determined to hold society in light esteem, and she had succeeded so well that her detachment was quite genuine. She enjoyed the compliments that were paid her and rejoiced over bouquets and invitations, but she had gone without long enough to know that they were not essential to her comfort. She was, then, in an enviable position: she did not hunger, and she was not beguiled.

Nonetheless, she enjoyed the days that followed with all her heart. After years of being a wall-flower, it was very agreeable to stand up for every dance, and she enjoyed the society of Laurence Feather and Sir Errol Gordion. If the knowledge that she had missed Lord Rune's call distressed her, she could comfort herself with the fact that he had remembered to lend her Herrick's poems. It was even possible that the book was a gift; it looked very new. Lucy stroked the crimson leather of the cover; she longed to ask Cassy and Grace if they thought the book was a present, but dared not let them see the poems. They were—some of them—rather *warm;* in showing them, Lord Rune was perhaps guilty of impropriety. Lucy rather hoped he was.

She hoped, too, that Lord Rune would call again,

though she was seldom at home. Her days were busy; she had some difficulty finding time to practice her singing. She attended two routs, an informal hop, and a dress-ball without catching so much as a glance of Lord Rune, and she began to look forward impatiently to Lady Curry's musicale, where he was to accompany her rendition of Rossini's "Cruda Sorte."

Lord Rune was growing equally impatient. After leaving the Herrick verses at his sister's house, he determined—half-consciously and without recourse to logic—to avoid Miss Saint-Clair's company. He spent the following week doing just that. He attended a few card-parties, where the company was exclusively male, and visited his club. He tried to reread *The Divine Comedy* and left off halfway through the *Inferno*. He spent some time cataloguing his glass collection, only to decide it was a dead bore.

It was no use; every gossip in town was talking of Miss Saint-Clair, and he wanted to see her. He wanted to watch her flaunting her Sybilline finery, and to tease her about the reclusive Sir Errol, the inane Mr. Feather. He wanted, most of all, to laugh with her. It seemed to him that their laughter would dissolve the strangeness of that curiously unpleasant moment in his sister's drawing-room. He began to wonder if he could wait for Lady Curry's musicale and decided that he couldn't.

This conclusion reached—again, without recourse to logic—he donned knee-breeches, and set off for the long-despised portals of Almack's.

It had been several years since he had visited London's self-conscious marriage mart, and a number of heads turned when he entered the room. He affected not to notice but gave his full attention to saluting Lady Jersey and Princess Esterhazy. This being done, he accepted a glass of champagne, assumed an indolent air, and leaned back against one of the marble columns.

It was a large room, and—Lord Rune considered— ill-proportioned. With its quantities of curled moldings, its columns and balconies, and its swags of musty velvet, it had a vaguely theatrical look. Lord Rune always complained that Almack's made him feel like an actor in a second-rate melodrama. He disliked, too, the atmosphere of settled wealth and respectability; it was at once complacent and oppressive. Nevertheless, the scene before him had some of the charm of a mechanical clock. Young girls dressed in fragile muslin and opalescent gauze swayed and glided and spun. Their cheeks were flushed, their lips curved in the prim smiles sanctioned by their mammas.

Lord Rune, scanning the crowd for a glimpse of Lucy, had not far to look. A set was forming for the quadrille, and she stood fanning herself and talking to Laurence Feather. She wore a white gown garlanded with ivy and a wreath of ivy encircled her dark hair. Her lips were parted in laughter, and she looked as if she were enjoying herself more than any one else in the room. Lord Rune's face softened as he looked at her.

The orchestra began to play, the music sounding thin and sweet beneath the hum of conversation. Lucy caught Mr. Feather's hand and began the quadrille. Her fan swung from the ribbon at her wrist; the scalloped hem of her gown flared as she pivoted. In the execution of one of the figures she glimpsed Lord Rune, and joy and recognition came into her face. She nearly crashed into Mr. Feather, drew herself up, and compensated by posing very prettily, with one satin slipper pointed. The gentleman on her other side narrowly escaped being kicked; he dodged, blinked, and fell out of step. Lucy tossed an apology over her shoulder, switched feet, and set off again, this time in the right direction. The corners of her mouth puckered in an effort not to laugh.

Lord Rune had no such scruples; he laughed aloud, and with his laughter came a rush of warmth that he interpreted—perhaps correctly—as relief. In spite of her satin slippers and festooned dress, she had not changed; she was precisely what she had always been. She was gauche, idiosyncratic, straight-forward; she was too stout and her eyebrows were absurd. There had been no reason to avoid her all week.

She did not look at Lord Rune again, but gave her attention to the quadrille and danced conscientiously, with a faint smirk lingering on her lips. As the music ended, he took a step forward, but it was no use; a fair-haired youth claimed Lucy's hand, and the pair began the contradance. Lord Rune resumed his post beside the column.

"You won't be able to dance with her," Tabitha said matter-of-factly, "She always has a partner."

Lord Rune bowed, inwardly congratulating himself as he suppressed a start of surprise. It occurred to him that he was seeing a lot of his sister of late, and he wasn't sure he liked it. He was, of course, very fond of her—he inquired after her health with charming tenderness—but she seemed always to be hovering about. Sisters, he thought, shouldn't hover. No one should hover, and family members least of all.

He finished his investigation into the family health and nodded towards Miss Saint-Clair, who was attacking the contradance with a good deal of mettle.

"You are pleased, I hope?"

Tabitha's gaze went to the circling figures. "Indeed I am," she answered. "Not that there's anything to be gained from that quarter—that's Jack Seddingham, you know—never a feather to fly with—but he's perfectly good ton, and he's called three times since the masquerade. And Sisleigh has called twice, which I never would have credited! He is usually so high in the instep! Not that I mean to suggest that he shows any inclination to dangle after Lucy—in fact, Lucy says he is in love with Millicent Gray—but his attention does Lucy a deal of good. And you needn't look scornful—" Tabitha's voice took on a combative note. "You know what society is, Ernest! One's consequence depends so much on one's intimate friends! Not that the Duke is intimate, precisely—that would scarcely be suitable—but he is very kind to Lucy. He says"—with a delicate shade of deference—"that she makes him laugh. Isn't that delightful?"

"Prodigious," responded Ernest.

Tabitha, never very quick at subtle intimations, went on. "And then, there is Sir Errol Gordion," she said. "Oh, not here—he doesn't dance"—she cast a sidelong look at her brother, and added formally—"in public. That is, not yet. Lucy is teaching him to dance, and he is teaching her to drive."

"A felicitous arrangement."

"Yes," agreed Tabitha, "although trying, of course, with all that scuffling about, and Sir Errol's boots not being the sort of boots that agree with the carpet." She produced an airy affectation of a sigh. "But he is a really good man, I believe, and Lucy likes him, and the Gordions are a fine old family. He would really"—Tabitha regarded her pirouetting god-child—"*do* very nicely."

Lord Rune, who had allowed his attention to wander, recalled it with a start.

"Do?" he echoed.

Tabitha's smile became benevolent. How handsome dear Ernest was looking tonight; he was really awake, and it became him wonderfully well. For once there were no circles under his eyes, and a certain tautness and energy in his face made him look ten years younger. Even his hair seemed to curl more crisply than usual. The muscles beneath the russet-colored coat seemed tighter, and the chin above the silk cravat was very firm.

"What do you mean—he would do?"

Tabitha, whose eyes had wandered to the admirable snugness of her brother's inexpressibles, had to think back a moment. "For a husband," she said. "For Lucy."

Lord Rune shook his head. "Don't consider it. I've known Rollo Gordion since he was a boy. He's not in the petticoat line. Never was."

He spoke dogmatically; his eyes, no longer annoyed, were expressionless. Tabitha did not reply at once; she had left off looking at his clothes and was studying his face. Then she ventured to protest. "But—"

"I'll grant you he may respect her as a woman of superior sense. He may even admire her." His tone of voice implied that nothing could be less likely. "But he's perfectly reconciled to a bachelor existence—and extremely fond of his nephew, who will inherit the estate. Moreover, I don't believe there's a woman alive he could love as much as he loves his horses—or his dogs— or his solitude. He'll return to his ancestral acres without a wife, I promise you."

Tabitha sighed. She was aware she had been indulging in a little wishful thinking with regard to Sir Errol; the dancing lessons, although convivial, did not seem to inspire sentiment in either the pupil or the pedagogue. Nevertheless, it was rather shabby of Ernest to be so discouraging, and she would not capitulate. Changing tactics, she said, "Of course, there's Laurence Feather."

She had supposed that her brother liked Laurence Feather, since very few people did not. She had enough mischief in her nature to enjoy it when he looked not just surprised, but appalled.

"He has paid her a very flattering degree of attention," she went on smoothly, "and I believe she is inclined to favor his suit. He is a little younger than she is, but it would be a brilliant match, and he is the most amiable young man alive."

"He's an idiot," said Lord Rune roundly.

Tabitha drew herself up. "Really, Ernest! He is no such thing!"

"He is," said Lord Rune.

Tabitha was forty years old; she had spent at least thirty-three of those years having quarrels with her younger brother, and she knew that when he resorted to that particular tone of voice he was irreclaimable. She drew in her breath and turned pointedly away. After a moment or two, she felt a warm hand grasp hers, and she turned back to face her brother's most blinding smile.

"I am very rude this evening, am I not?"

"Yes," said Tabitha, robustly. She tried to look disapproving, but failed; Ernest's charm, when he cared to employ it, was potent. She managed to free her hand and added petishly, "And I don't see why you came."

Lord Rune looked grave, as if her disapproval worried him. "Why I came?" He managed to sound at once hurt and amused and said wistfully, "Would you deny me the feeble dissipations of Almack's?"

Tabitha tried simultaneously to stifle a laugh and to sniff. The result was an indisputable snort.

"You can't bear Almack's," she snapped, her heart hardened by the mortification of having to snort when she didn't want to, "and you ought to leave Lucy alone."

Lord Rune, who had been trying to regain his sister's hand, stopped short.

"I don't mean to be ungrateful," Tabitha said, "but you know we agreed that Lucy was inclined to cherish a tendresse for you and that it oughtn't to be encouraged. I don't blame you—girls are what they are, and it was hardly to be expected that Lucy's sentiments would undergo a change when there were no other men to distract her, but—" She indicated the dancing floor with a tentative gesture. "There are others now. She has her admirers, and there *is* Laurence Feather, and I think you could—withdraw a little, without upsetting her. And"—Tabitha met her brother's eyes steadily,—"I think you ought to."

Lord Rune was no longer attending. It had often been his way, when he disliked the turn of a conversation, to gaze off in the distance, as if fascinated by something he saw there. Tabitha followed his glance, which was riveted to a dowager feeding champagne to her lapdog. It was a spectacle that everyone in London, including Lord Rune, had witnessed a thousand times before, and Tabitha felt an urge to pinch her brother, as she had when they were children and he wouldn't listen to her.

She restrained herself and tried to match his rudeness with her own, turning away from him to watch the dancers. The contradance ended, and she saw her godchild desert Mr. Seddingham with unflattering haste. Half-running, almost dancing, Miss Saint-Clair made her way across the floor. At last she reached Lord Rune's side and unfurled her fan with a snap. Her voice was breathless.

"Baron Baumfalk wants to waltz with me, and I told him I couldn't, because I was promised to you. You will dance with me, won't you?"

Lord Rune's features, which had been rather alarmingly still, relaxed. Mrs. Theale said, "Lucy," but without much conviction.

"I know I shouldn't be bold," Lucy said regretfully, "and I don't suppose I ought to say things that aren't true, but dancing with Baron Baumfalk is so horrid." She looked pleadingly first at Tabitha and then at Lord Rune. "You will dance with me, won't you?" she coaxed. "His hands are clammy, and he winces when I step on his feet and looks reproachful. And I can't help stepping on his feet." Her eyes brightened as Lord Rune's lips curved. "No one could help stepping on his feet. They're as big as—as flippers, and he *won't* keep them to himself."

Lord Rune laughed. He seemed to have forgotten his sister. "It would serve you well if I refused."

Lucy, unmoved by this threat, tossed her head. The leaves of the ivy quivered, and her curls brushed against her bare shoulders. Lord Rune had a sudden memory of her at the Gratham's musicale, looking sullen and dowdy and miserable in her tight dress. He bowed, one hand on his heart.

"I won't refuse you this time," he said, and Tabitha wondered if he spoke with a double meaning to his words, "but the next time—"

Tabitha did not catch the rest of the sentence. The musicians struck up the waltz, and Lucy stepped forward into the welcoming curve of Ernest's arms.

13

Laurence Feather was nineteen years old. His reputation was bad; it was almost as bad as he hoped it was. He was intemperate; he was profligate; he was luxurious. He squandered vast sums of money and was known to enjoy low company. His temper was hot—he was wont to indulge it in an occasional duel—and his disposition was volatile. In spite of this, he had not an enemy in the world, and Mrs. Theale was very well pleased to find him paying court to her god-daughter.

There were several circumstances that accounted for Tabitha's forebearance. The first and foremost was that Mr. Feather had an annual income of thirty thousand pounds. He had grown up in Dorset, a distant relation to the wealthy Sherrilton family. Then diphtheria attacked the Sherriltons and the sixteen-year-old Laurence Feather found himself sole heir to a vast estate.

It had been so unlikely that he would inherit that the Sherrilton lawyers were at a loss. A hastily drawn-up trust sufficed only to pay, and not to control, Mr. Feather's debts. For debts there were: a rash, a fever, an epidemic of debts. Laurence Feather liked comfort, and he liked pleasure. He liked gambling, too; he liked fast horses, and he found—as he grew older—that he liked the society of pretty women. A desire for fine clothes led him to London, where he immediately purchased a richly appointed town house, a suite of furniture uphol- stered in gold brocade, a watch set with diamonds, four match greys, a perch-phaeton, three snuff-boxes, and a gilded pianoforte.

It was uncertain, at first, whether so much lavish spending would brand him as a vulgarian. His father had been a gentleman, but his mother had been half German, and there was some question as to whether Mr. Feather was good ton. His servants, receiving their cheerfully tossed vails with astonishment, were the first to make up their minds: they liked him. In a little while, every one liked him, though few people took him seri- ously. He was as open-handed as he was light-hearted and the energy with which he set about amusing himself was exhilarating.

He lost no time in schooling himself to emulate the most dashing blades of London. The Viscount Sexton introduced him to White's, and he introduced himself to Tattersall's, Cribb's Parlour, and the Daffy Club. He hired a box at the opera and ordered an elaborate ward- robe from Mr. Stultz. This last disappointed him: Mr. Stultz was unable to give Mr. Feather the Byronic dash he coveted.

This was not entirely Mr. Stultz's fault. Mr.

Feather was neither tall nor slender. He had a round, ingenuous face and cheeks so determinedly pink that late nights and dissipation could not blanche them. His hair was a glossy but undistinguished shade of brown, and it curled, which made him look cherubic. No feat of tailoring could make him look wasp-waisted, and somber colors only drew attention to the freshness of his complexion.

It was perhaps this circumstance of sartorial disappointment that led to Mr. Feather's first duel. He left Mr. Stultz's shop in a state of fuming discontent and spent the evening insulting his closest friend. The next morning, he put a bullet through his friend's shoulder; the next week found him supplying the wounded with fresh fruit, lascivious on dits, and the more expensive patent medicines. The friend—the somewhat unlucky Jack Seddingham—did not take offense; Mr. Feather's bounty had rescued him from a number of mortifying situations. The wound healed, the friendship resumed, and Mr. Feather enjoyed the conviction that he was a devilish dangerous fellow.

He found himself well-suited to a life of idle amusement and cheerfully altered his own tastes to conform with the current mode. He sent flowers to the reigning beauties of each season and lashed himself into Byronic fury when the beauties became engaged. His rages were impressive, but a little hypocritical, since he himself had never proposed to any of the ladies in question. He was sufficiently shrewd to realize that his fortune might prove an overwhelming temptation, and he enjoyed his freedom too much to risk it. He supposed he would marry one day—but not yet. He was not without sentiment and often dreamed of a slim, golden-haired creature who would love him with a chaste and childlike ardor.

In the meantime, there were birds of paradise and bits of muslin—and Lucy Saint-Clair, who had just become the fashion.

He liked her enormously. Indeed, he liked her better than any of the aristocratic beauties for whom he had professed so much passion. She was good-natured; she received flowers and compliments with something perilously close to a grin; and she laughed when he tried to be witty. It was a real laugh, too, not an insipid little titter, but a rich, open-mouthed peal that made a man feel that his bon mots were worth something. He liked her clothes also—Mr. Feather fancied bright colors— and her sobriquet "the Gypsy." It had been deuced clever, the way she told fortunes at Lord Rune's masquerade, and he liked the mischievous look she wore when he teased her to do it again. She always said she wouldn't—but Mr. Feather thought that she would, eventually. And in the meantime, there was her singing to listen to; Lord Rune said that she had the finest soprano voice in London.

To do Mr. Feather justice, he might have admired Lucy's voice without his lordship's endorsement. In most matters of taste he bowed to whatever arbiter was at hand, but he was deeply and honestly musical. He was, after all, one fourth German and two halves sensual, and he loved music as ardently as he loved food and drink. It was not long before he began to visit the Theale house every day, not only to listen to Miss Saint-Clair, but to cultivate his own hearty tenor.

Mrs. Theale deplored the circumstance that made her the captive victim of Mozart, Handel, and Rossini,

but her matchmaking hopes soared. She steeled herself
to defend Mr. Feather against her brother's disparage-
ment, but unnecessarily; Lord Rune, when he next encountered Mr. Feather, was the soul of courtesy. Cassy
and Grace were more difficult to manage. For some reason their mamma could not comprehend, they found
Mr. Feather ridiculous, and any hint that he might serve
as Lucy's husband threw them into ecstasies of mirth.
As for Lucy herself, she said that she liked Mr. Feather
very well, but the idea that a boy of nineteen could
entertain a serious passion for her did not seem to enter
her head.

"You could have him," she offered, when Grace
teased her. "He'd be just the right age for you."

"He's fat," Grace said uncompromisingly.

"Only a little." Lucy held a pink rose under the
brim of her favorite bonnet and studied the effect judiciously. "Only in front."

Grace handed her a straight pin. "In back, too, I
should think. Besides, he doesn't like me. He likes you."

Lucy stabbed herself with the pin and stuck her
thumb in her mouth to keep from saying something
unbecoming.

"Mamma thinks you could marry him."

Lucy opened her mouth and examined her thumb.
"I wonder if that will bleed on my gloves," she mused
and then spoke to Grace. "You silly! He doesn't want to
marry me."

"Why does he come, then?" countered Grace.

Lucy pinned the rose successfully, tried on the bonnet, and tied the ribbons in a bow beside her left ear.
"Because I'm the fashion," she answered and grinned, a
little unwillingly.

Grace balanced herself on the footboard of the bed. "You're getting conceited."

"Am I not?" Lucy's eyes were alight with amusement. "It's very agreeable. If I had known how pleasant it was—being conceited, I mean—I would have tried it years ago. You ought to have told me." She laughed at the expression on Grace's face. "Oh, Grace, I'm only funning! I feel so giddy, and light-hearted—and—and as if I were going to have my own way," she finished boldly, and turned back to the mirror.

"Lucy!" Grace slid off the foot of the bed, and came to join her. "Has Lord Rune—has he *spoken?*"

Her voice was hushed with wonder, and her blue eyes were hopeful. Lucy gave a little shrug and turned away. "No," she admitted, "not—not if you mean—" She did not finish her sentence, but went on: "Really, Grace, you're as bad as your mamma! Always thinking of marriage!"

Grace blushed a little but spoke up with vigor. "But Lucy, you must get married. The Season's almost over, and your mamma wants you to come home. And Sir Errol Gordion has gone back to Devonshire, and you won't have Baron Baumfalk—"

"Grace Ermengarde Theale! *Nobody* could expect me to marry Baron Baumfalk!"

Grace considered. "No," she conceded, "but if you don't marry somebody, you'll have to go home, because your mamma wants to send Mina and Letty."

Lucy's face was suddenly grave, the fierceness of her scowl at variance with the rose-trimmed bonnet. "I shan't go home," she said, but so wretchedly that Grace didn't believe her.

"But if you don't—" Grace's delicate brows knitted in unconscious imitation of her friend. "Lulie, what will you do? You haven't any money, and you haven't any other relations you could live with. Of course, you could live with Cassy"—The memory of her sister's absorption in Mr. Bloomsbury made her sound dubious—"or you could live with me, when I marry, but it might be several years. I don't think I have a lasting passion for Viscount Sexton, because he is always talking about horses, and it bores me. And even that wouldn't be a home of your own . . . " Her voice trailed off as she contemplated her friend's future.

Lucy turned and put her arms around the younger girl, hugging her tightly. "Oh, Grace," she sighed, and the two clung together for a moment. "I wish you were my sister—you and Cass."

Grace snuggled against her. "You have Mina and Letty," she said, not dismissively, but helpfully; offering up the sisters for Lucy's delectation.

"Mina and Letty are twins," Lucy retorted, as if that explained everything. "They're not interested in anyone else but each other." She remembered that Grace would have the repudiated twins as house-guests next year, and added, as an afterthought, "You'll like them."

"I won't," contradicted Grace. "And Lucy, what are you going to do?"

Lucy sighed and went back to the mirror. "Perhaps I'll become a governess," she said. "Do you think I'd make a good governess?"

Grace pondered the question in earnest. To her mind, Lucy was much older, extremely learned, and—except for her recent butterfly behavior—very sensible. "Yes, but I think it would be horrid."

"Not horrider than home." Lucy's eyebrows closed ranks and then lifted as she heard voices downstairs.

"There's Rune—we're driving—I must go down-stairs—"

She caught up her gloves and reticule, kissed Grace absentmindedly, and ran downstairs, dismissing all fear of the future.

14

Whatever feelings of animosity Mr. Feather's avoirdupois inspired in Grace were destined to be short-lived. The following week, Mr. Feather met Mrs. Theale and her daughters in Bond Street and outlined a plan that met with Grace's heartfelt approval.

"Lucy!" Grace burst into the music room, slamming the door so emphatically that the sheet music flew to the floor. "Lucy, we met Laurence Feather and he walked home with us, and he says—"

Here she stopped. Lord Rune sat at the spinet, with his hands poised over the keys, and what Grace described as "a horrid, quizzing, look" on his face. Lucy stood beside him, with a pencil between her fingers; after a moment she stooped to gather up the sheet music.

"What is it, Grace? Has Mr. Feather come to call?"

"Yes." Grace reached up and coiled one of her curls

around her forefinger, a gesture that never failed to restore her composure, even while it made her look like a
fidgety schoolgirl. "I'm sorry, Uncle; I didn't know you
were here."

"Pray don't apologize." Lord Rune exchanged a
speaking glance with Lucy. "Nothing could be more
charming than the way young ladies rush and scamper
and slam when they think there are no gentlemen present. I much prefer it to propriety and pursed lips—and
artifice and insipidity."

Grace promptly, and quite unconsciously, assumed
the demeanor her uncle deplored.

"Mr. Feather is in the drawing room with
Mamma," she reported, "and he has been good enough
to invite all of us—Mamma and Cassy and Mr. Bloomsbury and me and you—to a gala night at Vauxhall. And
Lucy"—here the prim demeanor cracked before the excitement behind it— "Mamma says that we may go!
Only think, Lucy! He is going to hire sculls, and a box—
and he has ordered a splendid hamper from Gunthers—
and I shall see the grand cascade and the fireworks! I
have teased Mamma to take us scores of times, and she
always puts it off, but now we shall go!"

Lucy, who had seen the gardens several times in the
course of her Seasons, smiled with more sympathy than
rapture and then turned to Lord Rune. "I suppose I
ought to go downstairs and see Mr. Feather," she said
reluctantly, "though we haven't practiced that andante
enough. Will you come?"

Lord Rune began to shape an affirmative, but
Grace, offended by so blasé a reception, broke in.

"Oh, don't prose on about a horrid andante," she
said reproachfully, "No one ever really listens to music,
and you always sing better than anyone else. Aren't you

excited, Lucy? Mr. Feather is going to have a charabanc, so that we can watch the fireworks without a
crush, and he is going to have musicians—in another
boat, of course—follow us down the river. And then it
will be dark, and I shall see the colored lights—and
Viscount Sexton is coming—" For the second time, she
stopped and colored, wondering if Lord Rune knew
that the Viscount admired her and hoping that he did.

"It will be very romantic," said Lord Rune.

His voice was light; his intention was to tease his
niece, but he looked at Lucy as he spoke, with a look
that was quizzing without being—or so Grace told
Cassy later—altogether horrid. Lucy met his eyes and
then looked away; a faint current flowed between them.
Grace was aware of it without knowing what it was.
She said stoutly, "Well, of course it will be," and re-
newed her blushes directly after speaking. Her voice
sounded overloud.

Both Lucy and Lord Rune looked at her with mild
surprise, as if they had forgotten what she was talking
about. It was disconcerting; Grace had recourse to her
ringlets again.

"Are you coming downstairs?"

Lucy cast a final, wistful glance at the sheet music.
"Yes, of course." She arranged the music on the spinet,
stuck the pencil absentmindedly into the knot of curls at
the back of her head, and started to follow Grace out of
the room.

"Lucy—"

Lucy halted, turning her back to the door. "Yes?"

"Have you a tendresse for this Mr. Feather?"

It was an impertinent question; Lord Rune knew it
even as it left his lips. His position of privilege—as a sort
of half-uncle—did not justify it. No one could blame

Miss Saint-Clair if she chose to take offense; a stiffening, a regal chilliness, would be quite in order. Unfortunately, Miss Saint-Clair's sensibilities were not very nice; her face lit up, and she looked more roguish than embarrassed.

"He?" The monosyllable quivered; only indifferently did she manage to steady her voice. "He's very agreeable—"

The last syllable was lost in a splutter of laughter. It was infectious, and Lord Rune caught it.

"And very amiable," he said equably, and quoted, à la Tabitha: " 'The most amiable young man alive.' "

Lucy made a praiseworthy attempt to control herself. "He *is* very amiable," she echoed. "It's very wrong of me to laugh at him. I can't think why I do so, except that you look so provoking, and that sets me off. Indeed, I like him very much," she said, rather shakily but with passable composure.

"But you don't—" He began the question still laughing, but found himself unable to finish it with the same levity. He paused, searched for the words and found none; he rose and went to her, and her eyes met his.

"No," she said. "I don't."

She spoke resolutely but she sounded breathless; they were both breathing rather hard. He said, half-teasing: "What sort of gentleman—" and again did not finish, because the answer to his question was written on her face.

It was not the first time that a lady of Lord Rune's acquaintance had looked at him that way. He had been honored—or confronted—by meaningful glances quite often enough to know how to receive them. Ladies of noble blood, wives and widows had cast their lures to him; beauties had made use of their lovely eye-lashes to hint at still more lovely secrets. Many a bird of paradise, seeing in Lord Rune a rich protector, had telegraphed her willingness to display her plumage for her lordships' gratification. None of them had discomposed him in the least. He stared at Lucy, the vicar's daughter, and blushed to the roots of his hair.

She was smiling, but her eyes were moist. Her smile was both timid and rueful, but she held his gaze without faltering. Again something flowed between them, a current grown stronger and more hazardous than before. They were both flustered and a little hot, caught somewhere between embarrassment and intoxication.

"My dear Lucy—" Lord Rune heard his voice with some astonishment; it sounded so urbane. "You put me to the blush—!"

It was Miss Saint-Clair's turn to examine the tone their intercourse had taken; it was her turn to go red with mortification. Her hands flew to her cheeks; she uttered an incoherent "Oh!" of anguish and was unable to continue. How could she explain the boldness of her behavior? The thing was impossible; she would never be able to face Lord Rune again. She whipped round, turning her back to him, and pretended to examine her hair in the mirror. Her fingers shook; she fumbled for a hairpin and stabbed herself on the pencil. She looked as if she were going to burst into tears.

Lord Rune's embarrassment faded in the face of her distress. He followed her to the mirror and cupped his hands over her elbows, stilling her frantic efforts to destroy what was left of her coiffure.

"Miss Saint-Clair, I beg your pardon."

Lucy twisted around—not without some feeling of loss as he let his hands drop—and scowled at him savagely; a single tear shone on her cheek. Lord Rune lifted a hand to brush it away and then hesitated. Something —his indecision perhaps—changed his hand in its course; his fingers went to the ruined coiffure and began to loosen her disordered curls.

Lucy held her breath. His fingers were warm as well as skillful; she felt them brush her temples, her cheeks, the back of her neck; she felt them press against her skull. He plucked the pencil from the knot of curls and showered the carpet with hair-pins. His hands were strong, and her hair tumbled down and fell into a loose tangle. She closed her eyes, feeling a shiver run over her scalp and throughout her body. She wondered both at her pleasure and his presumption. She gave a little shudder of delight and then opened her eyes; he had taken his hands away.

"Now you are a gypsy again."

Lucy racked her brains for a witty rejoinder— something that would convey the fact that the liberties he had taken had not offended her and that, in fact, he was welcome to continue them. "Yes," she said idiotically, and gave him a cloudless smile.

"Shall I come to Vauxhall, too?"

His answering smile was warm, but he put his hands behind his back; he looked like a prisoner in custody. Evidently he had taken all the liberties he was going to take and she might as well compose herself for rational conversation. "You aren't invited," she answered, not meaning to sound rude.

Ernest took her hand and brought it to his lips. "What are exquisite manners for, if not to enable one to obtain what would otherwise be denied? I shall elbow my way in."

Lucy's laugh rang out. "Come, then," she com-

manded, and wove her fingers through his, leading him
downstairs.

"Cass."

It was a whisper, softer than most of Lucy's whis-
pers. Cassy turned over in the darkness and adjusted her
pillow under her elbow, so that she faced Lucy.

"What is it?"

"Is Grace asleep?"

It was one of Grace's least lovable traits to feign
sleep and eavesdrop while the older girls whispered, us-
ing the purloined knowledge in a number of dreadful
ways. Cassy held her breath and listened, "Yes. I can
always tell."

"Are you sleepy?"

"No." It was a lie, but Cassy could sense her
friend's urgency even in the darkness. "What is it?"

"Lord Rune. He—"

A long silence. Cassy strained to see her friend's
face. "He—"

Cassy, always patient, waited for the verb of the
sentence. When Lucy failed to repeat even the pronoun
for a third time, Cassy leaned close to her, and whispered very softly.

"Has he tried to kiss you?"

The sound of Lucy's curls rustling told her that
Lucy had shaken her head. "No. And if he had—oh,
Cassy—"

"Shhh."

"If he had," Lucy lowered her voice obediently, "I
—I wouldn't dislike it. If—if what you say is true, it isn't
disagreeable, and I would know that he wasn't indifferent to me—"

"He isn't indifferent to you." Cassy felt along her friend's side, found a hand, and clasped it consolingly. "He comes almost every day to play for you—"

"I know, but—" Lucy squirmed a little, and Cassy understood.

"You mean that if he kissed you you would know that he loved you."

Lucy nodded, and once again Cassy half-heard, half-divined, the gesture.

It did not occur to either girl that a kiss could be anything less than a declaration of love. For Cassy, who had not kissed Mr. Bloomsbury until after the engagement was sanctioned, a kiss was as good as a proposal of marriage. Lucy, whose experience was supplemented by literature, was not quite so rigid in her expectations, but she did believe that Lord Rune was too honorable a man to kiss his sister's god-child unless he intended to marry her. Lord Rune agreed with her on this point, which was why he had—strictly speaking—avoided kissing Lucy.

"He hasn't kissed me, but—" Lucy turned over on her stomach, unable to face Cassy even in the darkness. "He's been—I mean, he's done some things that were odd."

"Odd? Do you mean he's taken liberties?"

Lucy flexed her toes in embarrassment. "I don't think they're liberties, exactly," she said. "If they were, they didn't—offend me." She remembered the delicious chill of Lord Rune's fingers against her scalp and hastened to qualify her words. "I mean, I was a *little* bit offended, of course, but not very much, because, after all a gentleman doesn't take liberties with a lady unless he likes her. Of course"—her voice slowed reluctantly—"of course, there are men who chuck chambermaids under the chin and that sort of thing, but even then, they only do so when they like the chambermaids, don't you think so? I mean, an *old* chambermaid, with watery eyes, or hair growing out of her nostrils—"

With uncharacteristic rudeness, Cassy cut short this portrait of a chambermaid. "What has he done?" she demanded, and then cautioned herself, "Shhh!"

There was a brief pause, and then Lucy confessed, "He untidied my hair."

"He what?"

"He—today, when we were alone in the music room—I had my back hair in a loose knot, and the front—"

"Yes, I remember. Go on."

"He took my head between his hands and shook out my curls." Lucy rolled over on her side and strained her eyes to try to see Cassy's face. She knew that her description was inaccurate; it conveyed nothing of the intimacy, the sorcery of that moment, but she hoped that Cassy would understand these qualities through intuition.

"Did he remove the pins?" Cassy inquired, after a moment.

"No," Lucy shifted back to her stomach, thrown a little off-balance by this way of looking at the incident. "Or—rather—yes, I suppose he must have done. My eyes were shut. Cassy, has Mr. Bloomsbury—"

"No," whispered Cassy positively. "Never."

Lucy sighed and then, driven by a confessional urge she did not understand, asked, "Cassy, does Mr. Bloomsbury ever—" She stopped, suddenly aware of how strange her question would sound.

"Ever what?"

Lucy squeezed her eyes shut. "Ever—bite you? Not

hard," she added hastily, "not hard at all—just on the fleshy part of the hand, and not hard, you know. Rather like"—she found Cassy's somewhat resistant hand and bit it—"like that."

Cassy shook her head, very thoroughly.

"I never even *heard* of anything like that."

"No, neither did I." Lucy hugged her pillow and collapsed back onto her stomach in a melancholy way.

"You could tell Mamma," Cassy suggested and felt the mattress heave as Lucy jerked to attention.

"Cassandra Theale! If you ever, ever breathe a word—"

"I won't." Cassy shrank back, not in fear but in such a manner as might convey her entire submission and repentance. "I won't, Lucy, I promise I won't."

A rustle from the bed in the corner made them grip hands under the coverlet. "What are you talking about?" hissed Grace, her curiosity unmistakable even through her drowsiness.

"Nothing," chorused the bed-fellows, in censorious unison.

"It is so something," contradicted Grace and yawned. "I think you're both beasts."

Her invective went unreproved, since both Lucy and Cassy were pretending to be asleep. Grace turned her back on them and adjusted her blankets as noisily as she could, trying to express contempt in the very rustle of the bed-sheets. After a moment or two of straining her ears, she lapsed back into an agreeable dream in which she was teaching the Duke of Wellington how to knit.

Lucy lay still, open-eyed and reflective. After Grace's snugglings subsided, she spoke again, her lips close to Cassy's cheek.

"Of course, he often kisses my hand—"

Cassy gave a little murmur to indicate that she was listening, even that she approved of this more orthodox method of wooing a female of gentle birth, but Lucy was not deceived. Her friend was falling asleep. She rearranged her pillow and pulled the blankets up around her ears. She knew she herself would not sleep for a long time.

15

Day and night Lucy pondered the riddle of Lord Rune's intentions. Being constitutionally pale, she lost no color, and her appetite increased rather than diminished, but she began to assume the rapt, brooding, distracted air that Tabitha dreaded. She subjected everything Lord Rune had said to rigorous scrutiny and badgered Cassy and Grace for commentary. She sought to decipher every glance, every touch. When she could not speak of Lord Rune, she fell silent, chronicling the changes in her heart. Over and over she wondered what the future would bring, weaving fantasies so vivid they brought tears to her eyes.

Lord Rune indulged in none of these pastimes. It could even be said of him that he never thought of Lucy if he could help it—though the times when he could help it were growing less frequent. At the back of his mind, there lurked a suspicion that his behavior towards his sister's godchild was not "the thing." It was a humiliating suspicion. For years Lord Rune had flattered himself that he knew "the thing" as well as any gentleman in London. As a man of the world, he knew exactly what degree of familiarity might exist between a disinterested party and a young lady of breeding. And yet . . . the unpalatable idea surfaced: his behavior toward Miss Saint-Clair had been rather too warm. He had encouraged false hopes. He couldn't imagine what had possessed him.

He didn't blame Lucy. The worst—he thought—that could be said of Lucy was that she was too candid. No. He decided that it could be said with perfect truth that she was appallingly candid. Appallingly candid and awkwardly vulnerable—it was a dangerous combination. All the same, he had navigated more treacherous waters than these. He wondered why his usual expertise had failed him.

He sought to placate his conscience with the decision to see less of Lucy in the future. Only—unfortunately—it was not possible this particular week. He had promised to play for her at the musicale and contrived to join the party at Vauxhall. It would be shabby to leave Miss Saint-Clair without an accompanist and churlish to disdain the hospitality he had finessed. He would have to honor his engagements, but he would guard his manner scrupulously.

At the musicale, his behavior was unexceptionable. He dressed well and played well; he danced the quadrille with Miss Saint-Clair and let Mr. Feather claim her for the waltz. He carried lemonade and cake to all the ladies of the Theale party and wielded their fans with impartial gallantry. He flattered Lucy for her deft handling of Rossini's coloratura, but there was a facetious character to his compliments that disappointed her. They were never alone. Lord Rune examined his behavior during the drive home and decided that it had been quite the thing. The recollection gave him no satisfaction; he remembered the look of frustration in Lucy's eyes and felt guilty.

A woman who can make a man feel guilty in several mutually exclusive ways is clearly an undesirable companion. Lord Rune determined to lose himself in masculine pursuits and took himself off to Manton's. An afternoon of shooting did little to relieve his feelings; he was out of practice and his eyes were weaker than they had been five years ago. In another five years, perhaps, he would need spectacles. The fact that his interest in firearms had never been more than tepid did not console him for the last reflection. He left Manton's in a very bad humor.

He found Tattersall's more convivial. The rich smells of horse and leather and newly varnished wood were pleasing enough to banish, for a time, both his guilt and his dread of spectacles. He took a fancy to a grey hunter and spent some time haggling over the price. The recollection that Miss Saint-Clair liked grey horses better than any other kind struck him during the final stages of bargaining and goaded him into buying a strawberry roan instead. He was disgusted with himself. The roan was exquisite, but lacked bone; the grey was the better horse.

He left Tattersall's and took himself off to Weston's, where he ordered three waistcoats, an evening coat, and a Wellington frock coat. They were all very expensive, which gave him an obscure sense of satisfaction, as if by squandering so much money he had compensated for something irrevocably lost. As he set off

down Old Bond Street he noticed for the first time that
the wind was fresh and the sky was delicately blue; he
had been laboring under a sense of oppression and had
not noticed that the day was unusually fine.

Upon passing Sybil Rant's shop, he glanced at the
display window, expecting to see the watered silk, the
brisé fan, and the grim-faced doll. The silk was there,
but the doll was missing, and the fan had been shut;
evidently the window was undergoing refurbishment.
Lord Rune opened the door and walked inside.

A plump and golden-haired damsel presided over
the counter, where she was gathering a lace betsie with
enviable skill. She favored him with a smile at once
contemplative and inviting, but Lord Rune had no eyes
for her. He saw Miss Rant herself seated by the window, with the half-naked fashion doll clamped between
her bony thighs and an expression of sour contempt on
her face. He knew that Sybil hated the doll and it looked
as if the doll hated Sybil; it would be diverting to witness the battle between them. He realized, with some
wonder, that he was a little lonely and that he was
longing for someone to tease. He bowed low and embarked upon a miscellany of compliments, greetings,
and inquiries as to Miss Rant's health.

Sybil did not answer at once. She fixed Lord Rune
with a basilisk glare, blinking at him as if to accuse him
of bringing sunlight into her shadowy realm. Her mouth
was full of pins and Lord Rune was every bit as irritating as he meant to be. She bent her attention on the
doll's dress, detaching a minute frill of lace from the
doll's splayed fingers. At last she deigned to reply. "Oh,
I'm well," she said grudgingly. "We don't all of us have
the time to indulge every little ache and pain."

Lord Rune, appreciating the intended slight, realized with some surprise that he had not been ill for some time.

"Those girls would be pleased enough, if I was to be took ill," Sybil continued grimly. "They'd be cutting their cloth crooked and tossing pins and needles out the windows, if I weren't up and about. This doll"—Sybil made the monosyllable an unspeakable insult—"I even have to dress this doll for 'em." She nodded towards the curly-haired vision behind the counter. "That Florence dressed it last time, and tore the rose-point lace at the elbow."

Lord Rune glanced apologetically at the maligned girl.

"Point de rose," pronounced Florence, with a crisp French accent and an enchanting pout.

"Rose-point," corrected Sybil, in flat English. "You'd best go upstairs, Florence, and see if you can set the sleeves in that sprig muslin. She has no more idea of a sleeve," she informed his lordship, "than if she was a barnyard animal. I've told them—I've told them all—that it's a sleeve that gives proportion to a gown, but they want nothing of anything I can tell 'em."

Florence waited courteously until the harangue was over, gave Lord Rune a dimpled smile and a coquettish bob, and sailed out of the room.

"Not a brain in her head," Sybil said morosely. She unpinned a petticoat from the doll's unnaturally feminine form and for the second time subjected Lord Rune to a piercing stare.

"You're looking less bilious than usual."

Lord Rune, realizing that he was not going to be offered a chair, reached over the counter and appropriated Florence's stool.

"You flatter me."

Sybil sniffed, as if to declare herself innocent of all amiable intentions, and skewered a lace-trimmed petticoat in place. A miniature masterpiece in silver moiré followed the petticoat; with infinite caution Sybil eased the sleeves over the wooden fingers. Lord Rune seated himself behind her; in spite of himself he grew interested.

"That's very pretty."

Sybil drew the back of the dress together and gazed at her handiwork suspiciously. The sleeves were delicately puffed and pleated, the bodice was subtly shaped by a profusion of tiny, flattering tucks, and folds of the skirt shimmered like falling water. A faint grimace disfigured the stoicism of Sybil's face; she almost disgraced herself by smiling.

"Silk moray," she said, making the fabric sound like an eel. "Has a weight to it."

She lifted the doll's train, letting the light ripple over the fabric as she held it between finger and thumb. Her face was expressionless; her voice intended to convey that she had been forced to acknowledge the fabric's "weight" but would not be betrayed into further extravagances. Her hands, however, were the hands of a lover; reverent, lingering, keenly aware. Lord Rune smiled to himself but without mockery; at that moment he found her endearing. He couldn't help thinking that it was perceptive of him to be able to appreciate both her Medusa-mask and the artist beneath it, and he felt warm with affection, both toward Sybil, and himself.

"It'd make a handsome wedding dress for your Miss Saint-Clair," Sybil stated, and Lord Rune's affections cooled.

"Miss Saint-Clair," he said coldly, "is not going to be married." He realized that his tone of voice was unduly forbidding, and added, "As far as I know," in a more temperate manner.

Sybil took a threaded needle and began to sew the dress up the back seam, once again pressing the doll's sharp little feet between her knees. "Ah," she said, and added, obliquely, "And you would know, wouldn't you?"

It was unlike Sybil to be oblique, and Ernest found it unnerving. He knew that she was often aware of things before they became common gossip, and he found himself wondering if Lucy might have become engaged without his knowledge. He had not seen her alone for over a week. The image of Lucy waltzing with Laurence Feather rose before his mind's eye and would not be banished. Like many heavy people, Laurence Feather was light on his feet, and he rejoiced in waltzing. He had spun Lucy round the Curry ballroom until she was out of breath. It was a triumphant and festive performance, so obviously a pleasure to the dancers that the chaperones smiled in spite of themselves. Lord Rune's face grew pensive as he remembered. Then he recalled the way Lucy's eyes had closed when he touched her hair, and his forehead cleared.

"Yes," he said, "I would know."

Sybil did not argue. She finished her seam and looped the needle through the thread, making a small, secure knot. She looked toward her workbasket, and Lord Rune—who saw her scissors glinting in the folds of her skirt—forbore to tell her where they were. With swift and savage efficiency, she brought the doll up to her mouth and bit the thread. The wet end trailed from her mouth, and she stabbed the needle into a dark, hard pincushion in the shape of a heart.

It was a commonplace sequence of actions, but it

made Lord Rune uncomfortable. Unconsciously, he was remembering the spinsters of myth and fairy tale: hunchback crones with their spinning wheels; Clotho, Lachesis, and Atropos; thread and truth and knife. He felt, with a surge of uncanny certainty, that Sybil knew something he didn't, and he demanded, "Who told you she was going to be married?"

"No one told me," retorted Miss Rant, with composure and perfect truth.

So bland a response might have been expected to conciliate his lordship, but he didn't appear to find it soothing. He looked narrowly at Sybil's face, but her features told him no more than the doll's. He began to suspect that he was making a fool of himself, but this suspicion—familiar to all mortals—is like the prophesies of unlucky Cassandra; it depresses, but it is never believed and is powerless to change the course of events. "Does she confide in you?"

It was not quite so farfetched a question as it sounded. Sybil did not even annoy him by asking who "she" was—which was, doubtless, an oversight on her part. Over the years, Miss Rant had found that her profession was one that led her customers to confide. Dressmaker and client are engaged in a conspiracy; clients are forced to reveal the weaknesses of vanity and the secrets of the flesh. Other secrets, not essential to the making of clothes, often follow, and Sybil Rant's customers found that they were kept safe. Sybil Rant was unsympathetic, but she was as tight-sealed as any tomb.

If Lucy had told Sybil . . . Swiftly Lord Rune passed from thinking how indiscreet Lucy was to wondering what she might have said. He could imagine nothing that seemed likely. In fact, Lucy had said noth-

ing. In Cassy and Grace she had two soulful confi-
dantes; she did not need others. Also, Sybil was very
terrible—all three girls flinched from the lash of her
tongue. Sybil, then, knew nothing about Lucy's pros-
pects that all London did not know, but she chose not to
say so. She merely shook her head in a disgruntled way
and said that Lord Rune knew more about Miss Saint-
Clair than she did.

"Then why," demanded Lord Rune, "did you say
she was going to be married?"

Sybil rose. "I didn't say so," she retorted and glared
down at her scissors, which had slid to the floor. Lord
Rune knew his gentlemanly duty; he bent over and offered them to Sybil with the blade sheathed in his palm.
Sybil took them and turned toward the window. The
doll, and the upper part of her body, vanished behind
the curtains. A sort of growl came from the window
alcove.

"I beg your pardon?" said Lord Rune, but he heard
her quite well.

Sybil emerged from the curtains with her arms full
of watered silk. "You heard me." She subjected him to a
third and final look: a spectral and merciless scrutiny
that made the hair curl on the back of his neck. "I have
work to do, even if you haven't."

Against such rudeness only courtesy could prevail.
Lord Rune apologized for the length of his call with a
humility that revealed, to Sybil's demonic penetration,
that he was furious. He went through every formality
that he could think of to prolong his leaving and managed to keep her from her task for another ten minutes.
At last, she simply turned her back and ignored him,
and he went out of the shop and slammed the door. He

did not care if he broke the plate glass in the window; he wanted to shatter the certainty in Sybil's pale eyes, and to drown out the sound of her voice muttering, "But she is."

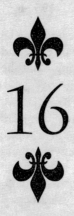

16

What is so tiresome as a young girl in love? So callous a question was never posed. If it had been, Mrs. Theale would have been hard put to find an answer that did not discredit her maternal heart. Tabitha's nature was affectionate, and her patience elastic, but the company of three young girls was beginning to take its toll.

Her sufferings were legion. The house was replete with company; the morning mail was choked with invitations and dressmakers' bills. The round of calls and balls became strenuous, and Tabitha began to look forward to the nights when she went to the opera, because she could sleep there without being rude. It never occurred to her that that she was insulting the present musicians or the absent composer, and this was a pity. The fancy that her snores struck a blow against Mozart and company would have afforded her no small degree of satisfaction.

Her worries were many. Cassy was the least of them; she was safely engaged and she was not—heaven be praised—the sort of girl to fuss over her trousseau. Her main shortcoming was that she spent too much time alone with her fiancé. Tabitha did her best to chaperone the young lovers, but they were cunning; they had ways of lagging behind or remaining in the next room, only to catch up a few minutes later, dreamy-eyed and guilty. Tabitha suspected that Cassy was indulging in osculation, even—she shrank from the word—in dalliance, but she was helpless to stop it. She found herself wondering if it would be very wrong to ignore her daughter's love-making, and decided that, wrong or not, it would be restful. She took comfort in the fact that Mr. Bloomsbury was the soul of honor and prayed that Cassy could be trusted not to sink herself beneath reproach.

The question of Lucy was more worrisome. Mrs. Theale watched the girl's moods plummet and soar and cursed her brother's charm. To be sure, Ernest was mending his ways—Tabitha, unlike Lucy, approved of his conduct at the last musicale—but she feared the damage was done. Lord Rune's attentions had done all that his sister had wished: Miss Saint-Clair was the fashion. If she were ever to receive an offer of marriage, it would be now. But would she have the wisdom to accept it? Tabitha found herself studying Lucy's face, hoping to see the shadow of reason but finding instead the unmistakable radiance of love. The girl was sick with love, and it would cripple her. At a time when she most needed to be expedient, she was going to be a fool. Tabitha tried to remind Lucy that time was passing; this was her last Season. She began to drop hints about the return to Yorkshire, speaking of the peace of the vicarage, of how Lucy would miss the opera. Her daughters stared at her reproachfully, and Lucy's eyes grew dark with panic, but Tabitha was ruthless. She knew her brother would not marry Lucy, and she was exasperated by the girl's constancy.

Grace was less worrisome than Lucy, but she was even more irritating. Inspired by Lucy's social triumph, Grace was determined to assume the role of a dashing young lady. She implored her mamma to let Sybil Rant make her gowns; she anguished over hair-styles; and she was funereal when she developed a spot. She was feverish to visit Vauxhall, and the fact that Viscount Sexton meant to go reanimated her fondest feelings. Grace was a practical young person, and she knew that springtime and a new gown are more pleasurable if one is in love. Rapidly, she fanned the embers of her recent fancy and her efforts were rewarded. By the gala night at Vauxhall, she had worked herself into a very promising little passion.

"He said he liked pansies," she informed her sister and her god-sister, "only he didn't know the name for them. Isn't that droll? We were walking in the park, and he pointed at them and said he liked those yellow things. Of course, I laughed at him and told him he was a great fool—but he didn't mind." She gazed fondly at herself in the mirror and straightened the pansies in her hair. "Do you think it's very bold of me to wear them, when he said he liked them? He may not remember, of course."

She waited for an answer but had none. Lucy sat before the mirror, gazing at her reflection with the desperate energy of a gambler about to stake his last shilling. Cassy was wandering back and forth; she had mislaid her diamond crescent and was beginning to fear it was lost for good.

Grace sighed in a manner that expressed how provoking it was to have to share a room with two such dismal females and went back to her toilette. Her gown was butter yellow, several shades lighter than the pansies, and made of thin gauze. Her reflection sufficed to make her forget her vexation, and she smiled, grateful that the spot on her chin had faded.

"I am so glad it's a fine evening," she announced, blithely and quite unnecessarily, for she had burdened the entire household with her anxieties about the weather. "When I heard the rain this morning I was quite desperate, but then it cleared up so beautifully, and even these thin muslins will be warm enough."

"It isn't underneath the bed," announced Cassy. "It's *lost*."

The despair in her voice was nearly enough to pierce Lucy's self-absorption. She looked down at the dressing-table, confused by a wilderness of hair-pins and trinkets and laces, of invitations and spilled powder, of pansies and pinks, of black hair combed from her hairbrush. "It isn't here," she said and pushed aside a fan to show that she spoke the truth. Three beads, two playing cards, a curling iron, and a sweet fell to the floor.

"I know that," answered Cassy, waspishly, "I looked there."

"I'm sorry," answered Lucy, humbly, but vaguely.

"It'll turn up," Grace said heartlessly. "Oh, dear! why must pansies have such brittle stems?" She plucked a stemless blossom from her wreath and looked accusingly at Lucy's wreath, which was woven of sturdy pinks. "I ought to have chosen some other flower, only—" She lunged suddenly, and pounced on the fan. "There it is! I thought you said you hadn't seen it!"

Cassy turned in a swirl of lilac jaconet. "My crescent?"

"No, my sandalwood fan." Grace unfurled the fan and admired the effect in the mirror. "Must you go on sitting there, Lucy? You've finished brushing your hair, and I want to check the folds of my sash."

Lucy mumbled something incoherent and rose from her seat.

"It's gone," Cassy lamented, in a manner that signified that she was thoroughly tired of searching and that someone ought to help.

Grace turned her back to the mirror and strained to see over her shoulder. "Where did you see it last?" she asked.

"I put it in my jewel-box last night," Cassy said tragically, "and it isn't there now." She threw up her hands, the gesture of the unjustly stricken.

"Did you look in your jewel-box?" demanded Grace, with enough patience to alienate a dozen sisters.

"I looked there a thousand times," Cassy retorted. "It isn't there." Her breath caught, and her eyes filled with tears. "Oh, how shall I ever tell Arthur?"

Lucy and Grace eyed each other. Silently they acknowledged that the crisis had become pressing and the time for preening themselves was over. "Now, Cass," Lucy said, in maddeningly maternal tones, "you mustn't cry and make your nose red. We'll find your crescent for you."

"It must be somewhere," Grace said brightly. "Did you look under the bed?"

Cassy raised her eyes to the ceiling. "I looked under the bed," she said, between her teeth, "and on the dress-

ing-table, and in my jewel-box, and under the rug, and
everywhere."

Lucy nodded, as if this catalogue effectively narrowed their search. "Did you look on the mantel?"

Cassy's eyes filled ominously; she had looked on
the mantel three or four times, and the implication that
she had not filled her with rage. "I *looked* on the mantel," she answered.

Grace sifted through her own jewel-box. "You
needn't be cross," she said, and slammed the lid to emphasize her point. "It isn't Lucy's fault your crescent is
missing. You should take better care of your things."

Cassy glared at her. Grace, realizing that she had
seriously offended her sister, devoted herself to rifling
through the chest of drawers.

"Did you look in your glove-box?" asked Lucy, in
the carefully colorless tone of a woman doing her best
not to offend anyone.

"Yes, of course, I looked in my glove-box," Cassy
snapped. "And my handkerchief drawer. I've looked
everywhere."

Lucy knit her bristling eyebrows but did not answer back; instead, she went to a pile of discarded
shawls and began to shake them out, one by one. Cassy
flung herself into an armchair and watched the others
search. She could tell they disliked her. She thought of
Arthur's face when he pinned it in her hair and was
betrayed into a sob.

Grace held up a stocking in one hand and something that glittered in the other. "Is this yours?" she
asked, with a sarcastic smile.

"Oh!" Cassy sprang from her seat, and grabbed the
crescent from her sister. "Oh, Grace, thank you!"

Grace's smile broadened and softened at the same

time. "It's of no consequence," she said. "People can always find things that don't belong to them."

Cassy hugged her, with the crescent clasped in her fist. "I suppose I didn't put it in the jewel-box, but on the chest, and then it fell into the drawer—oh, Grace, I'm so glad!" She wiped her eyes, and went to the mirror to pin the crescent in her hair, while Grace sat on the footboard of the bed and supervised the procedure.

Lucy folded the paisley shawl that Lord Rune had sent Cassy last Christmas and gazed at her friends' reflections. All day, they had annoyed her; Cassy was so smugly sure of Mr. Bloomsbury's love, and Grace had fretted over the weather until Lucy ground her teeth. Now she looked at them with hungry eyes. They were her dear friends, almost her sisters, and she would soon be parted from them—unless Lord Rune proposed. Tabitha's hints had not fallen on deaf ears; Lucy knew that her time in London was nearly up and that it was quite conceivable—not to be thought of, but conceivable— that Lord Rune would not propose.

She drew a deep breath and hugged the shawl, reviewing her chances for the thousandth time. He had stroked her hair; many times he had kissed her hand. Tonight they would be at Vauxhall. Surely, in the shadowy dusk, he would speak a few special words to her— something that would tell her that he cared for her—if he cared for her.

She swallowed hard and put down the shawl, giving herself one last look in the mirror. Her palms were sweaty, and her stomach ached with fear, but she looked pretty, as pretty as she ever looked. Again, she took a deep breath, and felt adrenaline course through her body. Tonight, she thought, tonight, and she dared herself to hope.

17

Lord Rune was ill.

That was the diagnosis of Lord Rune's valet, and Pudder was wise in the way of symptoms. Pudder's dream, never attained and never relinquished, was to be an apothecary; as Lord Rune's valet he had had occasion to practice medicine steadily, if unofficially. He heard his master's baritone deepen to a husky bass and nodded; he saw the flush on his master's cheeks and contemplated the possibility of influenza. He observed Lord Rune's indifference to the starch in his cravat and diagnosed accordingly: influenza it was, or a peculiarly malignant cold.

All of this the Argus-eyed Pudder observed, and he was thunderstruck when his lordship expressed a desire to be dressed for an evening at Vauxhall. No valet ever knew his place better than Pudder, but he was betrayed into uttering something that was almost a protestation;

he informed his master that the shrubbery at Vauxhall would very likely be damp.

"Damned damp," growled Ernest, and so serious was the matter that neither man smiled at the repetitive sound of the words.

In silence Pudder laid out his master's clothes and reconsidered his diagnosis: it could not be influenza, but must be a cold, and a mild cold, too. He noticed the languor of Lord Rune's carriage; the bent shoulders, the pathetic look in the eye. There was no doubt that his lordship was suffering; he had the look peculiar to men who catch colds—a look of animal bewilderment, of resignation and self-pity. Pudder had seen that look many times, and usually it meant lowered shades and lowered voices, beef tea and rum-and-water. That it could coexist with damp shrubbery and festive society was unthinkable.

It was no less unthinkable to Lord Rune. Even as he allowed Pudder to dress him, he tormented himself with the possibility of reprieve; it was not too late to send a polite note round to his sister's. Like his niece, Lord Rune had observed the rain that morning and supposed that the evening's festivities would be canceled. He trusted they would be, and he was crushed when the sky cleared and the wind sprang up. Now he reminded himself that he could still beg off. It would not be malingering, because he was really very ill; his head throbbed and his throat was raw. It was a long time since Vauxhall held any charm for him, and he found Laurence Feather tiresome. All in all, there was not the smallest chance that he would enjoy the evening; not one. Certainly he should send round a note.

Now, here is a mystery, and not an uncommon mystery either. Lord Rune knew that he would not en-

joy himself and that he could avoid Vauxhall without
incurring censure, and yet he dressed to go. All men,
and all women too, have been in his place, faced with a
social occasion that will certainly bring no pleasure and
may even bring pain—for there are degrees of boredom
that amount to real suffering. And yet, the carriage is
ordered; the cravat is knotted, nooselike, around the
throat; the tender feet are forced into the tight slippers.
No good ever comes of these occasions. And yet, like
wars, they continue to flourish, a tribute to human per-
versity and the wickedness of fate.

It was Lord Rune's destiny to attend such an occasion that evening, and dimly he knew it and was miserable. He found himself thinking wrathfully of Sybil Rant,
as if she were somehow responsible. Perhaps she was.
Since he last saw Sybil, he had engaged in a long series
of phantom arguments with her, in which he proved
beyond the shadow of a doubt that Miss Saint-Clair was
not about to be married and that if she were, he would
not suffer in the least. He argued his case logically and
painstakingly and quite exhaustively; he was the play-
wright who wrote both sides of the argument, and he
gave himself all the best lines. And yet the imaginary
Sybil never conceded a point. She was very nearly as
intractable as the real Sybil and every bit as irksome,
and Lord Rune was sick of the thought of her. The real
Sybil had filled him with an indefinable dread; he felt
certain that she knew something he didn't, and he was
threatened by it. He had no peace, either of body or
mind, and he was doomed to Vauxhall.

Never, thought Lucy, had Vauxhall been more picturesque; never had wind and tree, sunset and rising moon,

conspired to cast a more potent spell. The night air was as damp as Pudder had foreseen, but Lucy felt only its seductive coolness; she inhaled the scent of the river— by no means entirely fresh—as if it were the most luscious of perfumes. She had contrived to sit beside Lord Rune, and the seat of the boat was narrow; she could feel the warmth of his body though they did not touch. That phantom warmth was enough to sharpen all her senses; the tint of the sky was deeper, more significant; the sound of the lapping water more sonorous.

The evening had begun badly. Lord Rune's greeting was civil, but his eyes looked remote. There was nothing fond, nothing piquant, nothing provocative, in his manner. Lucy felt a sinking certainty that her slippers were too gaudy and her gown too low-necked; she should never have worn that ridiculous wreath in her hair. With a cold sensation in the pit of her stomach, she adjusted her shawl before Tabitha's lotus-carved looking-glass.

She had looked forward to the evening so eagerly; she could not abandon hope. She shrugged off her fears as best she could, trying to believe she had imagined his lordship's coldness. With energy born of tension, she joined in the conversation, executing her proper share of courtesies, quips, and raptures. It was a lively performance, and Laurence Feather, at least, found no fault in it. He coaxed his pink-wreathed gypsy into taking the ribbons of the charabanc and teased her about her driving as she piloted the unwieldy vehicle through London. If Lord Rune was silent and grim, it was possible— surely it was possible?—that it was jealousy that stiffened his features and stopped his mouth. Laurence Feather was merry and gallant, and several times in the course of the drive he contrived to touch Lucy's hands.

It was unnecessary and rather gratifying. Lucy hoped that Lord Rune had noticed and that Mrs. Theale had not.

Lord Rune had noticed but without taking umbrage; his attention was divided between a throbbing head and a strong disinclination for the company of his youngest niece. Grace was seated between her uncle and her mamma—a cruel privation for any flirtatious young lady—and she compensated by projecting her voice so that Viscount Sexton, who sat behind her, could hear it. Her discourse was sunny and sportive, and the viscount leaned forward appreciatively, but Lord Rune suffered. He knew, now, he should not have come.

By the time the charabanc reached the Thames, Lord Rune was beginning to hate himself and everyone around him. He failed to notice that Miss Saint-Clair was trying to catch his eye, and it never occurred to him that she was hoping he would press her hand as he helped her into the boat. He saw the end of her shawl fall into the river and he fished it out, squeezed the water from it as best he could, and nodded when she thanked him. That she smiled at him, instead of speaking, struck him as agreeable after Grace's chatter, and he returned her smile with real affection. It was the reassurance Lucy craved; she lowered her lashes in shyness and deep content. Her faith in silver slippers and rose-colored gauze was restored. She leaned back against the boat-cushions—they, too, were damp—and savored the romance of the evening.

Her reverie was short-lived. Laurence Feather had commanded a boat-load of musicians to provide all that was elegant in the way of entertainment. Since he preferred stringed instruments to horns, he had hired violins and cellos, two harps, and a lute. The dampness of the air played havoc with cat-gut and the result was a discord that made Lord Rune wince and reduced Lucy to helpless giggles. Even Tabitha, the least musical of mammas, broke off her conversation with Mr. Blooms-bury to say that surely the music should not sound like that? Mr. Bloomsbury, torn between candor and tact, was hard put to frame a response.

He was saved from replying. At no time was Lau-rence Feather's tact extraordinary, and his ear was of-fended; he bolted from his seat and began to shout at the musicians. The boat rocked, Grace emitted a dear little shriek, and the young viscount sought to reassure her. The musicians, fearing that they would not be paid if they left off playing, continued to saw and pluck, wringing a series of excruciating sounds from their in-struments. Laurence Feather grew red-faced with morti-fication, and Lord Rune was betrayed into a guilty smirk.

At last the musicians were persuaded to desist; Lau-rence Feather promised them an extra half crown each if they would go away without playing another note. Lucy regained control over her countenance and returned to her lovesick fancies. The boat-ride was brief, but de-lightful—for most members of the party. Lord Rune did not enjoy it, and Cassy was seasick. The sight of Vauxhall, which was Cytherea to Lucy, was doubly wel-come to Cassy because it was land. Lord Rune noticed his niece's wan expression and was moved to sympathy. Here was a fellow-sufferer; someone with the sense and sensibility to be ill.

Lucy, who had meant to walk with Lord Rune, saw that he was deeply engaged in a discussion of seasick-ness with Cassy and the hitherto disdained Mr. Blooms-bury. With a feeling of bewilderment, she accepted Mr.

Feather's arm and joined him at the head of the party. Behind her, Cassy murmured her symptoms and Lord Rune sympathized. Mr. Bloomsbury—as poor Lucy strained her ears to hear—had often been seasick as a child but had outgrown it. Cassy confessed, with a hint of perverse pride, that she had *not* outgrown it. With some enthusiasm, Lord Rune embarked on a description of some of the very rough crossings he had suffered on his travels.

Unlucky Lucy! The moon had risen and Vauxhall was shadowy and fantastical; the trees were ancient and dark, the grass dewy, the wind moist, fragrant, fondling. The avenues and groves were spangled with tiny lamps; there were temples and cascades, statues shining like ghosts in the twilight, flowers heavy with scent, painted canvasses of lolling cherubs and languishing nymphs. It was more stage-setting than garden, fashioned to nourish every amorous conceit; it excited the imagination as well as the senses. Lucy had seen Vauxhall before, but she had not yet loved; now, she felt its power tenfold. Behind her, Lord Rune had fallen silent. The erotic fairyland around him did not move him; he was imprisoned in a palace of pain. He shivered and felt a little dizzy; his throat hurt so badly that he wondered if he might have swallowed something sharp.

The likelihood of this last possibility occupied his thoughts for some time and served to deprive him of speech. He declined to compare seasickness with carriage sickness, and let Cassy and Mr. Bloomsbury go on ahead. Behind him, Mrs. Theale played duenna to Grace. She had noticed her brother's abstraction and heard his complaints; evidently Ernest had decided once more to play the invalid and discourage her lovesick god-child. It was very good of him, and well-timed; Mr.

Feather was clearly disposed to be attentive. Tabitha half-trotted a step to reach her brother's side and clasped his arm. Her manner was doting, but it made no impression; the marble statues in the Italian walk were not more insensate than Ernest with a sore throat.

As it grew darker, it became impossible for Lucy to see Lord Rune. The blue arch at the end of the trees turned violet and then faded. The pleached alley was black with shadows, and the fairy lamps no more powerful than fireflies. Vauxhall was a stage-setting, but its nightfall was real. Lucy and Laurence Feather, Cassy and Mr. Bloomsbury, Grace and her viscount all felt it: the atavistic fear that is felt in the dark, in the presence of ancient trees. Cassy nestled closer to Mr. Bloomsbury's solid shoulder. Grace's voice hushed. Lucy gazed at the moon against the smoke-dark sky and felt her throat close. For the first time she was aware of Mr. Feather's arm; the virile strength of it, the comforting warmth—

She began by being aware of Mr. Feather's arm and ended by being aware of Mr. Feather. He was talking— she scarcely cared about what—in his rich, jovial voice and he hugged her arm close to his body. It was clear that he meant to please her. Lucy responded with a show of vivacity and was touched to see his broad cheeks widen and his eyelids curl upward. He looked like a happy cat.

Like Lucy, Laurence Feather had been to Vauxhall before; had, in fact, been to Vauxhall often. He was not the sort of man who grew weary of things he liked, and he liked Vauxhall almost inordinately. He had enough German in him to be sentimental about anything pastoral, and enough satyr in him to have a history of erotic encounters in bosky groves. Vauxhall—as Laurence

Feather knew well—was very bosky. He had trysted there often, and the memories of those trysts warmed his blood.

So, when Miss Saint-Clair tilted her chin and smiled at him, he found himself liking her better than ever before. He had always considered her a good sort of girl, and he sensed that Vauxhall was having the same effect on her that it had on him. He thought too—as it grew darker—that she was prettier than he had realized. He liked pink, and he liked the scent of the wreath in her hair, and he found no fault with the expanse of décolletage that Sybil Rant had authorized. In short, he was susceptible, and he squeezed Lucy's arm ardently.

Lucy felt the squeeze and wondered whether she should do something about it. She supposed that a little maidenly shrinking was in order, but three years as a wall-flower do not prepare a woman for amorous advances; Lucy was unpracticed in prudery. Also, it was hard to imagine shrinking from Mr. Feather. As a seducer, he was miscast; his caresses were too innocent, his manner too affable. Lucy had always thought that lust was a serious thing, even a grim thing. She could not reconcile Mr. Feather's joie de vivre with depravity. She resolved not to shrink and then started as a woman in white darted out of the shrubbery, pursued by a stout gentleman in knee-breeches. The lady turned to face him, with her hands clasped in helpless entreaty. She waited for him to catch up, uttered a breathless cry, and fled.

Laurence Feather, who had done his share of woodland pursuing, assumed a virtuous air and patted Lucy's hand. "There, now—nothing to worry about. Sort of thing happens all the time here. Not but what—

bolting out like that—Looked like a dashed ghost, didn't she?"

Under cover of his distraction, Lucy endeavored to worm her arm free. "She did, didn't she?" She gazed at him wide-eyed, trusting that he would forgive her the worming. "He didn't, though."

Laurence Feather considered this a moment. "No, he dashed well didn't. Well—knee-breeches, you know —not but what pantaloons—" He broke off to consider the proper attire for a gentleman ghost, and chuckled. It was a rich and owlish chuckle—his sturdy arm quivered with it—and he recaptured her hand and gave it a whole series of little pats.

These pats, instead of being tender, were friendly; the sort of hearty petting one gives a favorite horse. Lucy was surprised to find herself wanting, very irrationally, to cry. Mr. Feather was so kind, so willing to be pleased, so eager to squeeze and pat. Whereas Ernest—

Lucy blinked and turned to look for Ernest. He stood at the end of the alley, beside a statue of the dying Adonis, and the light from a gold paper lamp shone over his face. He looked unnaturally pale, and his face was devoid of emotion. Lucy gave a little shiver.

"There, now," Laurence Feather said warmly, "if we haven't walked enough—! Your shawl is wet, Miss Saint-Clair, and you're cold. I daresay you want your supper. I know I do."

His voice was sympathetic, and his eyelids curled more cheerfully than ever. Already he was thinking of the splendid food he had ordered, the goose and oysters and rumpsteak pie. All his favorite dishes, and champagne as well. Miss Saint-Clair looked down and murmured something ladylike, but Mr. Feather was not discouraged. She was a girl with a good appetite; she would enjoy her dinner. He gave her a final pat and turned to retrace his steps, eager to shepherd his company to supper.

It was a magnificent supper. Mr. Feather rose in Lucy's estimation; he might strike her as ridiculous, but he understood food. Also, he understood comfort; there were extra cushions for the hired chairs, footstools, and a miscellany of shawls for chilly shoulders. Lucy, who had railed against the bland cakes of Almack's, found herself encouraged to partake of scalloped oysters and poulet Marengo, buttered crab and cheese tart. There were oranges and meringues and pastry tubes dripping cream; there were apricot tarts and charlotte glacé, and champagne, which Laurence Feather implored her to drink on the grounds that he had ordered it just for her.

Lucy cast a beseeching look at her godmother, who shook her head. "I'm not a gypsy tonight, Mr. Feather. I mustn't drink champagne."

"Stuff." Laurence finished filling his own glass and filled one for Lucy. "You're always a gypsy. Why, I feel like a gypsy myself, at Vauxhall. Could dance the what-do-y'call-it and tell fortunes. I don't suppose you'd want to tell my fortune, would you?"

Conscious of Mrs. Theale's repressive glance, Lucy nibbled an apricot tart and shook her head. "I would rather listen to the orchestra," she said evasively. "This is Mozart, I think."

The party honored her comment with silence, all of them pausing to listen attentively, as if they could distinguish Mozart from Gluck. Lord Rune spoke up. "I think it's Beethoven."

It was the first time he had spoken since dinner

began. Lucy leaned forward so that she could see him. "Do you? I suppose it might be. It's difficult to hear properly—I do wish people would stop talking—" She caught Mrs. Theale's eye and had the grace to look ashamed. "Just for a moment," she temporized, and, ignoring the rest of the company, "Do you admire Beethoven's music, Lord Rune?"

Lord Rune had passed melancholy and arrived at morose. He had been unable to eat Mr. Feather's food, which was almost uniformly rich, savory, and exotic; and he was alienated by the spectacle of his companions happily wielding their cutlery. He would have given a great deal for a pot of hot tea and a slice of buttered toast, but he couldn't very well say so. Lucy cherished the illusion that he was dashing, and he had come to cherish it too. Dashing men—Lord Rune erroneously assumed—never admit to yearnings for tea and toast. Nor do they complain of influenza at dinner-parties.

He was, therefore, reduced to anathematizing Ludwig van Beethoven, while Miss Saint-Clair listened intently and with so obvious a desire to please that a more sensitive man than Mr. Feather would have abandoned his suit on the spot. Van Beethoven, Lord Rune pronounced, was talented but doomed to obscurity. His music was not without merit, but he was too fond of novelty for novelty's sake; he sacrificed beauty to singularity. He had written little in the last several years, and —if Lord Rune's Viennese friends were well-informed— was now very deaf. It was a pity, but his music would almost certainly prove to be of no lasting importance.

Lord Rune delivered this speech in a rather hoarse voice, wondering, as he did so, why he was condemning a composer he admired. He sounded dogmatic, and he knew it; he also knew that Lucy's wide eyes and little nods of agreement were intended to appease his ill-humor. Her slavishness irritated him. He finished his lecture by apologizing to Cassy for leaning past her, thereby reminding Lucy of her own rudeness in speaking to someone who was not her neighbor at table. Lucy's brows snapped together, and she turned away without another word.

As Laurence had predicted, Lucy had partaken of Mr. Feather's supper with ladylike, but genuine, enthusiasm. Her appetite, which was always good, was sharpened by anxiety. Also, she was cold. She was too proud of her pretty gown to wear the drab-colored shawl that Mr. Feather provided, and her own shawl was wet. Dinner warmed her and heartened her; Lucy was of the sisterhood that finds comfort in food. Now she gazed down at the rum soufflé and considered Lord Rune's unkindness. Why was he so disagreeable? What had she done? She realized that Laurence Feather was looking at her and smiled so sadly that he, connecting her wistfulness with a passion for soufflé, served her another helping.

Lucy did not disdain it. She ate soufflé as Grace and Viscount Sexton excused themselves and went to the amphitheatre to dance. She scraped the dish and sucked the spoon as she watched Cassy and Mr. Bloomsbury draw their chairs together so that they could flirt with greater intimacy. Pensively, she gazed at the dancers and nibbled a meringue. The sweetness of it made her thirsty, and her lemonade glass was empty. She put her fingers to the stem of the champagne glass and saw Laurence Feather watching.

"I won't tell," he coaxed, and nodded toward Tabitha, who sat with her maternal eye fixed on Grace. "Won't you taste it, Miss Saint-Clair? I promise you

you'll enjoy it. And a gala night—well, it *is* a gala night. No getting away from that. One should always have what one likes at a gala night. I always do," finished Laurence Feather, with a guilty and highly pleasurable recollection of some of the things he liked.

Lucy opened her mouth to say that what she liked was lemonade and was interrupted. Lord Rune was quoting, with his sardonic glance fixed on the half-eaten feast:

> "Here every man may have his fill,
> Vauxhall-fashion, sup or swill,
> Every mother's son may cram
> Peaches, partridges and ham,
> While porter, hock, and iced champagne
> Pour more freely than the rain."

It was a popular ballad; Lord Rune supposed that Lucy had heard it before. That she had not was clear from the wrath that filled her eyes. Wrath and—Ernest observed ruefully—mortification. He had watched Lucy's steady consumption of sweets with a fascination akin to nausea, but he hadn't planned to humiliate her. He had, in fact, associated that dreadful word *cram* with his host—a man, he realized now, he had always disliked.

"It's a pleasure," remarked that host, as he witnessed Miss Saint-Clair's anguish, "to see a female who's not too missish to enjoy her food. But that's gypsyish, too. Isn't it, Miss Saint-Clair?"

Lucy could have wept. She felt as if the entire company were staring at her, made incredulous by her greed. She felt—she knew—that they were thinking that she was too fat, that she was bulging with fat; it was ludicrous to have thought, for one moment, that she looked pretty. With her last shred of self-esteem, she refrained from burying her face in her table napkin. She looked round wildly, trying to think how to draw attention away from herself, and saw the champagne glass. She raised it and said boldly, "Gypsies don't often enjoy such a feast, Mr. Feather."

Laurence Feather took up his own glass. "Are you toasting me, Miss Saint-Clair?"

"No, only roasting you." That was good, Lucy thought; the conversation was getting away from the subject of food. "Only I mustn't say so, of course. It isn't proper for females to use such language."

She spoke with oppressive primness, striving for a comic effect. Cassy and Mr. Bloomsbury did not smile, for the very simple reason that they were not paying attention—they were holding hands under the table. Tabitha was disapproving, and Lord Rune was impassive. Laurence Feather, however, had had a good many glasses of champagne, and his sense of humor was easily tickled. He indulged in another owlish chuckle.

"Propriety? You are roasting me, Madam Gypsy." He poured a little more champagne and touched his glass to hers, tipping a froth of champagne down the side of the glass. "There. Now I've toasted you, and it would be improper," he mimicked her primness, "not to drink."

Lucy reached for the lemonade glass and saw that it was empty. Lord Rune would not meet her eyes. She lifted the wine-glass, smiled as briliantly as she could over the brim, and drank to Mr. Feather.

* * *

Later—and for the rest of her life—Lucy was to blame the champagne for what happened in the shrubbery. In this she was deceiving herself; as Lord Rune had hinted, she had had a substantial dinner and no more than a glass or two of wine. Still, she concluded, those glasses had an effect; the vintage must have been a potent one. How else could she understand her deplorable conduct?

She might have felt less guilty had she thought to blame Sybil Rant, who was, in fact, partly responsible for the events of the evening. Faced with the exuberance of Lucy's bosom, Sybil Rant had decided that what couldn't be minimized might be celebrated. The result was the rose-colored gauze, with its off-the-shoulder sleeves and bodice *en coeur*. It was superbly flattering, and discreet in revelation, but it was a dangerous dress; not even Sybil Rant could make a gown capable of encouraging some admirers and repelling others. Laurence Feather had spent the evening contemplating Lucy's white, firm, and prominent bosom.

He was not a cold-blooded man. His heart was susceptible; his passions easily stirred. He was also, as Tabitha had pointed out, an amiable man, and it was clear to the dullest of sensibilities that Miss Saint-Clair was in need of attention. She had abandoned her deferential attitude toward Lord Rune. Instead, she listened to Mr. Feather as if he were the one man alive who could save her from boredom. Her carriage had altered subtly; her back was arched, her neck curved. Several times, she tossed her curls, and her laughter was softer and throatier than usual. In short, her manner was provocative, and Laurence Feather could not be provoked with impunity.

He was not in love with Lucy. She was the antithesis of the golden-haired maids he imagined when he

dreamed of love. But he was fond of her, and his appetites had been well-watered with champagne. With one
eye on Mrs. Theale, he asked if Lucy would enjoy a
stroll in the shrubbery. Lucy assented and accepted his
arm with a coyness that would have made Lord Rune
laugh, had he been feeling better.

He was feeling very much worse. Lucy's coquetry
was not inspiring, and her attempts to seem indifferent
were so transparent that he was embarrassed for her.
He had been ignored by many women in his time, but
always with a modicum of finesse. Miss Saint-Clair's
nonchalance would not have deceived a child. Nor did it
deceive Mrs. Theale, who glared at her brother accusingly; Tabitha, of course, blamed him for Lucy's indis-
cretions. It only wanted that, thought Ernest, and he
rubbed his aching head.

Now he watched Lucy lay her hand on Mr.
Feather's nicely-frogged sleeve. He turned to look for
Tabitha and found her greeting an elderly lady in
mauve. It was, in fact, a duchess; a kindly, affluent and
personable duchess. If Tabitha had a weakness, it was
for duchesses. Her three charges were forgotten.

Ready to clutch at the proverbial straw, Lord Rune
looked for Cassy, who might be induced to accept the
chaperone's role. He was too late; Cassy had noticed
her mother's interest in the duchess and was sidling
down one of the dark paths, accompanied by Mr.
Bloomsbury. Lord Rune rose, favored the duchess with
the curtest of nods, and made his way into the shrubbery.

His prey was not far to seek. Less than a hundred
yards away, Lucy and Mr. Feather were admiring a
charming grotto. Ernest was just in time to see Mr.

Feather turn to Lucy, clasp her to his waistcoat, and press his lips to hers.

It is a curious thing, but unless the gentleman in question is distinctly repellent, a woman seldom resists her first kiss. She is usually too curious and too astonished. The part of the mind that ought to worry over the logistics of defense is too dazzled—or too disappointed —for immediate action. Lucy had been very curious and was now much astonished.

For a moment, she froze, and Ernest hesitated. He expected her to pull away at once; perhaps even to slap Mr. Feather's rounded cheek. Instead, she stood with her hands at her side and her back straight. She began— Ernest could think of only one word for it—to squirm. Instead of wrenching herself from her assailant's grasp, she twisted and ducked, so that he had to crouch over her to continue kissing. This he was willing to do; he was not easily discouraged.

Ernest's lips twitched. Sick man that he was, he had a sense of humor, and the sight before him might have convulsed any man. Lucy grumbled and continued to squirm until the crown of her head pressed against Mr. Feather's shirt-front. Mr. Feather, moved as much by determination as by ardor, contorted himself and went on kissing. So vain were his efforts that he might have abandoned them, had not one hand, trying to encourage his Chloe to nestle closer, come in contact with Lucy's breast.

Lucy squeaked, a soft but panicky sound, and Mr. Feather, enchanted with the pliancy of the breast, tried to gather her closer. Ernest, no longer amused, stepped forward and shook the pair apart.

"Oh!" gasped Lucy, relief, embarrassment, and dismay combined in a single word.

"Oh, God!" groaned Mr. Feather.

Lord Rune let go of Lucy and turned his wrath on the unfortunate Laurence. He had forgotten that he was ill; if his throat burned and his head throbbed, he had ceased to notice it. He was wholly enraged; all of his senses were servants to his wrath.

"What in hell do you think you're doing?"

Mr. Feather gulped. At no time was he an eloquent man, and Lord Rune's fury was a bolt from the blue. "I—" he began and then stopped. He remembered what he had been doing, and it was indefensible. "Oh, God," he said unhappily, and looked to Lucy for help.

"He was kissing me, but he didn't mean any harm," Lucy said obligingly. She tugged at Lord Rune's hand. "Lord Rune, please! Don't tell Godmamma! I won't do it any more—it wasn't at all nice—but it's over, and I don't want to talk about it. Take me back to Godmamma!"

Lord Rune jerked his hand away. "You know my sister's whereabouts; I suggest you go in search of her," was all he said to her. To Laurence Feather he said, "Your explanation, sir, does not meet with my satisfaction."

He spoke the last word between his teeth, with an emphasis that Laurence Feather ought to have understood. Unhappily, he did not; for once in his life, he was too preoccupied to seize the chance to fight a duel. "No, I don't suppose it does," he said, and tugged at his cravat. "That is to say, I haven't—That is, I know I've been damned impertinent—"

"Lord Rune, he didn't *mean* it," insisted Lucy, her voice projecting in a way that made both gentlemen shush her.

"I suppose I could marry her," Laurence offered,

after a moment's reflection. "Not that it's what I had in mind, but I daresay it's what I ought to do. And I don't suppose I'll be any the worse for it. Lucy—"

"*No,*" Lucy answered, so forcefully that Mr. Feather actually flinched. "I don't want to hurt your feelings, Mr. Feather, but I would very much rather not marry you."

Laurence Feather was too relieved by her words to be hurt by her tone of voice. "Well, there you are," he said to Lord Rune. "As I say, I could marry her, but she won't hear of it."

"Certainly not," agreed Lucy, crossing her arms over her outraged breast.

"Thing is," pursued Mr. Feather, beginning to breathe a little easier, "there's not much I can do. Can't marry her. Can't unkiss her. Once a woman's been kissed, there's nothing to be done about it, that I can think of."

He tugged at his cravat again—an awkward gesture that would not have escaped him in more felicitous circumstances. He was breathing rather hard, but he tried to sound dispassionate, even offhand. This last was a mistake; it did nothing to appease Lord Rune. He swept a contemptuous glance over the younger man and spoke with deadly quiet. "Must I tell you?"

Laurence Feather stiffened. When he spoke again, his voice had changed: he was on familiar ground, and his manner was businesslike.

"I believe I understand you, sir."

"I hope you do."

"You have my address in Regent Square. I shall be at home tomorrow morning."

"Ernest," Lucy broke in on these rapid-fire exchanges, "I mean, Lord Rune—you're not thinking of fighting a duel, are you?"

Both gentlemen shushed her again.

"But you mustn't!" Lucy whispered frantically. "Godmamma would be shocked, and I'm sure it isn't necessary! It was all so silly—and it was partly my fault that Mr. Feather kissed me. And I'm sure he's sorry—" She nodded approvingly at the sweating Mr. Feather. "Just look at him! Anyone can see how sorry he is, and *I* forgive him! If I forgive him, how can you bear him a grudge?"

She spoke impulsively, but without undue heat; she was rational, tolerant. Neither of these qualities recommended her to her listeners. Mr. Feather's cherubic countenance darkened; her plea for pardon compromised his honor. He spoke repressively. "This is no affair of yours."

"But it is," Lucy argued. "After all, it was me that you kissed." She saw that reason could not sway Mr. Feather and turned to Lord Rune. "Lord Rune, this is nonsense," she said. "It's *wicked* nonsense—and he only kissed me a little—and both of you ought to know better than to stick each other with swords over—"

"Pistols," corrected Laurence Feather, automatically.

"That's no better," Lucy scowled at him. "In fact, it's worse. One of you dead, or wounded, and the other fleeing the country, and all over nothing. Well, not nothing," she corrected herself, hugging her breasts, "but nothing as bad as all that. Nothing worth dying for." An idea occurred to her, and she suggested to Lord Rune: "You could bloody his nose, if you like, but that's all it's worth."

This suggestion found no favor with either gentleman. Mr. Feather went so far as to snort.

"I must counsel you not to concern yourself with how these matters are settled," said Lord Rune, so coldly that Lucy was momentarily quelled. She twisted her hands and looked back at Mr. Feather.

"I must beg you to say no more," Mr. Feather said, emulating Lord Rune's lofty manner. He held up a hand, as if to silence all further protest, and concluded, "I cannot but agree with Lord Rune in this matter."

He followed this proclamation with a crisp little bow, a remarkably crisp little bow for a man who had consumed an enormous dinner and copious amounts of champagne. Then he bowed in Lord Rune's direction. "I shall await your instructions." With military precision, he turned on his heel and strode away.

Lucy opened her mouth to call him back and realized it would do no good. Instead, she turned to face Lord Rune. In arguing with him, she had forgotten her embrassment. Now it struck her afresh. She realized, with a clarity that made her want to cover her face, how foolish she must have looked; how clumsy, how coarse. The color rushed to her cheeks, but she braced herself and raised her chin.

For a long moment, nothing was said. Then Ernest stretched out an arm and pulled Lucy to him, massaging her shoulder with one strong hand.

Lucy promptly burst into tears and collapsed against his waistcoat.

"My poor Lucy!" Ernest's voice was tenderly amused; his arm was protective; he smelled of starch and cedar soap. Lucy burrowed deeper into the waistcoat and mumbled something that ended with " . . . not angry?"

"At you? No. Should I be?" Lord Rune produced a handkerchief handed it to her, and disengaged himself.

"No." Lucy sounded confused. "Yes, I don't know. It wasn't the thing—kissing him."

"You didn't kiss him. He kissed you."

Lucy shuddered. "Cassy said—" But Cassy would die of shame if she told what Cassy said. She faltered: "I —I shouldn't have let him, even for a moment, but I— we stopped to look at the grotto, and I said how pretty it was, and we didn't go on walking, even though we ran out of things to say about it, and then he started talking about the moon—but one can't even see the moon, because of all these trees—and I was afraid he was going to— Only I wan't afraid, exactly." She swallowed a sob and mopped her nose with Lord Rune's handkerchief. Her voice shook. "I don't know why I didn't stop him before he started."

"Don't you?"

Lucy looked at him with an almost desperate appeal in her eyes. He was smiling, and his voice was very gentle.

"I was *curious*." Her voice sank, as if she were confessing to an unspeakable crime. "And I—I think I flirted with him at dinner, only perhaps you didn't notice—"

"I noticed."

"And it seemed—pusillanimous," Lucy brought forth the five-syllable word with sharp-edged emphasis, "to flirt with him, and then not—not—" She wiped her eyes and spoke to the handkerchief, seeming to forget Lord Rune's presence. "But I didn't like it *at all*," she said with feeling. "Not one bit." She risked a glance at Lord Rune and saw that he was still smiling. "It wasn't the way I feel when you kiss my hand. It was like kissing

a—a raw chicken," she concluded, and added, for clari-
fication, "plucked."

Lord Rune had stood back from Lucy quite deliberately, but at that last word he gave a shout of laughter
and caught her to him once again. She snuggled greedily
against his chest, feeling his warmth, hearing his heart-
beat, catching his laughter through the vibration of his
body. She began to snicker and then to laugh. They
stood together, shaking with shared delight, and then
Lord Rune disengaged himself a second time.

"Now," he said, "I must take you back to my sister
and be civil to the lecherous Mr. Feather for the sake of
your reputation. And in the future, you must try to
remember that if you flirt with a gentleman, he is entitled to flirt with you. He is not entitled," Lord Rune
sounded stern, "to anything else."

Lucy nodded and rolled his handkerchief between
her palms. "Yes—but—" she faltered, "you're not going
to fight a duel, are you? Because if you are—"

"And if you should honor him with"—Lord Rune
offered his arm in his most stately manner—"anything
else, you must not hazard guesses as to what it is worth.
Such valuations are bound to be considered vulgar, and,
in fact"—he sounded surprised by his own conclusion—"are vulgar."

Lucy had intended to press the question of the duel,
but Ernest's last sentence made her blink. "Lord Rune,"
she asked plaintively, "do you think I am vulgar?"

Ernest actually stopped. He looked at Lucy for a
long moment. Then he grinned in spite of himself. "Superbly," he answered, and saw the confusion in her
face. He cupped her chin in one hand and kissed her,
not long, but thoroughly, and with tenderness.

That passion—and pleasure—may be shared in an

embrace is much celebrated; what may also be exchanged is knowledge. Neither Ernest nor Lucy was in the best frame of mind for passion; Lucy was agitated and Lord Rune was unwell. Both of them were having a difficult evening. In spite of this—or perhaps because of it—each found sweetness in the other's arms and learned what they hadn't known before. Lord Rune encountered his own hunger as well as Lucy's; he passed from affection to desire. With arms that trembled slightly, he gathered her close and drew her into the shadow of the trees.

Lucy gave a low murmur, a yearning, almost maternal sound. All evening, her senses had been hungry, heightened, frustrated; now, with Lord Rune's arms encircling her, her head cleared. She sensed, beneath the image of the hero who had kissed her hand, the presence of a lonely and affectionate man. She felt his vulnerability; he discerned her strength. They clung together, with warm mouths and sheltering arms, and then, by tacit consent, they fell apart. With a unity both comic and unconscious, they sighed and let their arms drop.

"I should not have done that," said Ernest, but without conviction; he foresaw that Miss Saint-Clair would not agree with him. He had insulted her, but she was not going to feel insulted. In fact, she was trying not to smile.

"We should go back," he said, and offered his arm.

"I suppose we should," said Miss Saint-Clair, and accepted it.

They retraced their way through the dark trees, deaf to the rustling of the leaves and the sound of distant music. With unutterable delicacy, they avoided glancing at the entwined couples they passed; if it occurred to them that they had just been similarly employed, they did not say so. Lucy's thoughts were tangled and unfocused; Lord Rune felt suddenly very tired. His evening was not over; there would yet be dancing, fireworks, the journey home. He sighed again, and Lucy looked at him and forbore to ask why he was sighing.

18

According to hackneyed tradition, a lover does not sleep. Miss Saint-Clair, whose appetite had remained indecorously active throughout her love-affair, was in this instance conventional. The night after the gala she was wide-eyed and restless; she lay awake long after Cassy and Grace lapsed into slumber. Was it not the night of her first kiss? And her second kiss? And was she not—preposterous though it might seem—the cause and object of a duel? Under such circumstances, no lady of sensibility could rest. She must lie awake; she must thrill and throb and sigh. Lucy's stock of sensibility was not prodigal but it was adequate to the occasion. She lay awake and brooded.

It had been an appalling night, an unforgettable night. Lucy writhed and grew hot as she recalled it: she had disgraced herself. She had been a glutton; she had flirted with abandon; she had known the mortification of Laurence Feather's paw on her breast. And yet—she squirmed and sought to bury a smile in her pillow—she had kissed Lord Rune. He had held her in his arms, and rubbed her shoulder; she tingled with the warmth of his touch. She could still feel the vibration of his laughter. He loved her. She could not believe it; she did not dare. And yet—Lucy shivered with emotion—and yet he must love her, just as she loved him. Feelings so strong must be mutual; sensations so heady must be shared—

So Lucy reasoned—and if her reasoning was faulty, she was too overwrought to realize it. Perhaps she ought not to be blamed. All young lovers have reasoned thus. They are usually wrong. And yet their faith—which makes their plight so poignant and absurd—is an enviable thing. It is easily lost and can never be recovered. The fish that bites the lure may survive, but forever after the sweetness of the bait is compromised by the cruelty of the hook.

Back and forth between the anguish of humiliation and the ecstasy of love did Lucy fly. She reviewed the evening in detail, giggling as she remembered the barcarole on the river, wincing as she recalled her behavior at supper. She should never have had those glasses of champagne; Godmamma was annoyed, and there would be a lecture in the morning. Lucy knew she deserved it; she had been brazen and ill-bred and vulgar. There. That word again. Lord Rune had said she was "superbly" vulgar. What did that mean? "Superbly," she whispered, trying to parrot his intonation. She did it so well that a vision of his face rose before her eyes. His lips had been tense with suppressed laughter; the creases in the hollows of his cheeks had deepened, making his face older, more angular, and at the same time more boyish. Vulgar. It did not seem like an insult, not the way he said it. And yet it would have been better, surely, if when she asked if he found her vulgar, he had answered, "Never." Lucy went back to the beginning of the scene, reworked it, and substituted *never* for *superbly*. It was more complimentary, but it lacked something. Any man, any ordinary mealy-mouthed man, could say *never*. Only a maddening, provoking, unpredictable man would say *superbly* in that caressing way. And perhaps Lord Rune had not meant that she was vulgar, not really vulgar, not in a vulgar sort of way. Lucy drew up her knees and curled herself round her pillow, meditating on Lord Rune's uniqueness—and on his anger.

His anger. Lucy remembered the look on her hero's face and shuddered with guilty pleasure. Lord Rune was jealous of Laurence Feather! She gripped the pillow so tightly that the old linen tore and a handful of feathers strayed into the darkness. Yes, Lord Rune was jealous. Why else would he be so icy, so implacable? She had been actually sorry for Laurence Feather. It could only be jealousy, she told herself, that made Ernest so stern with him, because it could not be moral outrage. Ernest was immoral. He had kept concubines—probably even foreign concubines, who were very likely worse than English ones. No, Lucy resolved, he must be jealous. He loved her and he was jealous because Laurence Feather had kissed her. Lucy remembered Laurence Feather's damp lips and dismissed the memory. That kiss had not counted. As Lord Rune pointed out, Laurence had kissed her but she hadn't kissed him. That, she decided, made Mr. Feather's kiss invalid. Lord Rune's kiss was really her first kiss, her first valid kiss, ineffable and delicious and officially first . . .

In the luxury of such musings, Lucy passed several

hours, but at last she put her lovesickness aside and turned to practical matters. As well as the more interesting points of the night's drama, there was something that must be dealt with: the duel. Lucy stuffed the torn pillow behind her head and concentrated on the problem. Few solutions presented themselves. One by one she eliminated them, until only one was left.

It was not, she realized, a very good solution. There were several drawbacks—one of them being that her scheme might not work. But it was the best idea she had, and it must be attempted. Very cautiously, Lucy sat up and drew aside the bed-clothes. It was well past midnight. She tiptoed to the door and soundlessly turned the knob.

It was nearly dawn when she crept back to bed. The warmth of the blankets was luxurious; it had been cold downstairs, and outside it had started to rain. Lucy snuggled down beside Cassy and closed her eyes. Her thumb and her two first fingers were liberally stained with ink.

19

Lord Rune slept heavily. The solicitude of Pudder had given birth to an elixir compounded of borage and laudanum. His lordship, shivering with fever and night air, tossed it off uncritically. He flung off his clothes and crawled beneath the blankets; he was as wretched and un-self-conscious as a sick animal.

Ernest disliked and feared pain. He was intolerant of all discomfort and sincerely afraid of illness; in the course of his flight from influenza, he was willing to poison himself a dozen times over. He did not question Pudder's ministrations; his attitude toward medicine was grateful and naive. He fell deeply asleep, and Pudder stood guard, forbidding the other servants to approach.

His lordship did not awaken until four o'clock the next day. By that time, the headache had grown in strength; it no longer ached, but pounded. His throat was raw, and he was both damp with fever and parched with thirst. His stomach was queasy, and there was a foul taste in his mouth. He swore. Or rather, he meant to swear—only a raspy whisper escaped his lips. The whiplash of invective that would have best expressed him was caught in his throat. He tried to cough to clear his throat, and tears came to his eyes. He could not speak.

He was really very ill. Ernest sat up in bed, shivering as his shoulders left the moist cocoon of blankets. He considered his symptoms and found a melancholy pleasure in their number and severity. Yes; he was ill. This was not a cold; nothing so trivial or undignified. This was influenza at the very least.

Then he remembered the duel.

Again he tried to swear and failed. He had said that his second would call on Laurence Feather, but he had not arranged it. He managed a spate of husky profanity, and pulled at the bell-cord. An affair of honor could not wait. He was going to have to leave his bed. He shoved aside the bedclothes and staggered to the window. What the hell time was it?

The curtains were drawn. He parted them with one shaking hand. Outside, the sky was slate-grey and rain poured down steadily.

Lord Rune's sense of ill-usage became acute. He was going to have to go out in that. He was ill, very ill, and he was going to have to suffer that appalling downpour. His clothes would be soaked through, and the carriage would be damp. It is only a short step, mentally, from influenza to pneumonia, and Lord Rune took that step without hesitation. He pictured himself trudging through the streets, his clothes heavy and slimy with water, while raindrops dripped down his collar

and off his nose. He saw himself wading through pud-
dles of dank, dirty water, while passing vehicles
splashed him and street urchins, seeing a beaten man,
pelted him with unimaginable filth. Once again, Lord
Rune sought to bring forth an oath; his voice sounded
so feeble that he pitied himself still more. No man with
such a voice should leave his bed.

The door opened, and Pudder stood before him.

"What time is it?" rasped Ernest.

Pudder did not answer at once. The sight of his
master out of bed seemed to rob him of the power of
speech. At last he cleared his throat, and suggested that
it was quarter past four.

"Why wasn't I awakened?" creaked Ernest. "I have
to make half a dozen calls. Now I'm late. Order the
carriage."

Pudder gaped at him. Unconsciously aping his master's whisper, he ventured to hope that his lordship was
not going out in the rain.

"Unless you plan to dislodge the clouds, yes, I am,"
snarled Lord Rune, sotto voce. "And stop that whispering, dammit. Go and order the carriage—and bring me
a pot of tea—and find me some warm clothes."

Pudder obeyed. Ernest stumbled back to bed and
wrapped himself in the bedclothes. His teeth were chat-
tering, and he wished he hadn't snarled at his valet. The
blameless Pudder would bear his master's anger sto-
ically, but the company of a long-suffering valet was
unlikely to prove exhilarating. Lord Rune sniffled, shivered, and rubbed his clammy toes with his feverish
hands.

It had not yet occurred to him that all of his woes
might properly be blamed on Lucy. In this he was heroic; many men would have realized this first thing.

That there are two sexes is a circumstance that provides scapegoats for both. Lord Rune was extraordinary. If he thought of Lucy at all—and few men are amorous in the throes of influenza—it was without rancor. She had been unwise to brave the Vauxhall shrubbery, and she had made a fool of herself flirting with the callow Mr. Feather. But Ernest, who had committed a great many peccadilloes of his own, was not the man to condemn Lucy's; he found folly sympathetic nine times out of ten.

That the tenth time would come before nightfall he did not suspect. He sat cross-legged and rubbed his feet and dreaded the moment when he would have to leave the bed and go out in the rain. The door opened, and Pudder entered with a tray. The smell of ham and buttered eggs filled the room. Lord Rune eyed his valet with hostility.

"Is that what took you so long?" A cough interrupted him, and he choked until the tears streamed down his cheeks. "I can't eat that, I'm *ill,* dammit."

Pudder did not answer. There was an awful patience in his silence. Lord Rune, who had just reproached himself for snarling, found himself wanting to snarl again. A triangle of paper, stuck to the bottom of the tray, gave him the excuse he needed. "For God's sake, can't Cheezum wipe the bottom of the trays every now and then? I don't say wash—that would be asking too much—" He peeled the paper off the tray, wincing as if the crackling sound hurt his ears. Then, seeing that the paper was a letter addressed to him, he slit it open with one finger—contracting a paper cut in the process.

Throughout this jeremiad, Pudder had maintained that silence, replete with moral superiority, which best becomes the martyr. He did not break it now. He stood and held the tray while his master read the letter. A look

of stupefaction crossed Ernest's face, followed by outrage.

"That cow-hearted—" Ernest heaved the blankets
aside, and rose unsteadily. "Don't just stand there looking like St. Sebastian. Go and find me something to
wear. And take that charnel-house of a tray out of my
sight—and tell Cheezum to wash it, or he's sacked. Do
you hear me?"

His voice was a whisper, but Pudder heard. He
took the tray and tiptoed out the door. His tiptoeing
served to irritate Ernest still further.

And Laurence Feather? The challenged party in a duel is
a dismal fellow, depressed by the imminence of his own
death, weighed down by the responsiblity involved in
taking the life of another. A haggard face, a trembling
hand, eyes that have seen little of sleep and blinked
away a tear—these are the proper attributes for the gen-
tleman-turned-swordsman.

Laurence Feather had fought three duels in his life
and his disposition was sanguine. He was an excellent
shot, and he enjoyed the theatricality of the thing. On
this occasion, however, his spirits were oppressed. For
one thing, he was ashamed of himself: he shouldn't have
taken liberties with Miss Saint-Clair. Moreover, now
that he thought of it, he hadn't especially wanted to take
liberties with Miss Saint-Clair. Inconveniently, he recalled that his other duels had been fought with amiable
young hot-heads like himself, eager to take offense and
loathe to kill. The coldness of Lord Rune's eyes haunted
him, and he began, most uncharacteristically, to worry.
In her gypsy mask, Lucy had predicted that he would
fight a fourth duel; had she also warned him against his

death? He couldn't remember. He was a superstitious youth, and the thought preyed on his mind. He even thought of offering Lord Rune an apology, but he shrugged off the idea. One did not withdraw from an affair of honor. Like Lucy herself, Laurence lay awake a long time, wondering how good a shot his opponent was and wondering if he ought to make his will.

And yet, by five o'clock the next afternoon, he wore a look of unclouded contentment. He sat in a well-upholstered chair, with his feet propped up on a tufted footstool. He had a crumpet in his hand and a smile on his face. A bowl of rum-punch filled the room with fragrance and a fire danced on the hearth.

He was not alone. Closeted with him were the young Viscount Sexton and a sweetly bovine maidservant with the stern name of Diligence. Diligence sat cross-legged before the fire, warming the small of her back, and the viscount—who had been given the title of Grave-digger by his quick-witted friends—was squeezing lemons into the punch.

"You're a deuced lucky fellow, Feather," the viscount was saying, as he scalded his fingers in the steam of the punch. "Rune's fought duels before—I b'lieve he killed a man, years ago, and left the country. Of course, that's only a rumor, but it might be true. No smoke without fire. He's traveled a sight, and that seems to fit with it. Wonder what made him cry off?"

Laurence Feather examined the sleeve of his red silk dressing-gown, and licked a dab of butter off the cuff.

"'E was afraid 'e'd be shot, that's what," answered Diligence, in her mellow contralto. "There's a lot o' gentlemen as don't like to be shot."

She smiled up at Laurence with ox-eyed admiration. Laurence nodded benevolently and passed her another crumpet. "Well," he conceded, "there might be something in that." He rubbed his buttery palms together. "I suppose I'm beginning to get a reputation as a good shot. After all, I did shoot Namby and Seddingham in the shoulder—which was just where I meant to shoot 'em. And Morley had the fever directly after our duel, so a lot of people thought I shot him, too."

"But you didn't," replied Grave-digger, with a reminiscent grin. "You both missed. Damme, Feather, I've never seen you drunker than you were that night. It's a wonder you didn't shoot yourself."

Mr. Feather grinned back lopsidedly and inquired as to the state of the punch.

"Just ready," declared the Viscount, with justifiable pride, "and first-rate. Only, Dill, you're not to drink it too quickly." He filled the glasses, scrutinized them to make certain he had dealt fairly all around, and passed them. Dilly took a sip, burned her tongue, and recalled Mr. Feather's love of toasts. She lowered her glass to her lap and pretended she hadn't tasted it yet.

"To good punch, and a warm fireside," Laurence proclaimed, "and to Lord Rune, who has given us leisure to enjoy them."

"Hear, hear," echoed Sexton, and Diligence murmured assent.

"Lord, that's good punch." Laurence Feather leaned back in his chair and flexed his stockinged toes. "I like rainy days, don't you, Dilly? Mind you, Grave-digger"—his voice became portentous—"I don't want the news about Rune's note to go any farther than this room. He wouldn't thank me for the rumor that he's cow-hearted." He passed the crumpet plate to Diligence, who looked at it sadly; there was only one crumpet left and it was cold.

"That goes for you too, Dilly," Laurence said, struck by the unusual thoughtfulness of his housemaid's face. "I don't want any gossiping below stairs. These things have a way of getting out. Have you said anything to anyone?"

Dilly paused with a full mouth and guilt-stricken eyes.

"I told Cook," she said, swallowing, "but she's deaf."

She meant that she had been obliged to shout the story at the top of her lungs and that the rest of the staff might have overheard.

"Oh, well, that's all right, then," Laurence answered comfortably. "A gentleman's honor is a queerer thing that you could guess, Dilly. And a duel . . . well, there's nothing that shows a gentleman's honor so well as a duel. I wouldn't want anyone hearing that I cried off. It's different for Rune. Not but what—well, some people might say that all that fustian in the note, about wishing to spare my youth, is just an excuse not to meet me."

"No 'might' about it," retorted Grave-digger, with a lusty swig of punch. "It's dashed well what they would say. I think it's damned good of you to hush it up."

Laurence Feather was modestly silent as a footman entered with a second tray of crumpets. He accepted the plate as if it were an accolade, chose a crumpet for himself, and passed the plate to Diligence.

"Oh, well," he said large-mindedly, "who am I to judge? Rune's over thirty, any way you add him up, and he's not the man he was. He looked dashed poorly last

night. Prosed on about seasickness and never ate a bite.
And then," he added, after an awkward flash of memory, "there's Lucy. Always liked her. No use dragging
her name through the muck."

"No," agreed Grave-digger. "No use at all."

Laurence winked at him and took a sip of punch.
"After all," he said, "friend of mine—makes good
punch—might be marrying into that Theale-Howard
clan. Wouldn't want any scandal in the family."

The viscount blushed. He was seventeen years old.
" 'M not going to marry her," he protested, around a
mouthful of crumpet. "Too young for parson's mouse-
trap! Besides, I've only talked to the chit once or twice."

"Seems deuced taken with you, Gravy."

Grave-digger shrugged, embarrassed but not ill-
pleased. "She does, don't she?"

The doorbell rang imperiously.

Dilly shoved the last bit of crumpet into her mouth
and jumped to her feet. She slid one foot into her slipper
and shook out her skirts with buttery hands.

"Ignore it," Laurence Feather covered her other
slipper with his foot and detained her by the simple and
agreeable method of cupping his hand over her shapely
bottom. "I've told Puffwort I'm not at home. Sit down
and finish your punch."

Diligence hesitated. By nature she was obedient,
but her instincts and her hearing were acute. Even as
Mr. Feather spoke, she heard the bell ring again and the
front door open. There was something contentious
about the sound of the bell, and the voices in the hall
were hostile. She dragged her left slipper out from under
Mr. Feather's foot and put it on.

The door opened and Lord Rune stood before
them.

Laurence Feather found himself at a disadvantage. He might despise Lord Rune as a coward, but he had no desire to be seen bootless and butter-stained by so nice an arbiter of taste. He noticed that Puffwort, who had followed his lordship, was looking helpless and that Grave-digger was chewing with more speed than elegance. Only Diligence retained her sang-froid; as the door opened, she picked up the tray and assumed the impassivity of the perfect servant.

"Er—Dill—that will be all," Laurence said to her, and Diligence glided out of the room with the stateliness of a duchess. "Puffwort, you can go, too. There's not much point in announcing Lord Rune, I know who he is."

Puffwort nodded and closed the door behind him. Laurence cast a wistful glance at his boots, which were lying under the sofa; he would not feel so ill at ease if he were wearing them. He took a firm hold of his punch-glass and spoke cordially. "Glad to see you, Rune. What's the matter at hand?"

Lord Rune did not answer. He was taking in the comfortable disorder of Mr. Feather's bachelor home, the rosy glow of the fire, the bowl of punch and plate of crumpets. It struck Laurence Feather that the arbiter of taste was not as fastidiously groomed as usual; he wore a heavy winter coat, and a wool comforter crushed the folds of his cravat. Also, he looked old; there were yellow shadows around his eyes, and his pallor looked greenish instead of aristocratic. For all that, Laurence Feather felt uncomfortable; he was reminded, somehow, of the last act of *Don Giovanni*, when the statue of the soprano's father comes to punish her would-be seducer. He sensed Lord Rune's contempt, and he flinched, even as he reminded himself that Lord Rune, and not he, had cried off.

"The matter," hissed Lord Rune, "is this."

His voice was at variance with the sternness of his demeanor. It creaked; it rasped; it wheezed. Laurence Feather was not a young man remarkable for self-control, and tense situations often struck him funny. He saw that Lord Rune held out a document of some sort, and he fixed his eyes upon it, half to oblige his guest and half to sober himself. He could not keep from grinning a little. It was a very faint grin, more an itch at the corners of his mouth than anything else, but it did not go unnoticed.

In a belated effort to hide his face, he reached out and drew up another chair, patting the seat invitingly.

"Happy to discuss anything you like," he offered, "entirely at your service. Thing is, you ought to have a seat. You're not feeling the thing, are you?"

"I'll stand."

The refusal would have been impressive, couched in Ernest's usual baritone. As it was, the whispery quality of his voice made for an effect at once grotesque and melodramatic. The Viscount Sexton rose discreetly and began to inch towards the door. "Ought to go," he explained. "Private matter. At least, I suppose it is." There was a distinct tremor in his voice. "Your most respectful, sir."

"No, don't." Mr. Feather, too, was having trouble controlling himself. "That is, I don't see what's so deuced hush-hush. Gravy—Andrew, I mean—s'my second. Friend of mine."

Lord Rune looked from one young man to the other and realized that they thought he was funny.

It was at that moment—the moment when he realized that these callow young puppies were laughing at him—that he began to blame Lucy for his sufferings. He had not thought of it before. If he had thought of it, he would have fought against it; he was a chivalrous man. But chivalry is fragile, and ridicule is harsh. At fifteen minutes past five, Lord Rune was querulous but patient, and Lucy was blameless. At sixteen minutes past five, the Viscount Sexton snickered, and Lucy became the authoress of Lord Rune's miseries.

He felt a surge of anger, and a shiver, born of passion as well as fever, went through him. Laurence Feather saw the shiver and managed to stifle a guffaw. "See here!" he said kindly, "you're as sick as a horse!" He picked up Dilly's glass, which was two-thirds full, and held it out invitingly. "Better have a drink," he offered and then jerked back. Lord Rune's fingers closed around the glass for only a second; then the hot liquid was hurled at Laurence's knees, and the glass shattered on the floor. Laurence twitched; the punch was still hot, and the noise startled him.

"*Now* will you meet me?" hissed Ernest.

"Meet you?" For a moment, Laurence was speechless; when he spoke, it was with a nice blend of incredulity and derision. "Do you hear that, Gravy? He's changed his mind again, and now he wants to meet me!"

"I have not changed my mind," Lord Rune whispered, so hoarsely that the words were half lost. "I have been of one mind since Vauxhall—and you may count yourself lucky that I mean to discharge the matter honorably. It would have given me great pleasure to toss that punch into your eyes and to thrash you like the school-boy you are—but I am determined to allow you the advantage of your questionable aim and your still more questionable honor."

Laurence stiffened. He turned to his friend, avoiding Lord Rune's eyes. "Here's a heroic fellow!" he jeered. "First he writes me a timid little letter of apology, and then he scalds me with my own punch!" He turned to Ernest, and mimicked the other man's raspy falsetto. "I will meet you whenever you like and wherever you like and with whatever weapons you like. Will that satisfy you?"

"What—?" The whisper was so faint that Lord Rune had to clear his throat and repeat it. "What letter?"

"You perfectly well know what letter," Laurence retorted, "and Gravy's read it, too—he was going to be my second, so it was his business as much as mine. So it won't do you any good to say you never wrote it." He bent over, and peeled the wet part of his trousers away from his knee, wondering if he had been scalded. It was an undignified thing to do, but he no longer cared for Lord Rune's opinion.

Lord Rune looked so confused and so wretched that the viscount sought to enlighten him. "The letter you wrote to cancel the duel," he said obligingly. "The one you sent this morning."

Lord Rune stared from one young face to another. Then he looked down at the paper in his hand and held it out to Laurence Feather.

"Read that," he commanded, "you'll see how I misjudged you."

Laurence took the letter between his buttery fingers and smoothed it out. At the sight of the handwriting, his color rose. At last he looked up from the paper.

"I never wrote this!" He looked at Lord Rune appealingly; he was suddenly a younger man facing the censure of an older one. "I swear it! I never saw this letter before! Who—"

"Lucy," answered Lord Rune, grimly.

"Lucy!" For a moment, Laurence Feather was too stunned to speak. "You think she sent this letter to you?"

"I think," said Lord Rune, "she sent letters to both of us."

Laurence nodded, his face taut with astonishment. "It's the same writing—the letter I had—I can show you—" He shuffled over to the mantel, avoiding the broken glass, and began to thumb through a stack of letters, invitations, and bills. "That interfering—"

"Yes." Lord Rune agreed. He was very pale, and he swayed alarmingly. Laurence, oblivious to his guest's infirmities, found the letter in the pocket of his dressing-gown and held it out.

"There. That's the letter I had this morning."

Lord Rune accepted it, even going so far as to sit down in the proffered chair. He read the letter, turned it over, and read it again. His posture, which had sagged, became rigid. At the end of the second reading, he folded the letter, shoved it in his pocket, and rose. He no longer seemed aware of Laurence Feather or Viscount Sexton. He strode toward the door.

"Wait!" Laurence took a step after him. "Where are you going?"

"To wring Lucy's neck."

So blood-thirsty an intention must find favor with Mr. Feather. "Damned good notion! I'll come with you!"

"I will, too!" The viscount, swayed by the martial

spirit in the room, began to divest himself of Laurence's second-best dressing-gown. He became aware that the other two men were regarding him curiously and he stopped short. "No, I won't! Come to think of it, not my place!"

Laurence Feather nodded approvingly and began to pull on his boots. "The gall of her!" he said, "Dammit, Rune, I can't think of anything bad enough to call her!"

Lord Rune closed his eyes. "Neither can I," he said, but without energy.

"I'll think of something." Laurence untied the belt of his dressing gown, shrugged himself out of it, and flung it on the floor. "By God, the sight of her will inspire me—" He added, somewhat anticlimactically, "May I come in your carriage?"

Lord Rune, with his eyes still shut, nodded again. He did not relish Mr. Feather's company, but he had sympathy for his rival; the letter that Lucy had written for Mr. Feather was worse than his. He leaned against the wall and swallowed while Laurence knotted a handkerchief round his neck and shrugged himself into a coat. At last the two men set off in the rain.

Viscount Sexton sat down to the rest of the punch. He felt rather lonely; it seemed paltry to have followed the ill-fated duel thus far and no farther. The thrumming of the rain was hypnotic. The viscount switched to the most comfortable armchair and stared into the fire. It occurred to him that the broken glass ought to be swept up. With rising spirits, he pulled the bell-cord.

His hopes were realized. That stern divinity, Diligence, came to sweep up the glass, and fold Mr. Feather's clothes. She was easily persuaded to help finish off the punch; she snuggled down beside the viscount's footstool and rested her glass on his knee. The bottom of the glass was warm and the warmth of her body was very sweet. Alas for Grace! She was destined to be forgotten in the viscount's pursuit of Diligence.

20

Bibble was downstairs, engaged in a pre-prandial dispute, when Laurence Feather rang the bell of Mrs. Theale's house. Lord Rune and Mr. Feather were obliged to wait on the doorstep, during which time Ernest steamed and shivered and Mr. Feather's anger seethed like the overflowing gutters.

The upstairs windows of the town house were lit, and the two men could look up and see Cassy silhouetted against the curtain. Her profile looked pure and serene and dry: she was reading aloud from *The Black Dwarf* while Grace embroidered and Lucy mended her torn pillow-case. Another man—Mr. Bloomsbury, for example—might have been softened by that demure profile, but Laurence Feather, already provoked, was inflamed. He was growing very wet; also, he regretted his lost punch and abandoned crumpets. Unlike his companion, he lost no time in blaming Lucy; he considered her guilty even of causing the rain.

The door opened. Bibble, red-faced from his battle with the cook, apologized for the delay. Mr. Feather interrupted him. They—he jerked his head to indicate Lord Rune—wanted to see Miss Saint-Clair, and they wanted to see her at once, and they wanted to see her alone.

Bibble quibbled. His mistress dined early this evening and Cook would not take kindly to two extra guests at table. Also, he had a conviction that the guests in question—both smelling of spirits—should not be inflicted on an unchaperoned young lady. He was accustomed to admitting Lord Rune to the household—even to ushering him into Lucy's solitary company—but that was when Lord Rune's manner was unexceptionable. This sodden gentleman, with his air of general wretchedness and specific ferocity, was not unexceptionable. Moreover, he was accompanied by one whom Bibble privately catalogued as a Loose Screw. Therefore, Bibble made tactful reference to the evening meal, adding cautiously that he would be happy to give Mrs. Theale the gentlemen's regards.

Laurence Feather interrupted again. Unhampered by Bibble's delicacy, he spoke impetuously. He said that he didn't care what hour it was; that he didn't want any dinner; that he wanted even less to see Mrs. Theale. He returned, *da capo*, to his first statement: he wanted to see Miss Saint-Clair, and he wanted to see her at once, and he wanted to see her alone.

Bibble listened. Upstairs, a door opened and closed and there was a sound of footsteps in the hall. He knew those footsteps and the rustle of bombazine that went with them. Mrs. Theale was coming downstairs. He awaited his deliverance with a grateful heart.

"Ernest, dear—" Tabitha halted on the steps, with one hand on the banister. "Is something the matter? What brought you here in such weather?"

Lord Rune did not reply. Laurence Feather closed his mouth and fixed his aggressive gaze on Tabitha. Tabitha inclined her head, eyebrows slightly raised. It was a gesture that granted hospitality and asked no direct questions, but it made Laurence feel that he had been certainly rash and possibly rude. He glanced at his hostess's brother, received no help from him, and carried on.

"We've come to see Miss Saint-Clair," he began, but without the heat that had inspired him before. "We—that is, I—know it's a dashed—a bad time—not the thing! But the circumstances"—he remembered Lucy's perfidy, and ground his teeth—"are unusual. Are very unusual, ma'am."

Mrs. Theale nodded again, and Bibble breathed a sigh of relief. His mistress understood that there was trouble, and she would deal with it.

"We will go into the drawing-room—we will be quite comfortable there," said Mrs. Theale. "Bibble, I should like you to go to Miss Saint-Clair, and tell her she is wanted downstairs. Oh, and Cook must set back dinner a little."

Bibble's "Very good, madam," was grave. His relief at having been spared the angry gentlemen was blighted by the prospect of a thwarted Cook.

Mrs. Theale, indifferent to the sufferings of her butler, led the gentlemen to the drawing room. One glance sufficed to inform her that her brother was too angry to speak. If explanations were to be forthcoming, they would have to come forth from Laurence Feather.

She turned to that fire-eating young man and addressed him crisply. Her voice was maternal—in the least tender sense of the word.

"I think you had better tell me what this is all about."

Laurence Feather stared at her dumbly. During the carriage ride, he had pictured himself reviling Lucy, reducing her to penitent tears, humbling her—at last—with his forgiveness. He had not thought of anything to say to Lucy's god-mamma. He realized with frustration that he could not expose Lucy's iniquities without speaking of his own. He blushed a little and replied, "It's a private matter," hoping to sound aloof, instead of sulky.

"My god-daughter does not entertain 'private matters,'" retorted Tabitha, icily. Like Mr. Feather, she was conscious of how she sounded, and two things struck her at once; she was expressing herself with unusual dignity and grace, and she was talking nonsense. "No young lady of quality has 'private matters.' I am entirely in Lucy's confidence, and I am sure that she will tell me what this is about, if you do not. And I must add"—she fixed her cloudy green eyes on Laurence Feather—"that your reticence does not predispose me in your favor."

Laurence Feather was conscious of a desire to squirm. It had been a long time since he had been scolded by a woman, and he found himself remembering the old nurse, now deceased, who was the nemesis of his childhood. Covertly he glanced at Lord Rune. Ernest had collapsed into one of Tabitha's Egyptian chairs and appeared more wretched than vindictive.

The door opened, and in walked Lucy.

Bibble's manner, when he summoned her, had been charged with innuendo; he had spoken the words "at once" so ominously that Grace fell to giggling and Lucy knew her hour was struck. She was nerved for battle and she looked it. When she entered the room her eyebrows bristled and she managed somehow to suggest the clash of sabers. Then she saw Lord Rune.

She stopped in mid-swagger. That her godmother might be shocked she had anticipated; that Laurence Feather might bluster she had foreseen. Lord Rune's anger was a wholly different thing. Never had she seen him look so forbidding; never before had she felt she was a stranger he did not care to know.

"Ernest?" She spoke as if they were the only people in the room. "Ernest, what is the matter?"

For a moment she stood hesitant, waiting. Then she stepped forward with outstretched hands. In the back of her mind was the certainty that he needed comfort, that by touching him she would solace him and learn what the trouble was. Lord Rune rose and turned his back, avoiding her touch with a brusqueness as explicit as a slap. Tears came to Lucy's eyes. She blinked them back.

"You're angry," she said slowly, "and you're cold and wet. Why, you're shivering!—" Enlightenment dawned. "You're not well! You're ill! Godmamma"— urgently she turned to Mrs. Theale—"we must have a fire lit. Lord Rune is ill."

"Lucy—" said Tabitha.

Her emphasis was sufficient to remind Lucy of the circumstances that had prompted the gentlemen to call. "Oh," Lucy said, irresolutely. Her eyes met Laurence Feather's. "I suppose you've come about the duel."

She spoke without heat, without shame. Laurence Feather, who had always enjoyed her theatrical qualities, found such coolness galling. At the same time, he was relieved; he had been given his cue at last. "I should think I have," he retorted, and doubled his efforts to sound fierce. "It was a piece of dam—of intolerable interference on your part, Miss Saint-Clair, and I'll be hanged if I—"

"What duel?" demanded Mrs. Theale.

Lucy sighed, exhaling patience and resignation with one breath. "Mr. Feather kissed me in the shrubbery at Vauxhall," she began, "and—"

"*Kissed* you?"

Laurence shifted uncomfortably. "I offered to marry her," he defended himself.

"Yes, but I wouldn't," Lucy went on, anticipating her aunt's next question. "And Lord Rune saw and wanted to fight a duel over it, only I thought it was nonsense—"

"Nonsense!" Tabitha echoed heatedly.

"Yes, and so it was." Lucy was becoming heated herself. "And I was determined to prevent it—the duel, I mean, so I wrote a letter to Mr. Feather—and to Lord Rune—"

"She wrote forgeries!" Laurence spat out the word vindictively. "Your god-child, ma'am, is no better than a common—"

"Oh, do be quiet!" snapped Lucy. "All I wanted was to save your wretched skin—and Lord Rune's, of course—and you make me wish I hadn't bothered." She turned to her godmother, and spoke pleadingly. "Don't you see?" she asked, clasping her hands and twisting her fingers. "I did wrong, of course, to let Mr. Feather kiss me, but I couldn't let them fight! That would have been beyond everything! You wouldn't have wanted"—she gulped—"Ernest—Lord Rune—to be killed."

There was an odd beat of silence. Then Laurence

was surprised to hear himself say plaintively, "*I* might have been killed."

"Of course." Lucy's voice was matter-of-fact; there was no doubt she would have considered this the lesser calamity. "And all over nothing. Did you really want to die for nothing, Mr. Feather?"

Laurence opened his mouth and found that he had nothing to say. To answer in the affirmative would be ludicrous; to answer in the negative would compromise his honor. He had no intention of conceding any points to Lucy, even though—he realized with disgust—much of his wrath was spent. He contented himself with saying, "It wasn't your affair," with all the height he could muster.

"You haven't answered my question." Lucy sensed that he was weakening and wanted to press her point. "Do you want to die for nothing, Mr. Feather?"

Laurence looked to Ernest for help. "Dash it all," he burst out, "haven't you anything to say? I thought you were going to wring her neck!"

"Oh, Lord Rune, were you?" cried Lucy.

Ernest did not answer. He kept his back turned, and his silence made Lucy's heart sink.

"I'm sorry," she offered, in a voice more hopeful than repentant. "I am truly very sorry, but I didn't know what else to do. I only wanted to keep you safe. Won't you forgive me?"

If she had spoken thus to Laurence Feather, he would have forgiven her on the spot; even Tabitha, hearing the quiver in her god-child's voice, might have relented. Unluckily, Lord Rune had reached the end of his forbearance. He turned away and spoke in a low voice. "No," he said.

Lucy burst into tears.

She was not, by nature, stoical; her passions were strong, and she usually preferred the relief of discharging them to the dignity of restraining them. The same physiology that gave her singing voice its ringing clarity affected her sobs. She wept stormily and without finesse.

It was rather an appalling noise; Tabitha deplored it, and Laurence Feather was aware of a growing conviction that weeping women were not in his line. Lord Rune, who had said no out of a general sense of malaise, found himself wishing he had answered differently. He wanted the noise to stop; also, there was a note of real anguish in Lucy's sobs that struck him as regrettable. He swallowed, opened his mouth, and managed the syllable "Lu—" before his throat caught. He began to cough violently, feeling his head pound with each movement.

"Oh, you *are* ill," wailed Lucy. "You ought not to have come. And I shouldn't have written those letters—but I didn't want you to be killed. Don't you see? It would have been my fault—your b-blood on my hands, and—" She gulped a little and, since Lord Rune had stopped coughing, offered into the silence, "But I shouldn't—I didn't mean—If you still want to fight the duel—after you're better—you may . . ."

Her voice trailed off. Her offer, which she thought generous beyond all reason, roused Lord Rune to an ecstasy of rage.

"Oh, may I?" His face, which had been crimson with coughing, was white. "How good of you to grant me permission! How kind of you to renounce your interest in my affairs!"

His voice was savage; his whole body shook with fever and rage. Tabitha rose, frightened, and the good-hearted Mr. Feather found himself pitying the woman he had come to castigate. There was no need. Lord Rune cold and silent paralyzed Lucy, but Lord Rune enraged did not. "Your affairs!" she shot back. "If someone kisses me in the shrubbery at Vauxhall, that is *my* affair—and if you hadn't meddled, you wouldn't be coughing and shivering and making a cake of yourself!"

Her retort went unheeded; Lord Rune had struck a vein of anger that gave him the force to continue. He sounded almost as if he were choking.

"Ever since I laid eyes on you," he rasped, "you have interfered in my affairs. You have interrogated me about details of my life that no lady should acknowledge, let alone discuss. You have pursued me in public, criticized my personal habits, and harassed my servants. You have made light of my infirmities—"

"Your infirmities!" flashed Lucy. She considered consigning Lord Rune's infirmities to the devil but did not quite dare. She contented herself with repeating "Your infirmities!" in a sarcastic undertone and biting her lip.

"And now"—Lord Rune went on without pausing for breath—"you seek to compromise my honor. Having none of your own, you seek to make a mockery—"

"I *do* have honor!" Lucy broke in hotly, "and it's better than your honor, because *I* have no need to kill anyone—"

"Of mine," finished Lord Rune. His voice died to a whisper. "And all"—he hissed—"in the name of—"

His eyes met Lucy's and she drew in her breath. They stood silent and frozen, both aware that what he was about to say would deepen the rift between them. Painfully Lucy waited, bracing herself to be hurt, but

Ernest never finished his sentence. Instead he choked, and a fit of coughing overtook him.

Tabitha put her hand to the bell-rope. Seldom had she encountered so dire a domestic crisis, and she had a cloudy notion that help ought to be summoned. Laurence Feather squirmed in his chair. He, too, felt the need of a *deus ex machina,* and he was very much afraid it would have to be himself. He cleared his throat.

"I say," he began, and no one stopped him. He glanced apologetically at the others, and realized that he had the floor. He would have to go on.

"I say," he repeated, "this whole business is beginning to . . . beginning to . . . Dash it all!" he said energetically, "when a man agrees to fight a duel, he agrees to fight a duel, that's what I say. Pistols," he elucidated, "or swords, it don't much matter, pistols or swords, and getting up early in the morning, which is devilish, but I'm willing to do it, because when a man fights a duel he does what has to be done, and that's what I was willing to do." He saw that his eloquence had captured his listeners' ears and went on with satisfaction. "But what I *didn't* expect," he continued warmly, "what I *wasn't* willing to do—because, if you ask me, it wasn't part of the bargain—what I *wasn't* willing to do, was have to read a lot of damned impertinent forging letters and listen to a lot of coughing and crying. Now, you may say"—he had glimpsed the enmity in two pairs of eyes and held up his hand to shield himself—"that it's my own fault that all this happened, because I shouldn't have kissed Miss Saint-Clair. And if you want to know what I think of that, then, what I say is: you're damned right. Well, there we are, I oughtn't have kissed her, but there's one thing: I didn't know there was any attachment between her and Lord Rune, and if I had I wouldn't have kissed—"

"Attachment?" Tabitha's voice was incredulous.

"Well, it's as plain as the nose on your face," Laurence told her staunchly. "When a man gets so angry that he challenges another man to a duel and drags himself out of a sick-bed to fight it and then acts the brute to her, and when a woman cries her eyes out because he's miffed, there ought to be an attachment. In fact"—he looked surprised—"if there isn't an attachment, you ought to be asking your brother his intentions. Half of London expects him to marry her by now. And what's more"—he turned challengingly to Ernest—"she expects it. And if you don't expect it, you're a fool. So there it is, the two of you, as good as engaged, and me not knowing anything about it. And if I had known, I wouldn't have agreed to a duel, because I'd have begged your pardon. Both your pardons. And that's what I'm doing now," he added, with a sudden switch from the challenging to the conciliatory. "Begging your pardon like a man. And if I were you, Lord Rune, I'd accept it—first of all because I'm sincere and second of all because you're not getting any younger and you shouldn't be fighting duels like some hotheaded young blood. It ain't the thing. Come to think of it, I'm going to stop fighting 'em. Hell, I've been angrier at Lucy than I've been at you for the last three hours. And if you won't accept my pardon"—he overrode an intake of breath that indicated that Lord Rune wanted to speak— "well, I don't care. Dammit, man, you're sick as a horse, and I'm not going to fight a man in that condition. And furthermore, furthermore and *finally*," he stressed the last word heartily, "I'm going to go home now, because I don't like it here very much."

If he expected applause, he was disappointed. A blank silence followed his words. Lord Rune had collapsed again and was staring dizzily at the carpet. Lucy was wiping her eyes on the backs of her hands. Her face was red with crying, and she looked so wretched and so unlovely, that Laurence spoke to her.

"Ah—Miss Saint-Clair," he said gently. "I'm sorry about Vauxhall and everything. You shouldn't cry so much, you shouldn't, really. He'll"—he nodded in Ernest's direction—"he'll come up to scr—I mean, he'll make you an offer. He's ill, that's all." He saw Lucy's eyes refill with tears and added, hastily, "Well, it's not my business. Never was." With intense relief, he saw the door open, and Bibble come in.

"Bibble," said Mrs. Theale wearily, "show Mr. Feather out."

Bibble conducted Mr. Feather to the door. He had to move quickly; Mr. Feather's desire to leave was urgent. The door shut, and Tabitha pursed her lips and tried to summon the energy to confront her god-child. Lucy was staring at Lord Rune, who had risen shakily and stood before her. All color, all emotion had drained from his face. He spoke without passion.

"Lucy," he whispered, "will you marry me?"

Lucy stared at him. Motionless, astonished, she stood and gazed at him. Tabitha uttered a wordless protest, but too late: Lucy sprang forward, as if a current of electricity had passed through her, and boxed Lord Rune's ears.

"How *dare* you?" she spat and burst into fresh tears.

Lord Rune swayed and caught at one of Tabitha's chairs; Lucy, too angry to notice his weakness, railed at him. Between plangent sobs, and gasps for breath, Tabitha caught the words "Never . . . condescend . . . inhuman . . ."

Tabitha rose from her seat. In the past hour, she had received several very unpleasant shocks and her head ached. Never had she felt less affectionate toward her brother or her god-child. She raised her voice and spoke sharply. She was surprised to hear how coarse she sounded.

"Enough!" The word cut through Lucy's hysterical babble. "There has been quite enough of this! Lucy, you are to go upstairs and go to bed. You are hysterical. Your conduct has displeased me more than I can say. I would not have believed you capable of such vulgarity, such deceit, and such ingratitude."

Lucy gaped at her godmamma, stricken. Her nose was running, her eyes were red, and her mouth was open in a wail of anguish. Tabitha thought, as Laurence Feather had, that she looked very ugly.

"As for you, Ernest," Tabitha continued, "I hold you grossly to blame. From the beginning you have trifled with Lucy's affections, and now you make a mockery of her. I don't altogether blame her for wanting to box your ears—although"—turning back to Lucy—"if she had the slightest delicacy of mind, the most rudimentary sense of principle, she would restrain herself." Seeing that this last reproof made little impression on her god-child—who by this point was quite incapable of self-restraint—she turned back to her brother. "I am disgusted with you," she said, and though her voice trembled, her face was hard. "You are no longer welcome in my house. I should like you to go—now."

Lord Rune did not seem to hear. With trembling hands, he touched his boxed ears and gazed beyond Tabitha to Lucy.

"Go upstairs," Tabitha commanded her god-child, "and get into bed. You are hysterical. We will discuss your conduct in the morning. I am far too angry to talk to you now."

Lucy put her hands over her face. Blindly, she turned and ran out of the room. After a moment, Tabitha followed, and Lord Rune was left to the dubious comforts of the Egyptian drawing-room.

21

That Lord Rune was very unwell he knew. That he had contracted scarlet fever he did not suspect. Nor did the sagacious Pudder realize the severity of his complaint; Pudder was still brooding over his master's incivility. Lord Rune had disdained his valet's advice; if his condition was worse he had only himself to blame. When Ernest staggered into the house, drenched and shivering, Pudder tucked him in bed without a word of sympathy.

Ernest didn't care. He thought only of bed, and warmth, and of being left alone; he was unaware of his valet's resentment and deaf to his silence. Pudder stood on his dignity for a day and a night. Then the urge to dose his patient overcame his pride and he drew up a chair beside the bed, all ready for a pleasurable talk about symptoms and treatments. Lord Rune wouldn't talk. For the third time in twenty-four hours, he demanded more blankets, only to throw them off again.

Slowly, Pudder's frustration turned to fear. His alarm reached its peak the day Lord Rune complained of a swollen tongue and a scarlet rash. Pudder gazed at the tongue, studied the rash, and sent Flintworm for his Lordship's doctor.

Flitworm was eager to obey. With one hand on the doorknob, he treated Pudder to a brief, agitated, and heartfelt speech. He spoke of the anguish he suffered on his master's behalf, his devotion to his duty, and his willingness to sacrifice himself to succor Lord Rune. Unfortunately, he was as useless as he was well-meaning. He returned at dusk with the intelligence that Lord Rune's doctor had left London and was practicing in Bath. He had not thought to find another doctor.

The virtuous Pudder refrained from shrieking at his fellow employee and went back upstairs to study the ominous rash. It had been an anxious day; Lord Rune had further unnerved his valet by proposing marriage to him. Pudder had declined and hinted that perhaps Mrs. Theale ought to be summoned to her brother's sickbed. Lord Rune's response was coherent, if profane. He had no desire to see Tabitha ever again. If Pudder wanted to do something for him, Pudder could remove some of those infernal blankets—couldn't the damned fool see how he was sweating?

Pudder obeyed, trembling. The possibility that Lord Rune might die was before him, and he was terrified he would be blamed. He went to his lordship's desk and after much cogitation composed the following letter:

Dear Mrs. Theale,

Your brother is ill, but doesn't want to see you.

Yrs. obediently, Erasmus Pudder.

The next day, Pudder posted the letter and found a doctor. The doctor examined the patient, admired the rash as an unusually fine specimen, and diagnosed scarlet fever. He relieved Pudder's mind considerably by saying that in his opinion the crisis was over and the patient was out of danger. He further elated Pudder by recommending a state of quarantine.

Quarantine! Pudder had yearned after it before; now, with his worst fears laid to rest, he settled down to enjoy himself. He burned aromatic pastilles and brewed a revolting draught that would prevent his fellow-servants from taking the fever. He sealed windows, and hung signs, and spoke in a hollow whisper. Lord Rune curled himself up in a ball and dreamed of Lucy.

He was beginning to recover. When Pudder suggested he eat and drink a little, the prospect no longer seemed untenable and he could bear to let the bedclothes slip off his shoulders for a moment or two. The taste of hot, sweet tea was comforting. He hoped that Lucy would hear of his illness and visit him, in spite of what had passed between them. When she did not, he mourned for her. He was still weak and a little hysterical; it took all his strength not to cry before the servants. He knew nothing about the quarantine. He knew only that he felt very sorry for himself and that Lucy Saint-Clair had boxed his ears.

Mrs. Theale read Pudder's letter and tossed it aside. Her brother did not wish to see her. Very well; she did not care to see him. She was still angry, and she was preoccupied with the crisis in her household. For crisis there was; the news of the stolen kiss and the aborted duel had leaked out. Mrs. Theale had troubles of her own.

It was not just that Lucy was despondent, though Lucy's misery pervaded the household. It was not even that Cassy and Grace had decided that Lucy was an ill-used heroine and that their mamma was wicked and cruel. These things were trying but manageable; Mrs. Theale had dealt with lovesick girls and sullen daughters before. What she had not dealt with, and never expected to deal with, was scandal. Mrs. Theale had spent her life avoiding scandal. Now it had come upon her, and she had no idea how to contend with it.

It was not, perhaps, a very grave scandal. If anything more interesting had been going on, Lucy's follies would not have constituted a scandal at all. Unluckily for Lucy, it had been a dull Season: the most depraved members of society had been behaving themselves with uncharacteristic propriety. The tale of the frustrated duel was novel and amusing. The discretion of Diligence had done its worst, and Lucy's reputation hung in tatters.

A letter arrived from Yorkshire. Mr. and Mrs. Saint-Clair had had a letter from Tabitha's sister Edith: Miss Howard wrote that their daughter was sporting gaudy clothes, telling fortunes, and provoking duels. Was this true? If it was—Fanny Saint-Clair waxed eloquent—how could Mrs. Theale have so neglected her duty toward their child? Lucy must return to Yorkshire at once. Fanny's tongue had always been sharp. Her pen was even sharper. Never had Tabitha received so unpleasant a letter.

She swore as she read. She used only the mildest of oaths, but they sounded thunderous; like most thoroughly nice women, she was capable of dreadful effect. She cursed her brother and her sister, and her old school friend, and Laurence Feather. In her heart, she feared Mrs. Saint-Clair's anger was justified. She had failed to find Lucy a suitable husband and allowed her too free a rein. Now the threat of scandal hung round the family name, and Lucy would never be married. It had been Lucy's folly, of course, but it was Ernest's fault, and after Ernest's, her own; she had asked Ernest to help Lucy, and he had ruined her. And yet—Tabitha clenched her teeth and reread the letter—she would not send Lucy home in disgrace. The girl was too wretched, and her parents loved her so little. Tabitha sat down and sought to write a letter that would pacify the Saint-Clairs and allow Lucy to finish her last Season.

Her effort was wasted. Edith Howard had written again, embroidering her tale with the most farfetched of the latest on dits. Before Tabitha's letter reached Yorkshire, Mr. Saint-Clair arrived on her doorstep, calling for his disgraced child. There was no use saying that Edith had exaggerated or that Lucy was not to blame. Mr. Saint-Clair had come all the way to London for his daughter, and he had no intention of leaving without her.

Cassy wept. Grace muttered under her breath. Both of the Misses Theales were so badly behaved, so really close to being rude that Tabitha was ashamed of them.

Lucy didn't seem to notice. Since Lord Rune's proposal, she had been guilt-stricken, lachrymose, and angry. Now she seemed stunned. She made no effort to defend herself against her father's accusations, and she accepted the fact that she must go home. Impassively, she began to pack. She would not look at Tabitha and shrank from the caresses of her friends. Tabitha thought she was trying not to cry. Almost before the family realized that Lucy was going to leave, she was ready to go.

She embraced her godmother, but kept her face averted. She mumbled something that might have been an apology. At the last moment, she stuffed her pearl necklace into Grace's hand and surprised Cassy with a book bound in crimson leather. Then she twisted free from her friends' embrace and stumbled toward the coach. The last glimpse Tabitha had of her was a sorry one: Lucy huddled by the window, as far away from her father as possible. She looked cold, in spite of the late spring weather, and her mouth wobbled. Once again she was crying, but furtively, painfully. For once she made very little noise.

It was all very disagreeable. The rumors of Miss Saint-Clair's wild behavior—which would perhaps have died down in another week—were fanned by her departure. Twice Tabitha saw herself pointed out, and a certain Mrs. Barrimoule, a toadeater of the lowest order, snubbed her in the Pantheon Bazaar. It was galling, and Tabitha was so unhappy that her daughters would have relented, if they had understood.

They didn't understand. They missed Lucy, and they blamed Tabitha for letting her leave, and they blamed Lord Rune for not loving her. They didn't care if he was ill. They moped and quarreled and stayed at home. And Lord Rune knew nothing of Lucy's exile.

His recovery was slow. His isolation was profound; he saw no one except the servants. During those weeks in quarantine, he had time and opportunity and even reason to forget Lucy Saint-Clair. She was many miles away and had scorned his proposal of marriage. There was no reason, save one, why he should ever see her again. And indeed, if that reason had not existed—if Lord Rune had not come to love Lucy very much—Lucy's exile would have been permanent, and her romance would have ended, as most romances end, in tears.

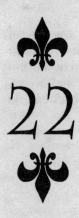

22

But Lord Rune did love Lucy, and he did recover, and, recovering, he ejected Pudder from quarantine and sent him to the nearest public-house. As his master intended, Pudder brought back the latest on dits; among them were speculations about Miss Saint-Clair's flight, Lord Rune's seclusion, and the frustrated duel. Lord Rune, still supine, set about thinking what might be done to salvage Lucy's reputation. Unlike Tabitha, he had more than a nodding acquaintance with scandal. He considered the matter ticklish, but not beyond his talents.

He determined first to send for Mr. Bloomsbury. The noble Arthur, hearing that his fiancée's uncle was ill, said all that was proper, and was eventually persuaded to say more than was proper. Lord Rune gleaned that Lucy was gone for good and that Mrs. Theale and her daughters were genuinely angry with

him. As to the nature of Miss Saint-Clair's sentiments,
Arthur could say nothing. Her departure had been pre-
cipitate, but—Arthur turned and addressed the bedpost
at this point—there was nothing in that. People were
often hasty; they lived in a rash and intemperate age.
He, for one, did not think that Miss Saint-Clair's departure compromised her in any way.

Lord Rune nodded astutely and ordered tea. He
told Mr. Bloomsbury to refresh himself while he penned
a note to the Misses Theales. He proceeded to compose
a short but poignant epistle. It alluded to an escape from
death so narrow as to be almost miraculous and
sketched his solitude in pathetic prose. It ended with a
plea for his nieces' company, and was signed: "Your
loving Uncle." In short, it was a masterpiece of manipu-
lation and the Theale girls called the next day.

Lord Rune brought forth the Sèvres tea-set, served
a magnificent tea, and set about his inquisition. It took
longer than he had expected, for Cassy was unexpectedly discreet. Her uncle's pallor had shocked her; she
shed tears upon seeing him, but she protested—albeit
feebly—that she had no knowledge of Lucy's heart.
Lord Rune asked her for another cup of tea and began
to interrogate Grace.

Grace was sixteen years old. Discretion, that autumn flower, had eluded her so far and would continue
to elude her for the rest of her life. She began by asserting that Lucy was well pleased to return to Yorkshire.
She hinted that a score of rustic suitors clamored for
Lucy's return, and she ended with the vindictive hope
that Lord Rune would see what he had lost when Lucy
was the bride of Another. Cross-examination about
"Another" reduced her to stammering equivocation. At
last she cast aside all pretense, divulging that (in her

opinion) Lucy's heart was broken and that the best thing her uncle could do would be to mend it.

Lord Rune had every intention of mending it, but it was another week before he left the city. He emerged from quarantine looking very shaky and set off for the most fashionable haunts of London. From White's to Almack's he wandered, dispersing reports of his infirmity and defending Lucy's honor. He led his listeners to believe that he considered the aborted duel a splendid joke. He professed the greatest admiration for Miss Saint-Clair's ingenuity. He managed, without quite saying so, to convey that Lucy's parents were humorless, provincial, and Gothic, and he implied that anyone who agreed with them was similarly humorless, provincial, and Gothic. Slowly, the wind of public opinion began to shift. Lord Rune, that arbiter of taste, continued to champion Miss Saint-Clair's originality; Lord Rune, whose honor had been impugned, was not angry but amused.

As Lord Rune had foreseen, it was a ticklish business. It was also grueling; his lordship, still convalescent, was on his feet all day, charming and conniving. At night, he fell into bed and slept deeply; in the morning he awakened full of new schemes and fresh resources. It had been years since Ernest had wanted anything badly enough to fight for it.

Between rounds of gossip, he daydreamed. He indulged in visions of a Venetian honey-moon and spent a whole afternoon choosing a harp for Lucy's wedding gift. He ordered a lavish dress-length of silver moiré from Sybil Rant, and he ignored her look of grim triumph as she wrote out the bill. Her manner reeked of I-told-you-so, but for once he did not care. He stuffed the bill into his pocket without reading it and went home to pack for his journey.

He arrived in Yorkshire late afternoon. It was Saturday, and a rainy morning had given way to an afternoon that was sunny and still. It had been years since Lord Rune had walked through the English countryside, and he found himself unexpectedly moved by the vigorous reaches of wild land, the green hills, the outstretched horizon. The air was sweet-scented and the light was the color of honey. Lord Rune, following his landlord's advice, took the road to the parsonage.

The road was winding but not long. The parsonage was a square, worn building, built of brick the color of dried blood. To one side of it was the churchyard, shaded by ragged yew-trees; to the other there was a labyrinth of walled gardens, boldly green and over-grown. The brick dooryard was unswept, and the door was shut. A dense silence hung over the place. Lord Rune felt a prickle of fear as he raised his hand to the door.

He knocked.

He knocked again, aggressively. He listened, not breathing, and watched the windows, hoping to see the curtains part, a shadow pass. No one answered. And still Lord Rune knocked. The parsonage could not be deserted, so close to a Sunday. In a moment, the door would open, and Lucy would stand before him. She would scowl her surprise at seeing him, and he would say—something, he knew not what—and her eyebrows would lift, and her paradoxical smile transform her face . . .

He had been knocking and waiting for fully five

minutes now. He could not bear his disappointment. He grasped the knocker and hammered his frustration against the door. The sound of it shocked him. He had been so sure she would be at home. He had believed, even, that she would welcome him. At their last meeting, she had boxed his ears, and yet he had allowed himself to imagine himself forgiven—to imagine himself beloved. He had bought the cloth for a wedding-gown without first making sure of a bride.

Then he heard a laugh.

He flinched, as keyed up as a shying horse. He had heard that laugh, or something like it, before. It was loud, ringing, resonant. It came from the churchyard. Lord Rune went to follow the sound.

Between the yew-trees, there was a flash of color: lavendar and rose. Lord Rune looked for the churchyard gate, missed it, and snagged his trousers climbing over the churchyard wall. The descent was painful; the old brick tore his coat. Ernest did not care. With eagerness, with trepidation, he hastened over the grass. And then his heart sank a second time, for neither of the young ladies in the churchyard was Lucy.

They were dark young ladies and curly-haired. Their curls, which were fashionably short, were like Lucy's, and their gowns were like Lucy's; their gowns, in fact, were Lucy's. Lord Rune remembered the rose-print—in that very dress Lucy had cautioned him against bad oysters—and the lavender-stripe had been worn in Hyde Park. These ladies were Lucy's sisters, the Mina-and-Letty twins Tabitha had mentioned. They were younger than Lucy and prettier. Their eyebrows were smooth and devoid of menace; although not slender, the twins were closer to being slender than Lucy

was. Lord Rune considered their hair insufficient, their flesh inadequate, and their faces insipid.

"Have you lost your way?" inquired Lavender-stripe, while Rose-print bit the corners of her mouth and tried not to laugh.

Lord Rune took heart. Lucy's sisters would lead him to Lucy. He felt surreptitiously at the seat of his trousers, realized with relief that only his coat was torn, and executed a faultless bow. "I hope not," he responded, and favored the twins with his most disarming smile. "I am Ernest Howard, Lord Rune. I should like to see Miss Lucy Saint-Clair. We were friends in London."

Two pairs of dark eyes met, telegraphing a message. There was complicity in that glance—Lord Rune suspected that the sisters had known at once who he was—and speculation. Then Lavender-stripe, who appeared to be the leader of the two, lifted her trim eyebrows and inclined her head, inviting him to continue.

"I should also like to meet Mr. Saint-Clair," Ernest added. It wasn't true; he had no desire to meet Lucy's father, but he was willing to go through whatever formalities were necessary.

Lavender-stripe said primly, "Papa is not at home," and Rose-print, anticipating his next question, added "Neither is Mamma."

Lord Rune arranged his features in an expression of hypocritical regret and tried again. "But Lucy—Miss Saint-Clair—?"

"She's at home," said Lavender-stripe, in a voice that wavered between a gasp and a giggle.

"She's not at home," said Rose-print, in the same instant.

Lord Rune waited. His silence was eloquent. The

sister in rose turned to her twin, and said reproachfully, "Letty, how can you?"

"How can you?" retorted Letty, shamelessly. "I only told the truth. It's wrong to tell falsehoods."

"It wasn't a falsehood," argued Rose-print, flustered. "It was a social convention." She turned back to Lord Rune, and suggested, "Perhaps you could call again."

Lord Rune did not answer. He stared at Lavender-stripe—or Letty—so pointedly that she blushed, poked her sister, and erupted in a fit of merriment.

"You mustn't tell him," Rose-print insisted and added cryptically, "You wouldn't like it yourself."

"Is Miss Saint-Clair at home?" repeated Ernest patiently.

He meant to sound icy; he sounded plaintive. The wistfulness in his voice gave the finishing touch to the sisters' mirth. They burst into fresh giggles, tried to stifle them, risked another look at him, tried to speak, failed, and burst out anew.

"She'll be angry," said Rose-print, but her voice shook with laughter and she was weakening. "It's horrid of us, Letty."

"We must," contradicted Letty, "and it serves her right, for being so cross." She drew herself up, gave a little cough, and said loftily, "My sister is at home."

"May I see her?" persevered Ernest, as the other sister fretted, "Poor Lucy!"

"She isn't poor. I don't pity her," retorted Letty and choked back another giggle. "She's in the kitchen-garden," she said, while her twin snickered.

"Behind the house," specified Rose-print—Mina by default.

Letty pointed toward the house. "There's a path" —she directed—"with a gate—"

"It isn't her fault," said Mina, in a belated effort to defend her sister. "Mrs. Simcock—she's our house-keeper—"

"She *was*," corrected Letty.

"Gave notice," finished Mina.

"Our servants always give notice," said Letty, "and I don't blame them."

"Letty!" cried Mina, in mingled disapproval and delight. "What he must *think*—!"

Lord Rune was already over the churchyard wall. He had no more interest in the twins. As he walked back to the parsonage, he heard Mina gasp, "We might have *warned* her—" but he didn't care what she meant. Lucy was near at hand. He would find her, and he would win her.

He made his way to the back of the parsonage, and followed a path of stepping-stones. Another wall sur-rounded the kitchen garden; the gate hung crooked on the hinges. Lord Rune lifted the latch and went inside. And there, on a rustic bench, sat Lucy, engaged in the unromantic task of plucking a fowl.

She did not look up. The task at hand held her concentration, and his feet made no sound on the wet grass. She sat with the dead bird across her lap and a basket full of feathers in the crook of her arm. Her brow was furrowed, and she looked forlorn and a little angry. Nor was she gowned to receive callers; it was this, Lord Rune surmised, and her menial task, that had aroused her sisters' mirth. Her curls were caught up in a scarlet kerchief, lightly sprinkled with feathers. Her dress was ill-cut and shabby, twice-turned. Perhaps in some dis-tant life it had been pink; it was now grey. It was also rather tight; adversity had not deprived Lucy of flesh. She had sought solace in the pantry; in the last weeks she had eaten rather too much bread and butter and jam.

Lord Rune stood spellbound, watching her. His gaze was ardent; his heart beat so fast that he half-hoped she would hear it and look up. He wanted her to see him, but he could not speak. His mouth was dry. At last, summoning all his courage, he took a single step forward. A twig snapped, and Lucy lifted her head.

He saw her face change. Disbelief first, and then hope: questing, tremulous. She leapt to her feet, and the dead bird dropped to the grass. The basket snagged, catching at her sleeve, and the feathers tumbled down the front of her dress. In another instant, she rushed to him, and he to her, and they fell into each others' arms.

They embraced so frantically that their heads thwacked together. Lord Rune saw stars, and Lucy bit her tongue. Neither cared; it did not matter. They clutched each other and kissed until they were breathless. The feathers whirled and drifted, settling on Lucy's shoulders, Ernest's hair. One feather clung to his eyelash, and Lucy reached up to stroke it away. Her kerchief had slipped, and her curls tumbled down. Ernest drew off the kerchief, and tossed it aside: a red flag lost in a snowdrift of feathers.

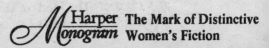

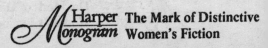

COMING NEXT MONTH

FOREVERMORE by Maura Seger

As the only surviving member of a family that had lived in the English village of Avebury for generations, Sarah Huxley was fated to protect the magical sanctuary of the tumbled stone circles and earthen mounds. But when a series of bizarre deaths at Avebury began to occur, Sarah met her match in William Devereux Faulkner, a level-headed Londoner, who had come to investigate. "Ms. Seger has a special magic touch with her lovers that makes her an enduring favorite with readers everywhere."—*Romantic Times*

PROMISES by Jeane Renick

From the award-winning author of *Trust Me* and *Always* comes a sizzling novel set in a small Ohio town, featuring a beautiful blind heroine, her greedy fiancé, two sisters in love with the same man, a mysterious undercover police officer, and a holographic will.

KISSING COUSINS by Carol Jerina

Texas rancher meets English beauty in this witty follow-up to *The Bridegroom*. When Prescott Trefarrow learned that it was he who was the true Earl of St. Keverne, and not his twin brother, he went to Cornwall to claim his title, his castle, and a multitude of responsibilities. Reluctantly, he became immersed with life at Ravens Lair Castle—and the lovely Lucinda Trefarrow.

HUNTER'S HEART by Christina Hamlett

A romantic suspense novel featuring a mysterious millionaire and a woman determined to figure him out. Many things about wealthy industrialist Hunter O'Hare intrigue Victoria Cameron. First of all, why did O'Hare have his ancestral castle moved to Virginia from Ireland, stone by stone? Secondly, why does everyone else in the castle act as if they have something to hide? And last, but not least, what does Hunter want from Victoria?

THE LAW AND MISS PENNY by Sharon Ihle

When U.S. Marshal Morgan Slater suffered a head injury and woke up with no memory, Mariah Penny conveniently supplied him with a fabricated story so that he wouldn't run her family's medicine show out of town. As he traveled through Colorado Territory with the Pennys, he and Mariah fell in love. Everything seemed idyllic until the day the lawman's memory returned.

PRIMROSE by Clara Wimberly

A passionate historical tale of forbidden romance between a wealthy city girl and a fiercely independent local man in the wilds of the Tennessee mountains. Rosalyn Hunte's heart was torn between loyalty to her family and the love of a man who wanted to claim her for himself.